To Elevate & Adorn the Mind

SET IN 1814 ALBANY, NY, THIS IS THE STORY OF ONE WOMAN'S
RADICAL QUEST TO GIVE GIRLS AN EDUCATION

Louise Copeland Marks

Louise Copeland Marks

Cover photo: Lucretia Foot, June 1807, unsigned painting,
courtesy of Susan B. Strange

Author photo by Genine A. Gullickson
Book design by Emma Schlieder

Printed in the United States of America

The Troy Book Makers • Troy, New York • thetroybookmakers.com

To order additional copies of this title, contact your favorite local bookstore
or visit www.tbmbooks.com

ISBN: 978-1-61468-187-8

For the master teachers in my life:

Rhoda Harris, headmistress of Albany Academy for Girls (1941-1964) and Dalton Stuart Marks, life partner (The Albany Academy, class of 1957). Your ability to awaken possibilities within others is beyond time and space. Blessed with intellect and compassion, knowledge and wisdom, you inform and inspire.

Acknowledgements

Many rivers flow to the sea.

Thank you to the family, friends, and professionals
who contributed to the fictional journal of Betsey Colt Foot.
Thank you to the librarians and archivists who protect
our earthly treasures from thieves, moths, and rust.

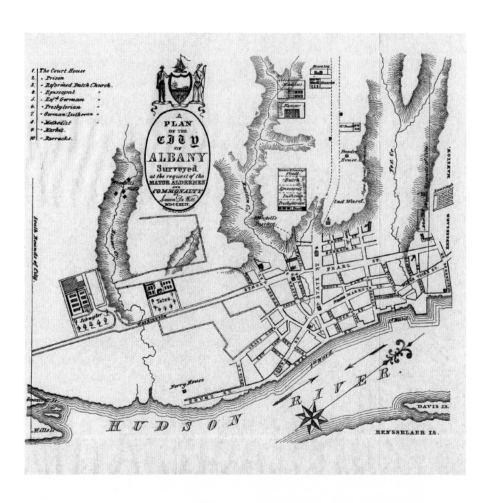

PLAN OF THE CITY OF ALBANY, 1794, SURVEYED BY SIMEON DE WITT.
LITHOGRAPH BY PEASE. COURTESY, ALBANY INSTITUTE OF HISTORY AND ART.

Friday, January 1, 1813

The first day of the new year, a new moon

A voice woke me early this morning, before dawn, the first day of a new year. I recognized it immediately. I knew the voice because I had heard it so many times. It was not a quiet whisper from far away and long ago, but close and clear, up and off to my right in my bedchamber in Albany, New York. My heart stirred. Ebenezer, asleep next to me, heard nothing.

"Betsey, dear. Take your first steps into the new year with intention. The new moon has great power. Whatever is planted at the time of the new moon will flourish. Mark your intentions. Make your choices Minerva-wise."

It has been more than ten years since I heard the voice of my Connecticut teacher, Miss Sarah Pierce. A tiny woman, she stands tall. She wears a gown the color of dark chocolate. She carries the scent of crushed raspberries. She presides over daily chapel at Litchfield Female Academy: a time for Song, Scripture, and Words of Inspiration.

While frost covers the window of my bedchamber, Miss Pierce's voice transports me to a warm, spring day in Connecticut. I do not see the snow covered hills across the Hudson. I see red-tipped buds on the sycamore trees along South Street in Litchfield. On Montgomery Street, the clop, clop, creak, creak of Mr. Lattimer's horse and wagon fades. I hear a piano.

Miss Pierce was not blessed with the gift of music. She only knew loud and soft. The pianist I hear is her sister Anna. She plays with flourish the first bars of the processional. It is the call for students to line up in pairs according to height. On cue we march into the front room singing the daily hymn.

> O splendor of God's glory bright,
> O thou that bringest light from light,
> O Light of Light, light's living spring,
> O day, all days illumining.

Following the amen, Miss Pierce takes her place on the dais at the front of the room. She bows to us and smiles. In her hand she holds a

1

rose-gold pocket watch hanging from a chain, the kind of watch a father hands down to his son. She checks the time then tucks the watch into a side pocket, scans the room, and waits for the students to become still.

"Girls, each one of you has been given a gift." She instantly has my attention. "Each one has been given a gift," she repeats, "a gift with your name, a different gift for each girl." I am struck by the news. I have been given a special gift with my name? I had never heard this.

MISS SARAH PIERCE

"We are one family, but just like the body has arms, legs, hands, and feet, we have different jobs according to the gift given to us. The Lord has placed within you a light to illuminate the path of your life. Cherish and protect the light and it will grow brighter each day. Use your gift to bring light to the world. Always and everywhere thank God for your gift."

Miss Pierce helped me understand the joy of using my own special gift, the gift with my name.

I have not thought about my gift of teaching since I left Litchfield Female Academy to marry Ebenezer. Would I be happier if I had stayed with Miss Pierce as her assistant? Today, in the midst of my family, I stumble. Was I mistaken about my gift? Can a gift be taken away if it is not used? Have I extinguished the light within? Was my gift given to someone else? Do I have a different gift now that I am a wife and mother?

Ebenezer and I have good neighbors in Albany. I meet weekly with the kind women at St. Peter's Society of Church Ladies, but there is no one in Albany with whom I might ask my questions, confide my concerns. Dare I write Miss Pierce and seek her guidance? She would reply that the letter I write must be to myself. She will remind me to listen to the still, small voice within. Her advice would be Gnothi Seauton: Know Thyself.

My intention is to take the first steps into 1813 and write letters to myself. Writing has more clarity than thinking. The pen is freer than the tongue. Prying thoughts out of my head and onto the page, I tell myself something I didn't think I knew. On private pages I will ask the troubling questions, clean out the clutter in my mind, and clarify my thoughts. I will confess how far I've fallen short of being a good wife and mother.

"I would never want others to know how I feel," my sister says. "They would think I'm crazy." I believe if I am thinking something, another person is thinking it as well. Writing will rekindle the light within and restore my footing.

Saturday, January 2, 1813
Cold and clear

Two of my most precious possessions are in the front room. A portrait of Lucretia, painted when she was two and a half, hangs above an exquisite cherry chest given to me by Grandmother Ely at my wedding. The chest sits on bracket feet and has four drawers. Each drawer has two brass handles and a keyhole. Only I have the key. Only she and I know the secret of the chest. There is a false bottom under the fourth drawer. This is where I have hidden the poem Miss Pierce wrote when I told her of my plan to marry Ebenezer. I never shared it with him.

> Her bosom beats; she knows not why
> She starts to think the hour so nigh
> When she her plighted vows must pay
> And learn that fearful word "obey."

Privately, she viewed marriage as a less-than-perfect union. She did not understand my willingness to neglect an intellectual gift and abandon the pursuit of teaching. She was disappointed in me, but I felt I was one of many that Miss Pierce loved whereas Ebenezer loved me more than any other. I wanted to be his wife. I wanted to have my own home and have many children.

Miss Pierce must have reconsidered her sentiments. Just before our wedding day, she sent a second verse.

> The word is not so hard my dear
> As our proud sex would make appear
> When love and friendship tie the band
> Ease the chain, light the command.

I have not heard from Miss Pierce since I left Litchfield. I never told her how much I admire her. I want to tell her about the band that ties me to Ebenezer. I want her to know about the love and friendship of our family. The truth is the band feels tight. The chain feels heavy.

I worry about Ebenezer. He labors over stacks of legal documents. His work takes him out until late at night. There is never enough income to cover our expenses. Will there ever be?

I worry about our boarder, Mr. North. His mind is sharp, but his body is frail. He is bone thin and bent over from coughing. Will he regain his health and resume his work as Ebenezer's law partner?

I worry about Ebenezer's younger brother who lives with us. Will Samuel pass the upcoming law exams? Will he return the money Ebenezer provided for the tuition at Union College? Ebenezer is impatient for Samuel to take over Mr. North's clients and increase his earnings.

I worry about our daughter Lucretia, now eight. Can I be a proper teacher for her? She is curious and asking to read my books, but she spends too much time on superficialities. During church she studies the fashions of young matrons visiting from New York and covets their furs, silks, ribbons, and plumes.

Hannah Scoville! Sixteen years old! What will become of Hannah? The Scoville's farm borders the Foot family farm in Connecticut. Her parents knew Hannah was not suited for the farming life and did not think she would benefit from further schooling like her older sister, Eliza, a student of Miss Pierce. Ebenezer and I agreed to bring Hannah to Albany in exchange for help with household chores. She is not suited for that either. She doubles my work and adds to our expenses.

I worry whether I have the strength for the ten thousand chores of the day. I became acquainted with work early in life. When father died, he left our mother with ten children and   my chores increased. That seems nothing compared to my current responsibilities as a wife and mother. I am forever judged by how efficiently I go round the mulberry bush.

I will not waste time or ink writing about the way I wash our clothes, iron our clothes, scrub the floor, mend the clothes, sweep the floor, and bake our bread so early every morning. I will create a record of my life. I will write about what I think about, what I do and see. I will include all the weeds and wrinkles. I will resist the temptation to make my thoughts prettier than they are. Letters to myself will ask the questions I cannot ask anyone else.

Long after I am gone, if my journal is discovered, my ordinary life will seem extraordinary. A future reader will be amused by my customs and dismiss my concerns as foolish. Perhaps they will know how my story ends. I trust if my writing is from the heart, others will recognize something of themselves.

Hannah has a head for numbers. I will teach her to measure the flour, yeast, and water for our bread. Lucretia will knead the dough. It will keep her busy while I slice parsnips and build up the fire.

Standing in front of a blazing oven, my face burns, but my feet are cold.

Sunday, January 3, 1813
The second Sunday after Christmas

She is not what you would expect to find in the city of Albany where even the dogs bark in Dutch. Standing at the top of State Street, the English Church overlooks the whole city. It was Divine Providence she did not retreat with the Loyalists after the War of Independence. St. Peter's Church was designed by Philip Hooker, architect of the Capitol, the New York State Bank, the Bank of Albany, Mechanics and Farmers Bank, and the Presbyterian Church. Our neighbor's husband, Reverend Thomas Ellison died before the church was completed, but Mrs. Ellison says, "From heaven, he looks at the finished masterpiece and is pleased." Ebenezer was on the church vestry before he became too busy with work.

We receive bread and wine from the Holy Communion Service, a gift to the parish from Her Majesty. It is an exact reproduction of the one she used at her coronation. Mr. Hochstrasser plays St. Peter's grand organ built by Mr. Redstone of Manhattan. The range of tones and harmonies are amazing. A steeple bell cast in London, another of Queen Anne's gifts, calls us to worship.

Ebenezer, Mr. North, Samuel, Lucretia, Hannah, and I collect Mrs. Ellison and together we walk up Steuben to Pearl Street. Today a frosting of snow covers the cobbles. On Sunday, there is a chain across Pearl Street to prevent carriage traffic from disrupting services at the Presbyterian Church further south on Pearl. We turn right at State Street and climb the hill.

The Second Sunday after Christmas, Reverend Clowes proclaims, "This is the year of the Lord's favor. God has poured upon us a new light." He tells us that the prophet Isaiah promises beauty from ashes, that we will receive the oil of gladness not mourning, and that a mantle of praise will replace a faint spirit. Ebenezer, Samuel, and Mr. North are buoyed. They believe 1813 will be a prosperous year, and are filled with hope.

New Light,
    Beauty,
        Gladness,
            Praise.

I pray for my own faint spirit and Isaiah assures, "Before you have asked, I have answered."

Wednesday, January 6, 1813

Even during times of war, men and women have the same everyday concerns: the high price of flour, rats in the cellar, and disputes with neighbors. Yesterday, we left our troubles behind to see Major Young from Troy lead his volunteer militia across the frozen river and up to the Capitol. He waved the British flag captured at St Regis. It was a spectacle to warm the heart on a cold January day.

Samuel, Hannah, Lucretia, and I, wrapped in thick mufflers, hats and mitts, joined other Albanians lined two deep along State Street. Samuel hoisted Lucretia on his shoulders so she could see the parade, not of men, but small, clean-faced boys not much taller than Hannah.

Congress declared war on Britain because of her interference with our merchant ships trading with France. American sailors are being impressed into service with the British Navy. Also, Major Young says,

Great Britain is blocking our expansion into Canada. He says we fight to protect the freedoms won in the War of Independence. According to Major Young, the victory at St. Regis means this will be a short war. A short war? Is that possible?

Major Young's speech was just what the audience wanted to hear, and he was rewarded with hearty huzzahs and hoorahs. The silent few understand there are no quick victories, no short wars. In conclusion we offered prayers for further victories and sang "The Old Hundredth."

> All people that on earth do dwell,
> Sing to the Lord with cheerful voice.
> Him serve with fear, His praise forth tell;
> Come ye before Him and rejoice.

I agree with Samuel. Those in favor of war should be the first to march into battle.

Thursday, January 7, 1813

Men like Major Young lead armies into wars, capture enemy flags, march in parades, and receive medals for bravery. They write histories about waging wars and negotiating peace treaties, followed by subsequent wars and new treaties. They make charts and maps and fight for land and power. Women's battles are in the uncharted territories of the heart. Our wars are waged alone and in private. There are no medals for the courage of women. What is my battle? What does victory mean for me? I do not talk to Ebenezer as I once did. I fear I will upset him.

Samuel scoffs at my writing. A better use of my time would be to replace buttons on his pants, the ones he popped since gaining weight. He tells me, "No one is interested in your trivialities."

> If you would not be forgotten,
> As soon as you are dead and rotten,
> Either write things worth reading,
> Or do things worth the writing.

He is confident he will do both, and I will do neither. None but the recording angel will ever know for sure.

I hush Samuel so I can concentrate on my correspondence. It is women who maintain social ties with distant family and friends. Letter writing is within our sphere.

Samuel is satisfied with my explanation and turns back to his book. Upstairs, Hannah and Lucretia are asleep. Mr. North is coughing. I resume writing and imagine Miss Pierce also sitting before a fire reading my thoughts. What does she think?

After Samuel bids me good night, I add wood to the fire and await Ebenezer's return. Finally, I blow out the candle and climb the stairs to bed, but not to sleep.

Saturday, January 9, 1813

The Hudson River has been closed to navigation since December 22. Mr. Cole will not take a sleigh across until the ice is thicker, but for a coin there is always someone else willing to try. A stage-driver fell through the ice last week. In the middle of the river, there is no chance of rescue and he, his horse, and a passenger drowned. I worry there will be more disasters because men feel their business on the other side will not wait.

Ebenezer dismisses my fears and crosses for his important business in Troy. He says the ice is strong as a street and he has no intention of falling through. The unfortunate stage-driver also had no intention. What would happen if Ebenezer fell into a watery grave? Our family, our house and everything in it would sink. It's too horrible to think about, but I do.

When I ask Ebenezer to wait one more week, he calls me foolish. When I beg him to think about the family, he demands I stop questioning his decisions.

I am accustomed to Ebenezer respecting my opinion. Lately I have learned it is better to hold my tongue and pick up the pen.

Sunday, January 10, 1813
The coldest day this year

Ice crystals laced the edges of my bed linen this morning. Frosty cobwebs hung in corners like fine silk netting. It was so cold the water in my wash bowl and the bread in our pantry was frozen. There will be no church. The Eucharist wine would be ice. When Hannah poured hot tea into my cup, it shattered. I mourned the loss of the beautiful cup Ebenezer's mother gave me, but cleaned up the mess without a word. Hannah cried, fearing I would punish her, and I admit I was angry. She is perpetually on a journey above the clouds.

Tossing the broken cup into the trash heap behind the house, I thought about my father's advice. "Never put off 'til tomorrow what you can do today, with one exception. Save your anger for tomorrow. When tomorrow comes, save your anger for the next day."

I will save my anger for tomorrow, and Reverend Clowes will save today's sermon for next Sunday when we will have a double half hour-glass sermon. When Hannah realized that added up to one whole hour, she started crying again and Lucretia joined in. She had been up early arranging and rearranging ribbons for her hair. She will miss her friends at church.

Samuel, happy to stay home, teased the girls chanting, "No church today! Double our pleasure next week!" This stirred up more outbursts from the girls. Ebenezer's stern look told me to take command. When a domestic tempest erupts, it is my duty to restore order.

Good manners and a bond of love and friendship unite our household. I am grateful we are not united with any others, including my dear mother in Hadley or Ebenezer's sweet mother living with his sister Esther in Ballston Spa. I could not endure the cheek to jowl conditions at the Allen Brown household. How does Mrs. Brown manage living in a small house with a husband, four sons, a troublesome mother-in-law, plus his cousin and baby? In our small household of six, when we sit down to a common meal, each one requests a different beverage. Ebenezer drinks coffee. Samuel prefers chocolate. Lucretia begs for the same. For Hannah and myself, I brew Souchong tea. I like it strong. She prefers weak. When my mother visits, she fancies Hyson tea. Ebenezer and Samuel's mother is grateful for whatever is served. She is quick to remind us, "We had only one pot of tea during the entire war, and the only molasses for the family was what I made from cornstalks."

After breakfast Samuel claimed the bank note he placed under his mattress is missing. He accused Hannah who denied knowing anything about it. She and Lucretia are not allowed in his and Mr. North's room. Anyway what could Hannah do with a bank note? The clerks at Mechanics and Farmers would never grant her entrance to the bank.

Samuel did not accuse Mr. North who is too weak to leave the house and whose integrity is impeccable. I assured Samuel he had misplaced the note and will find it tomorrow at work. He insisted he brought it home to deposit in the bank Monday morning. Eventually he conceded he might be mistaken.

Like the broken cup, I sweep up messy quarrels and harmonize the disparate personalities gathered around our fire. Regarding my own conflicts, I keep silent. Is this now the gift with my name?

Monday, January 11, 1813

Samuel was not out the door three minutes before he was back, uttering profanities. He insisted he was not calling the Lord's name in vain. It was for a good reason. When I saw the condition of his coat and pants, I understood. Five paces down Montgomery Street, Samuel slipped on the ice and fell into a fresh mess.

Hogs are fine on a farm, but they are a nuisance running wild in the city. Some say the hogs clean the streets of refuse. Most think they only add to the filth. There is a law in Albany that requires hogs be ringed, tied, and fed at home, but it is ignored. While he was constable, Elkanah Watson threatened to round up all hogs running free and deliver them to the public pound. The Dutch call Watson "that d.....d paving Yankee" because of his efforts to clean and pave our streets. The Dutch resent any interference with their freedom and pocketbooks.

I brush off Samuel's coat, find a change of pants and send him back out the door. He is like having a second husband. He needs to be ringed. He needs to be driven to the altar.

Just as I predicted, Samuel found the bank note in the top drawer of his office desk. He was certain he had removed it Friday from the bottom drawer. He is not usually forgetful about money matters. I think his mind is crowded with the upcoming law examination.

Tuesday, January 12, 1813

Worries circle my head in a well-worn path until I coax them out and put them on the page. I toil and spin, toil and spin, and worry. Mother's advice was simple.

> For every evil under the sun
> There be a remedy or there be none.
> If there be one, try to find it.
> If there be none, never mind it.

There is no remedy for Ebenezer's insistence on crossing the river, but thankfully Mother Nature intervened. The ice is now strong enough for crossing by sleigh.

Samuel takes the New York State Law Examination tomorrow. I do not worry about him because he is well prepared and, besides, it is outside my control. It is about Mr. North that I toil and spin and worry. Each cough slices through my heart. I have given him regular doses of butterfly root, but despite my efforts he is no better. I pray it is not the dreaded disease.

Mrs. Ellison has a remedy. Hanging in her kitchen is a pharmacy of dried catnip, boneset, elder blow, rosemary, pennyroyal, and tansy. She will mix an elixir to cleanse the lungs.

Thursday, January 14, 1813

Good News. Samuel passed the law exams. Ebenezer convinced his friend, Chief Justice James Kent, that Samuel's years at Union College should count towards the required seven-year law clerk apprenticeship. Judge Kent signed the license yesterday. Now Samuel can practice law in the State of New York. He will take over Mr. North's clients and be a full working partner with Ebenezer. Except for Ebenezer's counsel fees, Samuel will be entitled to half the total earnings of the law practice. This is a generous arrangement for a young lawyer. He can soon repay Ebenezer the college tuition.

There is more good news. Mrs. Ellison's herbs have quieted Mr. North's cough. He has been sleeping peacefully. Mrs. Ellison says rest will restore his health.

Saturday, January 16, 1813

A full moon

Mrs. Ellison was right. Mr. North felt well enough today to teach the girls and me about eudaemonia. According to Aristotle, the goal of life is the pursuit of happiness, achieved not through hedonistic pleasures but through reaching one's full potential in the service of others. Mr. North tapped his foot and turned the word into a chant.

> Euda mon ia.
> Euda mon ia.
> Euda mon ia,
> Da, da, dee.
> Da da. Da da. Dee.
> Da da. Da da. Dee. Dee. Dee.

Lucretia, Hannah, and I joined hands and performed a circle dance around the kitchen, sweeping the floor with our skirts and singing the eudaemonia song.

Mr. North makes learning fun. He instructed Lucretia and Hannah on the importance of listening carefully not only to what is said, but how it is said. They listened to his riddle and struggled with the solution.

> There was a girl in our town,
> Silk an' satin was her gown
> Silk an' satin, gold an' velvet
> Guess her name; three times I've telled it.

Mr. North recited the poem three times before Hannah correctly guessed the name ANN. Lucretia cried because she did not understand. She stopped when I served tea and molasses cakes.

"Silk an' satin, gold an' velvet" do not suit me. It is the mind I want to adorn. I want to live a life of purpose. I want eudaemonia.

My spirits are lifted to hear Mr. North plan a trip in the spring for the healing mineral waters of Ballston Spa.

Monday, January 18, 1813

When Ebenezer and I moved to Albany five years ago, I found an envelope hidden in the fourth drawer of Grandmother Ely's chest. Inside were twenty bills and a note.

Dearest Betsey,

Every woman should have money of her own. Use this for something of importance,

Your Loving Grandmother

Grandmother was well acquainted with laws covering "Baron and Feme," husband and wife. At marriage, women lose all rights to their personal property. When men asked Ebenezer to provide financial support for a theater in Albany, I told him about Grandmother's gift and agreed to give it to him for the Green Street Theater. In return he promised to obtain support for a school for Lucretia. Our neighbor Mr. Russell is on Albany's Common Council. He says there have been private discussions about an academy for Albany. Mayor Philip Van Rensselaer announced a meeting on January 28 to assess public interest.

The new theater opens tonight. I trust Ebenezer will soon honor his pledge regarding a school for Lucretia, especially after I read him Mother's recent letter from Hadley. Samuel Dickinson and Noah Webster have gained support for an academy for the boys and girls of Amherst, Massachusetts.

Tuesday, January 19, 1813

Mr. Bernard's theater on Green Street opened with Fortune's Frolics, a comedy about the tricks and reversals of fate. It is humorous when expectations are turned upside down. Good fortune turns into disaster and disasters bring good fortune. It is a bleak time of year. With war rumblings now getting louder, it is good to forget our troubles and laugh.

Before the performance, the street was jammed with patrons dressed in fur hats and scarlet capes. There are some Albany churches who preach theaters are monuments of depravity. They predict God will bring fire and brimstone down on the Green Street Theater just as He did with the Richmond theater two years ago at Christmas. Scenery caught fire and spread quickly. Virginia's Governor and many others, including women, perished.

Despite the dire warnings, all seats at the Green Street Theater were filled. Ebenezer paid two dollars for our box seats, elevated above the pit. A large glass chandelier dripped candle wax on those in the nickel seats below where I spotted the widow Henry's son Joseph. He is an aspiring actor.

The Kents, Ten Eycks, VanVechtens, our neighbors the Russells and Goulds, and many other Albany benefactors were seated when Mayor Van Rensselaer made his ceremonial entrance, bowing and waving to the cheering spectators. When the Mayor was settled in his seat, Mr. Southwick, the West Indian actor, swept aside the green velvet curtain and stood before the audience. He thanked the distinguished guests for their support. Precisely at 6:30, the heavy curtain lifted, and the first act commenced.

The audience roared at the buffoonery on stage, Ebenezer loudest of all. I believe he would have liked to become an actor. His parents released him from his obligation to take over the family farm, but they would not have condoned a career in the theater. The courtroom is Ebenezer's stage.

When the final curtain fell, there was a standing ovation, more for the promise of productions to come than the quality of the performance. Mr. Bernard, Mr. Southwick, and the other actors mingled with the audience to receive accolades. All agreed the costumes, the scenery, and lights were splendid.

An evening at the theater was just what Ebenezer needed to lift his spirit. We forgot our everyday concerns and returned to Montgomery Street lighthearted. I kept my promise to Ebenezer. Will he keep his promise to me and attend next week's meeting about a city academy?

Thursday, January 21, 1813

Ebenezer and I made the right decision to move from Troy to Albany. There are opportunities for him in New York's capital city. For Lucretia however, the school situation is deplorable. At the Society of Church Ladies, we knit hats and blankets for the poor, but mostly we talk. At yesterday's meeting we chatted briefly about the Green Street Theater. We were not sure if it was a proper topic for church, so we turned to the subject of Albany schools.

Mrs. Fowler says there was a free school in Albany. It flourished for four years under schoolmaster Seth Wells and schoolmistress Martha Wilson. Public support did not last and the school closed thirteen years ago. Martha Wilson now teaches Fanny Roorback, Sarah Davis and Jane Agnes Center at her home on Steuben Street. The three Henry sisters, Emma, Catharine and Mary, attend Catharine B. Thompson's School for Young Ladies on Columbia Street along with Mary Kent and Margaret Hutton. Mrs. John Nugent's Seminary for Young Ladies seems to be doing well. Except for Mariam Fowler, her students are all from the Presbyterian Church: Emma and Louisa Marvin, Sally Stearns, and Elizabeth Stewart.

Miss Brenton operates a Day and Boarding School across the street from our church. She advertises in the Albany Gazette that she teaches reading, English grammar, epistolary style, arithmetic, algebra, geography with the use of the globes, and history. She also offers a long list of ornamental subjects: drawing, painting in water colors and on velvet, embroidery, shell and wax work, artificial flowers, gilding, hair work, needlework, and plain sewing. How can she teach all this by herself? I have met Miss Brenton a few times at church meetings. She seems nice but aloof. She tutors Martha and Margaret Gill and Annabella Brown four hours a week. Her fees are high and I am uncomfortable that she has so many boarding students who, to me, seem poorly supervised.

Some in Albany send their children away to one of the New England academies. The Clarks' daughter Mary has been a student at Litchfield Female Academy since last May.

There is one small, all-age district school on Pearl Street, but it is not a healthy place for children for it is cold and smoky in the winter and blazing hot in the summer. A poorly paid teacher with a basic education teaches elementary reading, penmanship, and simple arithmetic. The current school master admits, "Tis little they pays me, and little I teaches `em." None of the teachers stay long.

Some teachers rely on brute force to pound learning into the skulls of their students. My Connecticut cousins told tales about the New London schoolmaster, Mr. Dow. He constructed a device to squeeze the fingers of an unruly student between two hinged boards. After the first victims, his students were well-behaved, though nervous pupils. Eventually the "corrector" was used only on the newly admitted, unsuspecting hooligans.

Here in Albany, Mrs. Fowler says everyone knows about the beer swilling teacher who fortifies himself before school with a tall morning mug. He believes it is his religious duty to whip the students regularly. Mrs. Fowler says,

> Mr. Crabb is a very good man.
> He goes to church on Sunday.
> He prays to God to make him strong
> To beat the boys on Monday.

The Mechanics have a school on North Pearl Street, but it is only for their sons. The Lancaster School, superintended by Mr. William Tweed Dale, is Albany's benevolent effort to provide for the elementary education of poor children. The instruction of four hundred boys and girls is delegated to an army of student mentors. It has economical appeal to the town fathers because advanced students teach less advanced ones. Physical punishment is not permitted, but in my opinion the school does little to instill a love of learning.

Friday, January 22, 1813

Why has it taken the town fathers so long to provide a proper school for Albany children? My brothers and sisters and I received an education in Hadley at the Hopkins School founded in 1644! Hopkins prepared my older brother Daniel for entrance to Harvard College.

It was Daniel who encouraged me to further my education to earn a living as a teacher. In 1795, the tuition at Litchfield Female Academy was five dollars per quarter, a financial hardship for middling families like ours. Wealthier families had no difficulty paying that amount plus additional fees for the ornamental curriculum of decorative arts, music, and dance. I was older than the other students. Most were between fourteen and sixteen. Some, as young as six, were orphans sent to Miss Pierce by their guardians.

Many in Litchfield thought matters of the mind were not suitable for girls, but Miss Pierce convinced fathers that daughters must be educated to assume their role as the social and spiritual guardians of the family and community. She stressed that although the home is a haven, enhanced by painting and needlework, women must also elevate and adorn the mind.

I loved being with Miss Pierce at Litchfield. It is the kind of school I want for Lucretia. Unlike the Clarks, I could not send her away. I have faith the Common Council will do the right thing and provide a good school for us in Albany.

Tuesday, January 26, 1813

There is now an Anti-Federalist paper in Albany, The Argus. The founder and printer, Jesse Buel, has a large farm west of Albany, but he is originally from Connecticut. The other paper, The Albany Gazette, is Federalist. Both papers report that the electoral votes are counted. James Madison with 128 electoral votes will remain as President. De-Witt Clinton had 89.

In Connecticut, there is nothing good said about Mr. Madison's War with England. Dominated by Federalists, Connecticut citizens say the war will destroy commerce, increase taxes, and result in terrible losses to life and property. Their Governor says the war is unconstitutional and he will refuse to allow his militia to leave the state. He threatens to impeach Mr. Madison or secede from the Union, but my Lyme cousins do not think it will go that far. In New York, the Anti-Federalists want to drive the British from North America because they are blocking our expansion into Canada.

How can Mr. Madison win a war against Britain? We are a small union of separate states. They are a rich country with the most powerful Navy in the world. What does the Lady Presidentress think? As a Quaker, Dolley Madison was a pacifist, but she has left the Society of Friends and attends the English Church with the President. Like me, Dolley spells her name with an added "e". Aaron Burr introduced her to "The Great Little Madison." She was twenty-five and Jemmie was forty. They were married one year after Dolley's first husband died.

Dolley dresses in the latest fashion: low cut, French gowns with small sleeves. Her favorite color, like mine, is yellow. She is fascinated with the Orient and wears a turban on her head. Turbans are now the style.

Everyone wants to be invited to her parties because she serves fried chicken and iced creams. She knows how to converse with all classes of people. To break the ice, she discusses her favorite book, Don Quixote which she usually carries tucked under her arm. Perched on her shoulder is her pet parrot, Uncle Willy. She enjoys snuff and keeps a snuffbox in her reticule. The Dutch in Albany love "snuftabak" so I also carry a snuffbox to offer it to others.

Dolley has special gatherings for women to discuss politics. She invites friend and foe to gather information and gain influence. Mr. Jefferson feels ladies should not upset their tender breasts with serious subjects, but Dolley disagrees. She says it will not deprive them of domestic happiness. It adds interest to the marriage. She believes men and women are intellectually equal. It is education that accounts for differences, not gender.

The anti-Madison people spread rumors about Dolley. They say when she was acting as President Jefferson's hostess their relationship went too far. People cannot imagine women's charms are more than physical. Gossip and criticism do not upset Dolley. She continues to express her ideas even if they are unpopular. I admire her spunk.

Thursday, January 28, 1813

Despite Mrs. Ellison's herbs, Mr. North has taken a sharp turn for the worse. Ebenezer decided he should be moved to Mrs. Ellison's next door. Her watchful eye and soothing touch has restored the vigor of many after their physicians have given up hope. I am sad, but tell Mr. North, "All shall be well." He will soon resume his place in our family. He looked at me with soft eyes that conveyed he appreciated the intention of my words. I sensed he has surrendered to the will of God.

After settling Mr. North with Mrs. Ellison, I returned home heavy hearted, but reined in my feelings and busied myself with chores. Our evening supper was a joyless meal.

Mr. North and I have had many discussions about what it means to live a life of meaning, a life of purpose, a life of service. He confessed he had regrets he did not pursue the ministry and wondered if it is now too late. He knew I was disappointed Ebenezer did not attend yesterday's public meeting about the proposed Albany academy. There was a large turnout in support.

Before moving to Mrs. Ellison's, Mr. North urged me to remind Ebenezer of the pledge we'd made a year ago. I confided that, "when things are going well, I do not want to spoil Ebenezer's rare good mood. When things are not going well, I do not want to upset him further."

Mr. North's response was puzzling. "Since I am not your counsellor, I cannot advise you one way or the other. The path is before you. In time it will become clear."

I will ask him to explain this cryptic message when he is stronger.

Friday, January 29, 1813

Mr. North always seemed a solitary man. At Mrs. Ellison's, he talked of a mother and brother who live on the River Road in Stillwater, four houses north of Harmanus Schuyler's home. He asked me to inform them of his condition. I promised we would write a letter tomorrow. Mr. North looked deep into my eyes, pressed a roll of bills in the palm of my hand and folded our hands tight together. "Thank you, Betsey, You have been my good family." He lowered his eyes and fell into a deep, peaceful sleep.

At home, I wrapped the bills in a handkerchief and locked them in the bottom drawer of the Ely chest.

Saturday, January 30, 1813

I have no words. At first, Mr. North appeared revived under Mrs. Ellison's care. He was breathing more slowly, but he was not coughing. Early this morning he exhaled his last breath.

It is the loss of a great man and friend. Ebenezer is thankful Samuel is handling Mr. North's work. For me, no one can replace Mr. North. Alone. Bereft. Deserted. Diminished. Adrift. Desolate. Empty. No words fit.

Like many men, Mr. North lived too much in his head. The brain thinks it is in command because it is on top, but the body always wins. My friend did not heed his own advice to take care of problems before they grew large. His cough became greater and greater and finally overtook him.

I will write the promised letter to Mr. North's family. Mrs. Ellison will prepare Mr. North's body for the wake. Until his family comes for his body he will repose in our front room under the watchful eye of Ebenezer, Samuel, and Mr. Russell. Tomorrow Reverend Clowes will say prayers for the departed soul of a good man. I pray God will take my grief and give me the peace of knowing my friend will receive all the heavenly blessings he deserves.

Tuesday, February 2, 1813

Candlemas day, a new moon

Mr. North's brother arrived midday to take him to Stillwater for a spring burial. Unfortunately, there were harsh words. The family is angry they were not informed of Mr. North's condition. "We would have brought him to our family physician. Dr. Chauncey Bull would have saved him."

I wanted to shout, "Mr. North never talked about his family!" Instead, I was quiet. Ebenezer expressed our condolences. He gave money owed Mr. North and agreed to accept Mr. North's collection of books on law and philosophy.

It is a dark day. In the church calendar, Candlemas is a day to celebrate light and hope. In Connecticut, flowers bloom through the snow on Candlemas. Snowdrops are the first sign of spring. I wish I could tell Mr. North that Lucretia will soon have her school. He would be pleased the Common Council met yesterday and resolved to pursue the development of an academy for Albany children. A school building will be erected in the Public Square to be renamed Academy Park. Archibald M'Intyre was named chairman of a building committee and trustees were appointed. Money to finance the building will come from the sale of the old city jail. It will still be necessary to raise thirty-thousand dollars through public subscriptions.

I expect the trustees will organize the Albany school in the same manner as the academy in North Carolina where Ebenezer's Uncle had a shipping business. Eli Foote was impressed with the New Bern school founded by the Anglicans before The War of Independence. The male and female departments, a common school, and recently, a Lancastrian department, are together under one roof.

On this dark Candlemas Day there are no flowers in Albany, but there is hope. The new Academy, like Plato's school, will be a garden to nurture young minds.

Wednesday, February 10, 1813

St. Peter's had been without a dominie for three years when Reverend Clowes appeared one year ago. He is a tall, ungainly man, plain speaking, direct, sometimes even blunt, but he is energetic and creative. Many church members feel he is more approachable than previous rectors.

"If there is a big job to be done, give it to the ladies," Reverend Clowes announced this morning. He is a single man who ordinarily shows little interest in "the ladies," or they in him, but today he addressed our meeting to say he has big plans and needs our help. He wants to open the church on Wednesday evenings, special Saints Days, and on all Holy Days.

After Reverend Clowes left, we discussed the tasks involved in opening the church for additional services. This concluded, Mrs. Hochstrasser led us in a rousing hymn.

Soldiers of Christ, arise,
And put your armor on,
Strong in the strength, which God supplies
Through his Eternal Son.

The ladies sing softly and without emotion. I restrain myself from the urge to arise, trumpet the words, and march around the room with gusto!

Saturday, February 13, 1813

For a second time Ebenezer's colleague Abraham Van Vechten was appointed State Attorney General. The two men spend evenings together. Tonight they will put business aside and celebrate. Mr. Van Vechten is a trustee of the planned Academy in Albany. I have only a nodding acquaintance with Mrs. Van Vechten and am looking forward to knowing her better.

Monday, February 15, 1813

A full moon, the snow moon

I am stunned. There are no plans for a female department in the new Academy. The Common Council has no intention of including girls in the school. Mr. Van Vechten confirmed the news with Ebenezer two days ago. If my husband had prior knowledge of this, he has not shared it with me.

The Academy will be for boys. The school will enroll boys. The school will prepare boys for college. Ebenezer had to repeat the words three times before I could comprehend the meaning. When I did understand, I felt as if a key bolt and screw at the hub of my whole being broke loose and sent me spinning off the road and into a ditch.

I can hardly breathe.

Wednesday, February 17, 1813

Cloudy, looks like snow

The one who loves words has none for the despair I feel. In last night's dream, I asked Mr. North to take me with him. He responded, "Betsey, your earthly business is not finished."

I turn for comfort to my worn leather volume of Anne Bradstreet's poetry: The Tenth Muse Lately Sprung Up in America, By a Gentlewoman of Those Parts.

Like many women, Anne left the comforts of home in England and settled in America with her husband, an associate of the Massachusetts Bay Company. Well-born and well-educated, she was not prepared for the barren and lonely life she found in New England. Anne studied theology and wrote poetry, but kept her intellectual and artistic life secret because it was not proper for women to feed their minds and express themselves. From Anne Hutchinson's banishment, she knew the consequence of violating the Puritan code of conduct. Anne Bradstreet's solace was a personal relationship with God.

> He chased away those clouds and let me see
> My anchor cast i` th` vale with safety.
> He eased my soul of woe, my flesh of pain
> And brought me to the shore from troubled main.

Anne's poetry lifts me above the mundane. She frees me from my own petty concerns. Why can't I accept what cannot be changed? What can I change? How do I ease my own "soul of woe?" If I am delivered from the troubled main, can I survive on shore? Is it true, as Ebenezer warns, if I speak about educating girls I will jeopardize his position in the community?

Friday, February 19, 1813
Cold and blustery

My mind is peaceful in the morning before others are awake.

"Only one child, and it's a daughter." My neighbor Mrs. Russell pities me for having only one child, but truthfully, I do not know what I would do if I had more. With all the daily interruptions, I cannot complete a thought of any complexity. I cannot finish the simplest task.

Yesterday was the day to label household linens. Just as I began, Ebenezer returned to the house for a letter he'd forgotten and misplaced. I found it under the bed. That settled, I asked Hannah to fetch onions and potatoes from the cold cellar and slice them for a meat pie. I assigned Lucretia letters to copy, expecting it would keep her occupied. She soon needed a new project. I gave her buttons to sort by size and color and resumed my sewing. I was not settled more than a minute before Hannah interrupted with one of her "Where is this, and where is that?" questions. I helped her find the thing that is always in the same place.

Back to my needlework, I had lost count of the stitches and needed to start over. I finished marking initials on only one towel before Hannah called for help with the fire.

What if I declared my independence and decided not to cook? What if I sent Hannah to buy a pie from Lansing's bakery?

It is peaceful in the morning with all asleep. I write, read Scripture, and sing:

> O splendor of God's glory bright,
> O thou that bringest light from light,
> O Light of Light, light's living spring,
> O day, all days illumining.

When I hear stirrings from upstairs, my heart falls. My quiet is disturbed. The daily dogtrot of domestic duties begins.

Monday, February 22, 1813

OVER AND OVER

A poem by Betsey Colt Foot.
Dedicated to Anne Bradstreet.

Washing, drying, sweeping, scrubbing,
Polish, mend, and press.

Over and
     Over and
          Over.

Creaming, cutting, grinding, grating,
Pick, pound, and squeeze.

Over and
> Over and
>> Over.

Marking, mending, quilting, tatting
Knit, pearl, and plait.

Over and
> Over and
>> Over.

It is not the muscle strain that wears me out. It is the mental.

Learning, loving, dancing, singing,
Read, write, and teach.

Over and
> Over and
>> Over.

If my mind is free, I am free.

Wednesday, February 24, 1813

Mr. William B. Winne, known to all as Penny Postman Winne, is our letter carrier. Despite prominent missing teeth, he has a perpetual grin. His large eyes are set wide apart, almost to the sides of his head. Walking down the center of the street, he can see both sides at once to quickly match letters to addresses.

Rain and shine, through the cold blustery months and hot, Penny Postman Winne delivers our letters AND the weather forecast. Show the

SILHOUETTE OF
PENNY POSTMAN WINNE

slightest interest and he will also entertain you with the story of his missing teeth or the latest neighborhood news: who is doing what with whom. Today he reports the flying iron horse on Mr. Vanderheyden's weathervane gallops toward Greenbush. Tipping his hat, bowing, and handing me three letters, Mr. Winne warns,

A weather vane that swings to the east
Proclaims no good for man or beast.

VI. Vanderheyden Palace.

FLYING HORSE WEATHERVANE, VANDERHEYDEN PALACE,
85 N. PEARL, IN 1805. JAMES EIGHTS, 1850.

There are two letters from Manhattan for Ebenezer and one for Mr. North from Aldridge's Hotel in Ballston Spa. We will send it on to his brother in Stillwater. Before moving on to the Russells, Mr. Winne's cheery thought is,

If February gives much snow
A fine summer it doth foreshow.

Friday, February 26, 1813

Bad news travels fast. Robert Livingston died early this morning at his home in Clermont. It is impossible to believe the esteemed gentleman from one of New York's oldest families is gone.

Citizens gathered at Webster's Corner to grieve under the Elm tree planted by Robert's cousin Philip Livingston, a signer of the Declaration of Independence.

Robert Livingston is remembered in Albany for his benevolence and generosity. Last July he donated five hundred dollars to the Society for the Relief of Indigent Women and Children.

Steamboats are a common sight on the Hudson now, but I will never forget the shock at my first sighting five years ago. Mrs. Ellison, the Groesbeecks, the Russells, the Roorbacks, and many of our Montgomery Street neighbors packed baskets of bread, cheese, and berries and paraded to the docks to await her arrival. It was a hot August day without a breeze, and we waited patiently in the sun, peering out from wide brimmed hats. Each one wanted to be the first to spot the boat's tricolored pennant on the forward mast, the glorious stars and stripes flying astern.

We felt the dock shake and heard the roar before seeing the North River Steamboat round the bend. She did not tack from side to side, but headed straight toward the dock. No one had seen anything like it. She looked like a monstrous dragon roaring and snorting volumes of black smoke from deep within a dark belly. She was five times longer than any other boat on the Hudson and wider than our house. The water trembled and parted on either side of her bow and her wake ripped at the shoreline. She was equipped with two sails, both furled when she approached. Paddles on either side of the boat turned like wagon wheels propelling her forward at great speed. We were afraid the captain would not be able to stop and we prepared to run, but she slowed just in time and turned alongside the dock. Deckhands threw lines and used four piers to secure her.

Her maiden voyage must have been a terrifying sight for small boats and spectators who had not heard about the invention. Some were convinced it was the Apocalypse and she was the beast from Revelation. There were stories that riverboat skippers steered away from the devil boat, headed straight to shore, and ran for the hills!

The Governor publicly acknowledged Captain Brink's skill navigating around the river's bends, rocks, and shallows. He praised the steamboat's passengers for their courage making the risky voyage and commended Robert Livingston and Robert Fulton for the incredible invention. Livingston graciously accepted the accolades and announced his intention to offer daily steamboat service between Albany and New York. He promised investors a lucrative commercial enterprise. Men and women applauded. Boys cheered. Girls danced.

Some in Albany greeted the new invention with delight, others with scorn. Mr. Groesbeeck shook his head and called it, "a fool's fire ship." He was not impressed the trip to and from New York Harbor took less than three days. "What's the hurry?" he asked anyone who would listen. "It is ridiculous! Fulton's Folly will never replace the sturdy sloop. What is this world coming to?"

NORTH RIVER STEAMBOAT

Captain Arthur Roorback standing nearby knew the answer, but did not share it with Groesbeeck. Roorback recognized an opportunity. After the ceremonies, I watched him walking arm in arm with Captain Brinker to the Tontine Coffee House and, I later learned, to a new career for Roorback: steamboat captain.

Wednesday, March 3, 1813

A new moon

St. Peter's vestrymen have approved the purchase of a hearse and harness. The cost with all the fittings is one hundred sixty dollars and thirty-seven cents. One by one, the hearse will take parishioners to their final resting place.

March is a gloomy month in Albany. Today, as every other day, I face ten thousand chores. Each one of the ten thousand is the same as yesterday, the same as last week, the same as last month, the same as last year! Ebenezer and Samuel hear ten thousand legal concerns, prepare and plead ten thousand defenses. Each one is different.

I direct Hannah and Lucretia to create a well-organized home, but my orchestrations are invisible. It all appears to happen without effort. Every day I spend hours procuring our food, preparing it, and presenting it to the family: corn bread soaked in butter, hard cheese and slices of salted beef. In minutes, nothing remains but the refuse. I clear and clean table and plate over and over and over. I have nothing to show for my labors.

What would Ebenezer and Samuel think if each evening their legal papers were shredded? How would Philip Hooker, Isaac Hutton, or Ezra Ames feel if each night their creations were reduced to rubble? Before St. Peter's hearse carries me away, I yearn to create something of lasting value.

Thursday, March 4, 1813

It is official. The Albany Academy was granted a charter by the New York State Board of Regents. I did not believe the wheels of government could move so fast. It is not surprising since four of the Regents were among the initial proponents of the school. It is official. It will be a school for boys. The Academy will prepare boys for college or business, which are not within the female sphere. Construction of a school building will begin soon. I think they hitched the horse behind the cart. I would first begin classes. Miss Pierce taught in her home for six years before she had a proper school building.

Monday, March 8, 1813

Mrs. Russell wants me to teach Julia to cross-stitch a sampler. She is not good with needlework and has lost patience. The truth is her eyesight has become poor. Unlike her older sisters, Julia has a mind of her own about needlework. She hates it! This upsets Mrs. Russell who says she should not hate and, besides, she needs to count to ten, write her name, and read the Bible and almanac. Julia agrees and says she should not waste her time with a needle. She wants to write with a pen and read books. Should I tell Mrs. Russell Julia is right?

Working with Lucretia on a sampler was also a battle of wills. Lucretia won. I ripped out each of her stitches at least two times. Cleverly, she would ask me to show her how to make each letter and number and the next and the next until I had finished the whole row. All the stitches in the fourth and fifth row are mine. Lucretia had no interest in stitching fancy flowers or birds and the piece remains unfinished, packed away. It was not a good use of her time or mine.

Grandmother Miriam was a skilled seamstress. Orphaned as a young girl, she supported herself in the needle trades. This is not one of Julia's, Lucretia's, or my gifts. In Romans 12, teaching, healing, and prophecy are examples of the gifts God gives. There is no mention of sewing.

I will help Julia with her needlework, and if Mrs. Russell agrees I will have Julia join Lucretia and Hannah for reading, writing, and arithmetic lessons though Ebenezer fears it will give the appearance he is unable to support the family.

Wednesday, March 10, 1813

One gloomy day after another

While the Fowlers support The Albany Academy for William, Mariam will continue attendance at Mrs. Nugent's Seminary for Young Ladies. Emma and Louisa Marvin, Sally Stearns, and Elizabeth Stewart are her other students. Ebenezer believes she would be a good teacher for Lucretia, so yesterday I visited her at her home on Van Schee Street.

She met me at the door wearing a g
shawl. At her throat was a large cabocho
blood. Behind her, I glimpsed, but did
turned his back, retreated into a side roo
behind him. She ushered me to a room fi
and a threadbare carpet.

Mrs. Nugent seems to be a good wo
tion (she did most of the talking) I was su
cational background is weaker than my o
is sparse. She has no globes, no maps, a
the Bible and Webster's Spelling. I did n

Of greater concern is Mrs. Nugent's b
riority, especially over the growing numbe
horrified to hear she called them "the dipp
ture at her seminary, specifically the Presb
and I believe Scripture should be studied
church. There is no "higher and lower" reg;
The road to heaven is open to all.

I was shocked to hear her hold forth
for young ladies. Maintaining an erect p
and smiled. "Mrs. Foot, I'm sure you agree
for girls is to boost their matrimonial valu
today are in danger of becoming too indep
laws of nature remind us women are depe
physically. With too much education, girl
ried. Even worse, too much thinking stimu
to epileptic seizures."

I was stunned. I wanted to say, "I do
lepsy, but I am quite sure it is not from th
independence and marriage, Mrs. Nugent,
toward marriage more by the body than by
better choices if guided by the latter. In a
I want an education for Lucretia that wil
mind I want to adorn. The heart and the r
to women and men."

It v
silent. I
female e

Mr
her pres
tea. Sho
Lucretia

At
door sla

Thursa

The
fireside
fold larg
copyboo

Luc
and gigg
progress
sentence

The
gree

She
Luc

Hast

Tom

Wast

Friday,

Isaa
Bank. H
to subscr

31

ld have felt good to get that off my chest, but no, I kept
uld be futile to engage Mrs. Nugent in a dialogue about
ation. She has no room in her head for new ideas.

Jugent expected to keep me prisoner for a second hour of
ation, but I begged my leave before accepting a third cup of
g me to the door, she said she looked forward to welcoming
o her seminary.

bottom of the steps and on the street, I heard an inside

, *March 11, 1813*

ssells agree to have Julia join Lucretia and Hannah for the
ons. We will not do needlework. I will teach her how to
heets of paper, cut pages and sew them together to make a

ia pulled her chair close to Julia, and the two whispered
d. Hannah fears the younger girls will interfere with her
Once the books are finished, I will assign Hannah a long
ith seven two-syllable words.

d is my shepherd, I shall not want; he maketh me to lie down in
astures: he leadeth me beside the still waters. He restoreth my soul.

nished the sentence quickly and asked for another.
ia and Julia struggled over their sentence of one-syllable words.

nakes waste.

rrow they will finish the sentence.

brings want.

March 12, 1813

Hutton was elected president of Mechanics and Farmers
sons will continue at the Mechanics School, but he plans
e to the new academy. His daughter Margaret will remain

at Catharine B. Thompson's School for Young Ladies along with Judge Kent's daughter Mary and the three Henry girls. Ebenezer thinks Miss Thompson would be a suitable teacher for Lucretia, however she is not accepting new students. I will call on Mrs. Martha Wilson. She has a good reputation.

Tuesday, March 16, 1813

Martha Wilson was the schoolmistress during Albany's short-lived effort at a publicly supported school. She is a widow and lives alone in the same Steuben Street boarding house as Mr. William Tweed Dale, superintendent of the Lancaster School. At one time Mrs. Wilson had many students. Currently only Fanny Roorback, Sarah Davis and Jane Agnes Center are enrolled.

I met with Mrs. Wilson after the girls had left for the day. She is reed thin with skin like onion paper. She held a square of worn flannel over her mouth into which she coughed. Around her neck she wore a pudding cloth the color of mustard.

The sparsely furnished room where we talked is her classroom. A shabby floor cloth covered the bare wood. In the middle of the room there was a pair of straight chairs. She indicated I was to sit in one of the chairs. Since she remained standing, I stood as well.

Along the back wall was a shelf of tattered books on Spelling, Composition, and Geography. Opposite the door was a couch or bed without arms or a back. On a crude table in front of the heavily draped front window was a globe, an abacus, and four hand sewn composition books. She did not invite me to examine them.

I admired the chronometer displayed above the globe and Mrs. Wilson's face brightened. "It belonged to my father, a ship captain from New Bedford."

When I began to tell her of the sea-goers on my side of the family, her smile faded and her eyes narrowed. She wanted to return to the purpose of my visit.

Mrs. Wilson's ideas about educating girls are quite different from Mrs. Nugent's, but just as disturbing. Mrs. Wilson says, "After years and years of experience, I have observed matters of the mind are hard for girls. There are some who are intellectually capable of studying the same academic subjects as boys. Most are not. For those who are capable, higher learning makes it difficult for them to fulfill their role as wife and mother."

Once again I responded silently. "Yes, Mrs. Wilson. I agree. Matters of the mind are hard for children. Both boys and girls require good instruction. Yes, Mrs. Wilson, men prefer women who are obedient and who provide cheerful service for them when they are young and who become a comfort to them when they are old. Yes, for men, children, and the elderly, it is best when women are agreeable caregivers (more accurately caretakers) without a mind of their own."

I remember father lovingly told me I would make some man very happy. As a little girl, I dreamed of doing as he said.

After summarizing her philosophy of education, Mrs. Wilson turned toward the door. "Well, Mrs. Foot, the sun is westering. The day is fading." She had no candles. It was so dark in the room I could barely see my way to the door. "I won't detain you. I would be pleased to teach Lucretia elementary reading, writing, and ciphering."

I feel compassion for the world-weary woman, but I will not subject Lucretia to her schooling. I will not hire Mrs. Wilson to do what I can do better.

On the walk home, I was grateful for an afternoon wind shift that blew away some of Mrs. Wilson's gloom. To clear what remained, I knocked at Mrs. Ellison's door. She is one of the "stop by anytime and tell me all about it" people.

She heard the details of my disappointing visits with Mrs. Nugent and Mrs. Wilson and their belief that educating girls would make it harder for them to adjust to the female role.

Mrs. Ellison was astounded. "Gracious! It is the joy of books and learning that sustains us. Books feed the mind. Learning frees us."

Just then, Mrs. Ellison's boarder appeared. I did not know Mr. Haney had been eavesdropping on our conversation. "Next thing you know, they'll be educating hens and chickens," he announced before slipping out the back door. I looked at Mrs. Ellison for her reaction.

There was a smile then a chuckle then snorting then a horse laugh. It was contagious. We each laughed louder and harder than the other.

"Stop. Stop," we both begged, but it was useless. We laughed 'till it hurt.

Home alone, I was visited by laughter's cousin, despair. Mr. Haney expresses the opinion of many who are not so blunt.

> I am obnoxious to each carping tongue
> Who says my hand a needle better fits.

Anne Bradstreet

Wednesday, March 17, 1813

A full moon, the sap moon

No need for a candle tonight, the moon lights my page. I pen my thoughts in a letter to Miss Pierce. This one I will post.

Thursday, March 18, 1813

The Hudson River is beautiful in summer, framed by mountains and rolling hills. In winter, the frozen river creates a highway for horse and sleigh. The treachery of the river is with the change of seasons, especially winter to spring when a sudden thaw creates a freshet from the mountains.

Waiting for Ebenezer to return at night, I listen to the sound of cracking ice. The rumble is like thunder except deeper, more intense, and unrelenting. Shoreline ice thaws first, then large heavy plates of ice crack and separate. Wind and the current drive the ice blocks to the banks of the river and create a wall. Water spills over the pile up and there can be flooding.

Monday, March 22, 1813

Wind and rain

Lucretia told Penny Postman Winne she saw a robin on Saturday. His response?

The March wind doth blow and we shall have snow,
And what will poor robin do then, poor thing?
He'll sit in a barn and keep himself warm
And hide his head under his wing, poor thing.

March is well-named after the Roman warrior god. It is hard to believe this cold, stormy day is the first of spring. Three days ago, blocks of ice broke free and sailed recklessly down river and out to sea. The river is open to navigation for those brave enough to fight wind and waves plus dodge the flotsam and jetsam from upstream: tree trunks, carriage wheels, and barn boards.

Saturday afternoon we escaped from the homes that held us captive all winter. Unfortunately our freedom was short-lived. Mother Nature toys with us. She tests our patience. She sent us back, to sit in a barn and hide our head under our wing.

For me, the problem with bad weather is first suffering through the rain, cold, sleet or heat. Then suffering through tedious conversations about the weather. "Brrrr, it's cold." Really? I didn't notice. "Did you ever hear such wind?" No. "Will we ever see spring?" I doubt it. "Will it ever stop raining?" Yes. "This weather is killing me." No reply needed.

March should be

A host of golden daffodils
Beside the lake, beneath the trees
Fluttering and dancing in the breeze.

There are no March daffodils in Albany. The city is behind in everything, including the weather. In Albany, March means six more weeks of dirty snowdrifts, rutted roads, and heavy coats.

I yearn for the true harbinger of spring, the bluebird. "Girls," Miss Pierce said, "notice that the bluebird only shows her colors when she flies."

Tuesday, March 23, 1813

General Stephen Van Rensselaer, President of The Albany Academy's Board of Trustees, has pledged two thousand five hundred dollars to the school. More donations are expected.

STEVEN VAN RENSSELAER, PAINTING BY GILBERT STUART

Thursday, March 25, 1813

If we had no winter, the spring would not be so pleasant;
If we did not sometimes taste of adversity,
Prosperity would not be so welcome.

Anne Bradstreet

We thought this would be the year without spring. Finally, the walls of winter collapsed and Zephyr, the fragrant soft wind of Spring, revived us. Fern fronds have broken through the shady portions of our garden. Neighbors open their doors and we look at each other in amazement. It feels like the first spring we have ever experienced.

Heavy rains cleaned the streets. Dutch women will perform the ceremonial sweeping of State Street, a tradition I will leave to them. I have enough spring cleaning inside 36 Montgomery Street, but will wait until the leaves have finished blossoming. Mother Nature has set us free. I want to admire her handiwork.

Saturdays when Ebenezer and I were students in Litchfield, we would put our books aside and ride to Mother Hoy's beer and cake shop, north of town on the Goshen Road. We talked of his latest idea or mine. I thought Ebenezer would always seek my opinion on important matters, but lately his head is bent over stacks of legal papers. He wrestles with "whereas and wherefores."

"He needs a break," my friend Mrs. Allen says. "You and Ebenezer should hire a carriage and ride to the Cohoes Cataract. Spring is the best time of year to view it." She showed me a small book of poems by the Irish poet Thomas Moore written when he visited the Falls. "Keep the book as long as you wish," Mrs. Allen said. "His poetry is in my heart."

COHOES FALLS 1778

Saturday, March 27, 1813

Sunny and warm

I was surprised Ebenezer agreed to set his papers aside and hire a carriage to take Lucretia, Hannah, Julia, and me on an excursion.

Nothing created by humans is as magnificent as the Cohoes waterfall. Cascades of white water drop straight down with such force that the spray creates mounds of froth. Behind the mist are rainbow prisms. Standing before the spectacle, my ten thousand concerns washed away and I felt at peace. Lucretia, Hannah, and Julia had ten thousand questions.

Hannah wanted to know where the water comes from. Ebenezer explained, "When the snow melts in the Adirondacks, water rushes into brooks, streams, and the river."

Julia asked, "Why is it so tall?" Ebenezer replied a cataract is created when water descends from a great height to lower ground.

Lucretia was puzzled. "Are there waterfalls across the river in Greenbush?" Ebenezer told her, "Greenbush has many brooks and streams flowing into the Hudson, but a real waterfall occurs only when water descends from tall cliffs of hard rock onto softer rock below. The higher and wider the rock, the more dramatic the waterfall."

The girls wanted to know where the water goes.

Ebenezer used a stick to draw a map in the soft dirt. "The water flows down from the mountains into the Mohawk River and the Hudson. It continues past Albany to Manhattan and out to the Atlantic Ocean." While he was speaking, the trunk of a giant tree that had been stuck at the top of the falls, suddenly broke free and crashed into the fast moving water below. Hannah wondered if the Hudson River could rise and wash us away.

Ebenezer placed a round stone on the back of his hand to demonstrate gravity. "Albany is at the same level as the Ocean. There is no drop."

"Why does the water keep coming? Will it ever stop? Could the ocean rise, overflow, and flood the world?"

Ebenezer launched into an explanation of the cycle of water, but the girls had lost interest and turned to my basket of biscuits, boiled eggs and hard cheese. Hannah wanted to feed the dappled horse hitched to our hired carriage, but Ebenezer warned her away. "Don't go near that horse. He could kick you in the head and knock you senseless." He is afraid of horses.

Before returning home, I recited Thomas Moore's poem Written at the Cohoes Falls of the Mohawk River. The first one to memorize my favorite stanza will receive an award.

One only prayer I dare to make
As onward thus my course to take;
Oh be my falls as bright as thine!
May heavens' relenting rainbow shine
Upon the mist that circles me,
As soft as now it hangs o`er thee!

Wednesday, March 31, 1813

At the Ladies Church Society meetings we do not stray off a narrow path of proper topics: the Holy Bible, Reverend Clowes' sermon, caring for our husbands, teaching Christian values to our children, service to those less fortunate, the recently deceased, and the weather. On rare occasions, the ladies veer off the path and talk about the absent ones. This explains why our meetings are always well attended.

Miss Brenton is the absent one today. "Undoubtedly, she forgot," said Mrs. Brown. "Miss Brenton forgot about Annabella's lessons on Monday and this was not the first time. She is probably fine, but I will check on her this afternoon."

Further discussion was halted when Revered Clowes arrived and directed the ladies to begin preparing the church for Holy Week. Seats in church are reserved by the status, age and financial generosity of parishioners. Work assignments are made in the same manner.

-Sweep the floors (Mrs. Brown) with special attention to the nave and altar (Mrs. Henry).

-Clean the mahogany pews (a big task for Mrs. Fowler and myself).

-Polish the Redstone Organ (Only Mr. Hochstrasser's wife can be trusted with this job).

-Arrange greenery for the Altar (Mrs. Ellison).

-Shine the Queen Anne Holy Communion Silver (The honor always goes to Mrs. Gill).

Before the closing hymn Mrs. Brown left to check on Miss Brenton. We later learned she was visiting her elderly sister who lives south of the Van Rensselaer home at Cherry Hill.

The ladies (even Mrs. Gill, whose hauteur can be intimidating), are very nice, but they do not share what they think about matters of importance such as President Madison's War, church finances, or expenditures of The Common Council. It is not polite to disagree. Do fathers, husbands, and the church plant all their opinions? Are differences permitted? It is impossible to know what is behind the cloaks of propriety that women wear into society. We do not invite each other into the back rooms of our homes, heads, or hearts.

I share back rooms with Mrs. Ellison. I trust her with my opinions about educating girls. She is a "judge not lest you be judged" person.

Her advice today is, "Take one small step. Gather your neighbors with daughters. Begin the discussion about a school. There may be others who feel as you."

Thursday, April 1, 1813

A new moon

I saw a bluebird this morning. Penny Postman Winne promises it will be sunny and fair all day.

> When wooly clouds come this way,
> There'll be no rain to spoil the day.

When the weather in Litchfield was terrible, we complained to Miss Pierce who would reprimanded us saying, "Keep it sunny in your head, and rain will never spoil the day."

Hannah received the prize for memorizing the stanza from the Cohoes Falls. I placed a crown of blue plaited ribbon on her head. "May you continue to adorn your mind with beauty."

I think about what is in my head the way others think about furnishings and fashion. Sir Joshua Reynolds' portrait of Maria, Duchess of Gloucester, is in my mind this morning. The Duchess leans against a Corinthian column and gazes toward heaven. Her thick copper hair is coiled on her head in the style of a laurel wreath. Her face, hands, and throat glow. What great thoughts does she ponder?

MARIA DUTCHESS OF GLOUCESTER

In my mind, I examine the delicate brush marks of the British painter. I imagine stroking the folds of Maria's velvet gown the color of terra cotta. I inhale the fragrance of the warm riverbank soil. The gentle river current soothes my soul. Will she follow the path to the water? Does she understand the courage of the cypress that leans into the coming cold or the young oak that does not fear losing its golden leaves with the approach of winter? Does she have faith in the benevolent cycles of nature? Does she fear her future?

Sir Joshua Reynolds' painting elevates and adorns my mind. I remember Mrs. Ellison's advice, "Gather your neighbors with daughters. Begin a discussion. There may be others who feel as you."

Saturday, April 3, 1813

I first saw Penny Postman Winne when he turned onto Montgomery from Steuben. He took forever stopping at the Goulds, Roorbacks, the Browns and Mrs. Ellison who rarely receives a letter.

This morning, it was the glorious weather that explained the delay. Pointing upward, Mr. Winne noted,

> The higher the clouds
> The better the weather.

He doffed his hat and bowed before me as if I were the Queen of England. When I saw the envelope, my heart jumped.

Mrs. Ebenezer Foot, 36 Montgomery Street, Albany, New York

I looked at the letter for a long time before opening and reading it in private.

South Street
Litchfield, Connecticut
March 20, 1813

Dearest Betsey,

I received your letter of 18 March. Thank the Lord we are well. Our winter was severe, but weather is part of God's plan which we do not question. I appreciate the kind words to your dear instructress. As you know, it is the student who makes the teacher.

I am happy to learn your family is well and Hannah is slowly adjusting to your home. I remember her sister Eliza was an eager learner, unlike her brothers, and expect this is true of Hannah.

Please accept my sincere condolences at the loss of Mr. North. You must thank God for the time you were blessed with his friendship and inspiration.

You have asked my advice on the school situation in Albany. At Litchfield Female Academy we are united like sisters so I am not surprised you are confronting a diversity of opinion regarding female education. I understand your challenge. I am aware how tall our New England girls stand above the unfortunate Dutch girls in the Hudson Valley. Litchfield Female Academy attracts girls from many geographic areas that do not believe in the democratic value of education. Two years ago Mary Clark came to us from Albany and has made remarkable progress.

Women do not want to usurp the role of men in business or politics. They want to exert a moral influence within the home. Although our sphere is domestic, it has great value. It is women who teach the ideals of The Democratic Republic to husbands and sons who are now or will soon be the military, political, and business leaders of The Union. Europe's leaders predict our Republic will fail. It will succeed because of her women.

I know you remember Mabel and Idea Strong from Addison, Vermont. Do you recall Mabel's husband invited Idea and me to set up a Female Academy in Middlebury? I am sorry to give you the sad news that Idea passed away not long after launching the endeavor. Emma Hart took over, but closed the school after her marriage to Dr. Willard. It was his financial reversal that inspired Emma Willard to reopen the Middlebury Female Academy in their beautiful brick home on Main Street. The Middlebury bank Dr. Willard owned had been robbed and he was duty bound to repay the depositors. At first it hurt Dr. Willard's pride, but eventually he became supportive.

Your boarding sister Almira Collins now teaches art for our girls. Louisa Wait is our music mistress. Reverend Beecher's daughter Catharine has advanced from student to division head and will soon be an assistant teacher. In a few years we will enroll Catharine's younger sisters, Mary and Harriet.

Betsey dear, look within for the guidance you seek. There are solutions when the cause is noble. Be patient. Prejudice dissolves slowly. Pushing against tradition meets resistance. An uphill climb requires small steps. Mr. Foot and many other industrious men are swarming from New England into the frontier states. They want their children to have the good schools they left behind. I am sure there are others who feel as you do. Begin the discussion.

You must be fearless in your efforts on behalf of Albany girls. Serving God requires the intellectual and emotional courage you gained at Litchfield Female Academy. Please let me know of your first steps. The job that's never started takes the longest. I stand by ready to help you any way I can.

Warmest personal regards to you, Mr. Foot, Samuel, Lucretia, and Hannah.

Semper et in aeternum,
Sarah Pierce

Monday, April 5, 1813

I read the letter three times before locking it away. First, it was a quick reading to be assured Miss Pierce was happy to hear from me. The second reading was later in the evening. That was a mistake because then I could not sleep. My head was filled with images of Almira, Louisa, and Catharine teaching with Miss Pierce. After the third, deep reading this morning, I am thinking about "A Noble Cause" and "Serving God" and "Small Steps."

Miss Pierce is right. Fear is the enemy I battle. At Litchfield Female Academy we were a perfect union. I have not learned how to respond to differences of opinion.

Tuesday, April 6, 1813

"Begin, be bold, and venture to be wise."

Today's letter in The Albany Gazette is from a citizen who has the same advice as Miss Pierce. He urges the city to BEGIN; be generous to the new Academy. He asks that funds be designated for a decent school building and salary provided for a qualified headmaster. A few large donors, such as Stephen Van Rensselaer, have stepped forward, but most citizens have been slow to subscribe.

I believe it is the parents' responsibility to educate their children. What if the parents are not financially able? What if the parents have daughters? Should citizens without children contribute because it benefits the whole community? What are the qualifications of a principal teacher? What is a proper salary? Who decides? How important is the school building? Do important buildings need impressive architecture?

The citizen's advice is to "begin" and "be bold." Boldness is bred out of ladies. We are taught to address our concerns in the private sphere. St. Paul says women should not speak out in Church. He says nothing about speaking up at home. This is where I will begin.

Thursday, April 8, 1813

It took courage for me to invite my neighbors Mrs. Gould, Mrs. Scrymser, and Mrs. Groesbeeck for afternoon tea. They have all lived on Montgomery Street for several years, but I do not know them well. I decided to begin with them because their daughters are not being tutored outside the home. What are their beliefs about educating girls?

All, except for Mrs. Groesbeeck, accepted with pleasure "my kind invitation." Her daughter Catharine returned my note with "regrets" scribbled on the back. It's strange I have not seen Mrs. Groesbeeck since late last summer. Mrs. Gould asked if she might bring her friend Mrs. Knower. She is often alone since Mr. Knower has a hat factory west of Albany.

The ladies arrived together. Before opening the door, I said a silent prayer. Be strong. Be of good courage. Be not afraid.

While I poured tea, Mrs. Gould grumbled about the weather and the terrible condition of the streets. Mrs. Knower admired our Lucretia portrait. "Such a pretty girl, but she looks so serious. When she learns to smile she will be a beautiful young woman. She will make some fortunate man very happy."

Mrs. Scrymser was quiet.

Mrs. Gould seized upon a short silence to talk about her son Charles. "Mr. Gould and I plan to send Charles to The Academy. He is not interested in the hardware business. He wants to become a doctor." Mrs. Gould questions the expense of an education for Eliza. "Why spend money on tuition for her when I can teach her at home? After she marries, her husband will take care of her."

Mrs. Gould does not think about the plight of widows. It has been over ten years since Mrs. Ellison's husband passed. She still worries whether she will be able to keep her home. My own mother was widowed at age 39. Families in Hadley helped our family before she married John Walker. He is a good provider, but I'm sorry to say, he adds little to the happiness of the family.

Mrs. Knower agreed with Mrs. Gould that her daughter will enjoy the protection of marriage. She wants Cornelia to be an asset to her husband. "Mr. Knower and I are considering Mrs. Nugent's Seminary for Young Ladies. I plan to visit the school before Easter."

When I heard the Nugent name, my hands trembled. My knees became weak. I had trouble following the ladies' conversation. Fortunately, I had returned the pot to the tea table or there might have been a spill.

Mrs. Scrymser told the ladies that Katrina is helpful at the grocery store. "She loves numbers. She sometimes corrects her father's mistakes."

Mrs. Gould could not withhold her disapproval. "Women should not be smarter than men. Strengthening Katrina's mathematical mind could draw attention to her father's deficit."

I wanted to shout, "The solution is to educate both, not keep both ignorant!" Instead, I cleared my throat and accepted compliments for my scones. Nothing was settled. I did not talk about my desires for Lucretia. I lost my resolve to bring up the school subject. I retreated to the family recipe for scones. The secret is to not over-mix the dough.

THE COLT RECIPE FOR SCONES

2 cups flour, 2 teaspoons baking powder, 1/2 teaspoon salt, 5 tablespoons sweet butter, 1 egg, 1/2 cup cream. Shape the dough to resemble The Stone of Destiny, the coronation throne of Scottish Kings. Bake in a hot oven until done.

After the ladies departed, I sat in the front room, alone with my questions. The Groesbeecks' view about educating girls remains a mystery. Does Mr. Gould agree with his wife about Eliza? Is Mrs. Knower aware that I visited and rejected Mrs. Nugent? Is Mrs. Scrymser proud of her daughter's abilities? Is Mr. Scrymser? Would Katrina like to pursue the study of mathematics?

Looking closely at the Lucretia portrait, I suddenly had doubts. I always viewed her expression as one of confidence. Is she too serious? Am I wrong about an academy education for her? Should I teach her to smile and make her husband and children happy?

Six years ago, a painter came to Troy from the Berkshires. I think his name was James Brown. Families with means commissioned him for a family portrait. We did not have the money for this extravagance, but he made a persuasive appeal to Ebenezer.

"I do not need to remind you, Mr. Foot, that your lovely daughter will not be two years old forever. For the modest fee of five dollars, you can have a portrait you will treasure forever. It will become a Foot family heirloom. It will be handed down from generation to generation."

This was an appealing idea to Ebenezer since there are no heirlooms in the Foot family. More convincing was what Mr. Brown said next. "A painting of Lucretia will elevate your status, Mr. Foot. It will adorn the walls of your home."

I did not support the expenditure, but admit that today the painting is one of my most treasured possessions.

Lucretia stands on a hilltop with one foot forward. Like an angel, she is halfway between heaven and earth. She towers over the trees and hazy landscape behind her. A stream meanders to the fertile, unspoiled valley below. Rosy cotton-clouds float above a distant blue mountain. "Mount Greylock at the dawn of a day in spring," Mr. Brown explained. "The cloudless sky above promises the day, and her future, will be fair."

A petite Josephine, she holds a garland of pink roses, careful to avoid the thorns. Two of the roses are in full bloom. One is in bud. Lucretia's glossy auburn curls are arranged in the latest French style. Her cheeks glow, and Mr. Brown highlighted the dimple on her chin "where an angel kissed you." She wears a gossamer dress embroidered with tiny flowers. Under the ruched neckline is a pink sash tied in the back with a bow. I let down the hem on that dress four times. Just last year it became too tight and I packed it away with the pink satin slippers.

Lucretia's dark eyes penetrate the viewer. Her lips are closed. She is not posing for the artist; she is at one with the viewer. Mr. Brown captured her inner light, a spirit in harmony with nature. I pray she will forever radiate love, beauty, and kindness.

Friday, April 9, 1813

Julia makes slow progress on her reading and writing. Her mind wanders. She distracts Lucretia and annoys Hannah with descriptions of the fashions she sees in church. After copying the day's sentence, she sketches the dress and hat she dreams of wearing for Easter. The design is shocking.

To be a la mode, even on the coldest days, grown women wear dresses so thin they resemble a petticoat. Necklines have dropped and waistlines have crept up to just under the bosom. Men satirize them:

Shepherds, I have lost my waist,
Have you seen my body?
Sacrificed to modern taste,
I'm quite a hoddy-doddy.

Hats for church are decorated with exotic plumage. Weekday hats are made from braided straw. According to the popular ditty, people and animals will go hungry if crops continue to be used for adornment. We might end up having to eat our hats!

What a fine harvest this gay season yields!
Some female heads appear like stubble-fields.
Who now of threatened famine dare complain
When every female forehead teems with grain?

Have we gained freedom from the British only to be enslaved by the tyrants of French fashion? The treasures of the world can be ours if we put them in, not on, our head.

My mind also wanders. What will Mrs. Knower think of Mrs. Nugent? Will they enroll Cornelia? Could I tutor Katrina Scrymser? Would Ebenezer agree? Would I be the subject of Mrs. Gould's ridicule? Is something wrong with Mrs. Groesbeeck?

Saturday, April 10, 1813

For a second time Cousin John has been elected to the New York State Assembly. This time he will move Abigail and the children from Greenville. Albany is a good location while he is serving as a surgeon with New York's Fifth Cavalry Regiment.

I look forward to their move. Maria, age twelve, is currently at a school in Goshen and boarding with her Elliot cousins. She will return to Albany at the end of the spring term. John says Reverend Clowes has a tutor for Maria. I wonder who he has in mind? Edwin will attend the new Academy. Adelaide, their "late in life chick" is only two.

Sunday, April 11, 1813

Palm Sunday

Palm Sunday begins Holy Week. When Jesus made his triumphal entry into Jerusalem at Passover, his followers waved palms, the Roman symbol of victory. Since there are no palms in Albany, we wave willow branches.

Thursday, April 15, 1813
Full moon, the pink moon

Mrs. Hochstrasser calls Maundy Thursday "Grundonnerstag," or Green Thursday. The foods she serves are green: peas, spinach, and string beans. Church vestments on Maundy Thursday are green, the symbol of renewal and transformation.

There will be no work on Good Friday, the most solemn day of the church year. I bake rolls for breakfast and decorate them with icing in the shape of a cross.

Sunday, April 18, 1813
Easter Sunday

Easter is the first Sunday after the full moon following the spring equinox. Since the date is different every year, it is called the Moveable Feast. It is a day of celebration unlike any other! At sunrise, church bells ring. St. Peter's Queen Anne Bell is the loudest and most beautiful.

In every neighborhood, mothers, fathers and children spill out of their homes to greet one another and call out the Good News: "Christ is risen! Christ is risen!" Men put business aside. Women are freed from their over and over tasks. From villages near and far, carriages, filled with scrubbed clean families, roll into town. Single men, also washed and brushed, ride in from the country and hitch their horses to posts along State Street. Albany's population is double what it was the week before.

People head to different churches, although some spend the morning at the Tontine Coffee House. After church, everyone gathers on Market Street to exchange greetings and catch up on news from family and friends, some of whom we have not seen since Christmas.

It would have been a lovely day except for one unpleasant incident, too insignificant to write about except that it continues to hang in my head. After church, our family left St. Peter's and joined the parade to Market Street. At Websters' Corner, I spotted Mr. and Mrs. Nugent coming from The Presbyterian Church. They were not arm in arm like other couples. Mr. Nugent walked briskly ahead of his wife. She lagged behind, head down. He did not notice me, but her eyes and mine locked when we came face to face. When I wished her "Good Easter Morning," a strange thing happened. She stopped abruptly and stared at me as if she did not understand what I said. An invisible but palpable force rose up from deep within her soul and pierced my whole body. Painful seconds of silence passed before she looked away and hurried on. When the blood and breath in my body returned, I caught up with Ebenezer. I did not mention the experience. He would have said it was my imagination and a distant witness would draw the same conclusion. I know it was real. I felt like she had thrown a shroud around me.

At the end of the day I tried to furnish my mind with the memory of church bells, Easter flowers, and happy families, but nothing could dislodge Mrs. Nugent.

Thursday, April 22, 1813

Spring, like fall, is one long chore. Half through scrubbing off the winter grime inside, I stepped outside to catch a breath of fresh air. Instead, I got an ear-full of gossip from Mrs. Gould about Mrs. Van Antwerp. Mother taught me to not pry into other people's business. She said, "If you wait long enough, you will find out."

It is true what many of us privately suspected. Mrs. Brown told Mrs. Gould that Mrs. Van Antwerp, who runs a grocery on North Pearl Street, is in the state of ladies who love their lords. The only trouble is her lord passed away two years ago. Tongues wag. How could this happen? She is not known to be free with her favors. Why? Who is the father? Now what? People claim to be concerned about Mrs. Van Antwerp and the children, but they do nothing more than talk.

When a neighbor brings me unfortunate news, I recoil. I do not want to join the parade of talebearers. I will help Mrs. Van Antwerp by giving her an order for groceries.

Tuesday, April 27, 1813

Mrs. Knower had the same idea as I, to support Mrs. Van Antwerp. After completing our purchases she asked to speak with me in private. Mrs. Knower seemed upset, and I assumed it was about Mrs. Van Antwerp. I did not want to be drawn into ugly gossip and backed away, but she steered me out to the street and began to tell me of her visit to Mrs. Nugent.

"It was awful," Mrs. Knower said clearing tears from her throat. "I arrived early and was at the bottom of the steps when I heard Mr. Nugent shouting. He was shouting terrible words. He was so loud I heard him on the street. There was a banging noise and muffled sounds from a woman. I cannot be sure if it was Mrs. Nugent because I had never spoken with her. The whole incident was frightening, and I left without rapping at the door. Mrs. Fowler told me you visited Mrs. Nugent. That is why I am telling you about this. "

I thought about my visit with Mrs. Nugent in early March and the encounter with her at Easter. I decided not to share it with Mrs. Knower but listened to what she had to say.

"I was not prepared. No one told me about Mrs. Nugent. I learned later that Mrs. Fowler's daughter had revealed nothing of what was happening at the Nugent home. Mrs. Fowler said in mid-March Mariam resisted going to school and acted strangely when she returned. At first Mrs. Fowler thought it was a case of spring fever after the long winter. Eventually Mariam told her of Mr. Nugent's outbursts and how he terrified his wife and the girls. The Marvins, the Stewarts, and Dr. Stearns have all removed their daughters from Mrs. Nugent's Seminary."

Before I could reply, Mrs. Knower continued. "Mrs. Nugent has no students left. I know you are searching for a school for Lucretia so I thought you should know. Mr. Knower and I want

Cornelia to be successful in her sphere, but we do not know what to do or where to turn."

I could console Mrs. Knower, but offer no solutions. I have none.

Thursday, April 29, 1813

I have not told Ebenezer or anyone about Mrs. Nugent. When I bring up the matter of a school for Lucretia, Ebenezer responds absent-mindedly, "In good time, in good time." For the past month he has been preoccupied with the race for Governor. Tompkins and Tayler are running against the Federalist Stephen Van Rensselaer. Samuel is unsympathetic. He rolls his eyes and says, "Save your breath to cool your porridge." He pledged twenty dollars to The Albany Academy.

Yesterday Mrs. Russell inspected Julia's copy book and was impressed with the improvement she has made in six weeks. The verse the girls copied yesterday contained three two-syllable words. Mrs. Russell could not believe it was her daughter's hand that wrote,

> Lay not up for yourselves treasures upon earth, where moth and rust doth corrupt, and where thieves break through and steal.

She did not ask where one should lay up treasures. She is pleased Julia is being educated to read Scripture and to write legibly, but she has the same fear as Mrs. Nugent.

"With too much education the girls may not want to marry. Confidentially," she whispered so Julia and Lucretia could not hear, "higher education might damage their..." I had to read her lips to understand that she said, "damage their reproductive organs."

She closed her eyes, inhaled slowly, sighed deeply, shook her head, took my hand and lifted her eyes towards heaven. "How sad," she said. "How sad," she repeated, "the Good Lord only blessed you and Mr. Foot with one child. And, how sad your only child is a daughter."

I confess the Good Lord blessed me with the ability to stifle a laugh. Now I pray He blesses me with courage to persist with Ebenezer about a school for girls.

Friday, April 30, 1813

The second new moon in a month is a black moon

The votes have been counted. Daniel D. Tompkins with 43,324 votes will be our next Governor. Stephen Van Rensselaer received 39,718 votes. It was close. There are disputes about the ballots and final count.

Saturday, May 1, 1813

May Day

The first of May has magical properties. A splash of dew this morning keeps the face beautiful all year. Lucretia and her friends join other "Mayers" to fill small baskets with lilies and violets. They tie them on doorknobs, rap on the door, and hide to watch the look of delight when the door is opened.

Mrs. Gould planned a May Day celebration. The girls will dress in white and wear a crown of flowers. They will dance around a maypole wrapped in pale pink and fern green ribbons.

> Ho! The merry first of May
> Brings the dance and blossoms gay
> To make of life a holiday.

Some view May Day as the heathen worship of the Goddess of spring. Instead, they say,

> Take the Bible in your hand
> Read a chapter through
> And when the Day of Judgment comes
> The Lord will think of you.

I do not worship Flora, but I believe the Lord wants us to celebrate spring, the first season of the yearly cycle; the sowing season.

Tuesday, May 4, 1813

Matthew Gill informed Cousin John about a vacant four-story brick home north of the Market House. When Abigail saw it she was shocked. She thinks it odd there is no front garden. "The house sits smack on the street with the gable end in front. It is perched so close to the neighbor, it practically touches. Our front window looks directly into the window of the house across the street. Can you imagine? There is no privacy. The alley between the houses is so narrow two stout ladies cannot walk side by side. Our neighbors are merchants," she explained as if I did not know. "They live behind their store with a warehouse above. Cargo is hoisted to the upper floors with a creaking, groaning pulley system! There are horses snorting and men shouting orders. All day long there is a racket of carts and wagons rattling up and down the street." Abigail dramatizes her comments clapping her hands over her ears, snorting, shouting, groaning, and rattling.

She did not mention the smells. At the Market House, butchers hang slabs of meat on hooks and farmers sell chickens, eggs, milk, and cheese. Buyer and seller haggle. In the afternoon, men gather in small groups to smoke and argue about politics.

Abigail moans, "Where are the white clapboard houses with a pretty green door in the center and a proper brass door knocker? Where can I have a kitchen garden? Where is the stately Congregational Church with its spire? Where is the town green?"

Abigail is outgoing. She will adjust when she makes friends in Albany and when Maria returns from the Elliott's in Goshen. She will like the social life of the front stoop. There is always someone to talk with.

Thursday, May 6, 1813

Old Mr. Scrymser is like many folks removed from the world of work. He plants himself on his front stoop where there is a good view of life passing by. To anyone who stops, he tells tales of the way it was in the good old days, with the good old church, and the good old king. He is not clear about the details of current events. Whatever the issue, he is against it. He criticizes the cartmen who drive too fast, Mayor Van Rensselaer's profligate spending, gutter laws, and street boys out of control. He has all the solutions and hands them out for free!

Today he groused about the cost of the new Academy. "All that money and it will only be for boys. My granddaughter Katrina is smarter than her brothers and all the boys in Albany put together. She is even smarter than her father, my own son." Before I had a chance to reply, Mr. Scrymser spotted Mrs. Brown's mother-in-law coming toward us. "That woman is a contrarian," Mr. Scrymser said. "If I think a door is too wide, she will say, 'That's ridiculous, it is too narrow.' The truth is all doors are too narrow for Mrs. Brown!" He couldn't stop laughing. Old Mrs. Brown thought he was laughing with delight to see her.

It's true. Mrs. Brown's song is an Oratorio in D minor of unleavened bread and bitter herbs. She is the principal mourner at every funeral. She praises The Lord and notes every detail of corpse and coffin. I decided to continue on my errands.

Mrs. Ellison, widowed for many years, is different. She collects the driftwood of society. Her current boarder is Jacob Haney who washed ashore last autumn. He is now a restored man.

Yesterday's Gazette announced the marriage of Mr. Lewis Grant to Mrs. Bussee of Guilderland. Both are 70 years old, proving it is never too late for love. I hope the union will add to their mutual pleasure and give them many, many years of happiness.

I do not want to become the old woman who wags a finger at the world going by. I do not want to entertain myself and bore others with the details of a neighbor's downfall and demise. I want to live a life of purpose.

Saturday, May 8, 1813

"What if I put good money into Wilhelm's education and he dies?" This is Mr. Groesbeeck's response when asked to contribute to The Albany Academy. He is known for his thrift. Wilhelm is known for his pranks. At The Albany Academy, it is likely he would learn about the hijinks of previous students. Peter Gansevoort's friend, Mr. James Fenimore Cooper is still remembered at Yale for capturing a donkey and tying it to the lectern at the front of his classroom moments before the ceremonial entrance of a bombastic lecturer. When he was Professor Silliman's lab assistant, Jemmie learned of the explosive qualities of heated potassium and charcoal. Igniting gunpowder at a fellow student's door caused President Dwight to dismiss him from the college. Fortunately, no one was hurt, but there was extensive damage to the newly refurbished Connecticut Hall.

Judge Kent admits although he was at the head of his class at Yale, the "test of scholarship at that day was contemptible." Four out of five of his fellow classmates died in midlife as drunkards.

Perhaps Mr. Groesbeeck is smarter than I thought. He could save money by letting Wilhelm skip college and go straight to the bottle? Or, Mr. Groesbeeck could educate his daughter Catharine. Her head is aways in a book and she does not imbibe.

Monday, May 10, 1813

The Seldens are visiting from Saybrook and we saw them at church. They say the war is heating up along the Connecticut coast. Earlier in the spring, British warships entered Long Island Sound to blockade ports and burn ships. The Seldens assured me the Ely family, who live at the ferry landing in Lyme, are safe.

They attacked New London and this is the second time. No one can ever forget the terrible scoundrel Benedict Arnold who was born in nearby Norwich. He was an officer in the Continental Army and a hero at Saratoga, but he turned coat and joined British forces against his countrymen when he plotted to betray West Point. His raid on New London was against his own family and friends. After torching ships anchored in the Thames River and warehouses along the wharf, the traitor commanded, "Soldiers, do your duty." He ordered his men to "rout out residents, ransack their homes, and set fire to the remains."

Soldiers do your duty? Is it your duty to burn and kill? Eighty men were slaughtered. Widows and orphans were left with no means of support. War is a perpetual go-round of attack and counterattack. Is war ever justified? God forgive me, but sometimes I think only when the blood in men's veins is replaced with water will there be an end to war, or when it is mothers who make the decision to fight.

Saturday, May 15, 1813

A full moon, the flower moon

If Mother Nature shows her temper in March, she repents in May. Our garden lilac is in full bloom. The aroma is intoxicating.

This afternoon Ebenezer, Samuel, Lucretia, and Hannah walked to Quay Street to admire The Lady Richmond. Built by the New York shipbuilder Charles Brown, the steamboat is breathtaking. Her hull is painted green with flourishes of gold. The wheelhouse is mahogany. She is one hundred fifty-four feet. On the dock she takes the space of five sloops and is wider than our house!

I looked forward to a rare and precious afternoon alone. I took out my company teapot painted with bluebirds and set it on a tray next to the teacup I use for special occasions. Hand-painted on the cup is a Japanese lady wearing a blue kimono. She sits under an umbrella of cherry blossoms. I poured Souchong tea into the cup, rearranged the cushions on Ebenezer's chair and was about to sit down with a book when there was a knock at the door. Puff. My plans evaporated. Dear Mrs. Ellison had seen everyone leave the house and thought I might be feeling lonesome.

I am never lonely when I'm alone.

When she handed me her hat and shawl, I knew the visit would be a long one. I offered her a cup of tea hoping she would decline. She accepted. I returned my precious cup to the back of the cupboard, took out two others, and led Mrs. Ellison to the front room. She settled herself in Ebenezer's chair.

About this time every year, Mrs. Ellison talks about her husband who died eleven years ago. Reverend Ellison was a respected preacher, teacher, and scholar. He prepared many students for entrance to Yale College. He died at the age of forty-three and is buried in the Episcopal section of the cemetery.

As predicted, after the conventional pleasantries, Mrs. Ellison steered the conversation in the direction of her late husband. I resigned myself to an afternoon of plain and grave conversation about his great character, sharp mind, and good deeds. I feared she would extend her stay way beyond my patience. She does not know how to end a visit. In the afternoon there is no ringing of a "time to go home" bell.

Mrs. Ellison shocked me by saying she wanted to share a troubling secret about her husband. I was not sure I wanted to hear it, but she persisted. Late in their marriage, Reverend Ellison confided he had been married in England before coming to New York. He left a wife in Newcastle. His hazy past and sudden appearance in Albany had always been a mystery to the parishioners.

Mrs. Ellison said she and her husband enjoyed a happy marriage. They promised to be with each other throughout eternity. His secret had not bothered her until recently. She is thinking about her own mortality and is distraught.

"Is the other Mrs. Ellison still living or has she joined my husband and taken my place at his side? Did he pledge to spend eternity with her? Has he confessed to her he is wed to another? What will happen when the three of us meet on the other side?" Mrs. Ellison wept. "You wouldn't believe that at one time I was a beauty. My hair is thin and completely gray. My face is so wrinkled that he will not recognize me."

I did not know how to reply. She has told me many times that her husband looks down on St. Peter's Church from heaven. I wanted to tell her if this is true, he has also watched her age. He will recognize her. I held her hand, but could not allay her fears. No mortal can answer her questions.

I cannot imagine discovering the man you have married holds a secret so powerful it reaches beyond the grave. What secrets of my own or another could so dramatically change my future?

The visit ended abruptly when my family returned home. They were bubbling with excitement about The Lady Richmond. Hannah was filled with how, when, and why questions. Ebenezer told her the steam engine has the equivalent power of many horses. Lucretia was more interested in the people she saw and what they were wearing.

Tuesday, May 18, 1813

In a day, anything is possible. I never expected what happened today. The Scrymsers were also at the docks on Saturday. Mr. Scrymser mentioned to Ebenezer that his father had told him I had been a teacher in Connecticut. He asked Ebenezer if he would permit me to tutor his daughter in arithmetic. He wants Katrina to help with the credits and debits at their store. Apparently Ebenezer said, "It would be an honor," but it must have slipped his mind because he never mentioned this to me. Mrs. Scrymser's visit to make the arrangements was a surprise.

I will meet with Katrina once a week on Thursdays. After Mrs. Scrymser left, I made a hasty visit to Mrs. Ellison. She still has her husband's ledger. I will try to make sense of it, at least enough to assign problems for Katrina.

Tuesday, May 25, 1813

There is a small notice in today's Argus that Captain Skinner, commander of the artillery in the Albany Volunteer Regiment, has been acquitted of all charges against him from an incident at Sacketts Harbor on Lake Ontario. The paper never published details about the incident, but gossip mongers maligned him with conjecture. Last October at Ladd's Coffee House he was praised for recruiting eight companies of volunteers. Who will pass on the news that his good name has been restored?

Thursday, May 27, 1813

I have four students. Hannah, Lucretia, Julia, and Katrina. Wrestling with numbers with Katrina strains, strengthens, and excites my brain.

Friday, May 28, 1813

A new moon

Terrible news. The British at Sacketts Harbor killed Colonel John Mills, commander of the Albany Republican Regiment. In his final hours, was he afraid? Did he suffer? Does he believe he died for a good cause? When his body is returned to Albany he will be buried in the Presbyterian section of the Capitol Park cemetery.

All knew him as a brave man and a good husband. Everything he owns will pass to their oldest son, who just turned eighteen. Mrs. Mills will be dependent on him. If he is kind, he will be generous to his mother, brothers, and sisters. Dutch laws are more favorable to women than English common law.

Tuesday, June 1, 1813

I cannot believe Mrs. Allen has passed. I did not know she was sick.

At five o'clock last evening, mourners met outside Solomon Allen's home just before he and Moses carried out her coffin. The woman who once carried the boys was in the end carried by them. The bereaved processed to funeral services at the Second Presbyterian Church and then up State Street to her final resting place in Capitol Park.

Dear Mrs. Allen. I met her when we first moved to Albany. Neighbors told me the Allens' store had a wide selection of goods and they were most accommodating with special orders, especially books. On my first trip to her store, she seemed sincerely interested in me. She was happy to hear of my childhood in Hadley because she and her husband were born in nearby Northampton. She knew my brother Daniel and was delighted to hear of my education in Litch-field. She wondered if I knew Martha Henshaw from Albany who was with Miss Pierce around 1798. I did remember her. She studied piano with Anna Pierce. The world seems big, but really it is small.

Mrs. Allen loved books. We had many good conversations about her favorites and mine. She leaves a hole in my heart. Although it was a mild evening, I felt a chill in the cemetery where we left her. The headstone next to hers was carved with these words:

> The rose is red. The grass is green
> The days are past which I have seen.
> As you are now, so once was I.
> As I am now so shall you be.
> Prepare for death and follow me.

When a person leaves us, I think about the grief of those left behind, the love given and the love lost. I think also about a life incomplete. What might she have contributed if she had been an educated woman? Mrs. Allen was a woman with an unblemished reputation. Was she happy with her life? Was she prepared for death?

"Do not ask questions for which there are no earthly answers," Ebenezer says. He is right. I cannot answer questions about Mrs. Allen's life, but I can search for answers about my own. One thing is certain. Our time on earth is precious.

Sunday, June 6, 1813

Pentecost

Monday, June 7, 1813

Unseasonably hot.

Negro people can turn a funeral into a festival. Despite their dismal circumstances, there is no gloom and doom for them. They worship with fiddle and tambourine. They sing the Psalms. Their preacher calls out the Gospel and they jump to their feet calling back, "Amen, Amen." They turn their faces up to God, their one true master. They love Him like a kind father.

Sunday was Pentecost, which the Dutch call Pinksteren. In our church it is a solemn holy day. For the Negroes, Pinkster is a time to forget their troubles and celebrate spring. Freed by their masters from work, they gather on Pinkster Hill. A few years ago the Common Council banned drinking, drumming, and dancing at Pinkster, but to no avail. It is still a Saturnalia.

> Rise then, each son of Pinkster, rise
> Snatch fleeting pleasure as it flies.
> See Nature spreads her carpet gay,
> For you to dance your care away.
>
> While every bird on every tree,
> Proclaims our happy jubilee:
> Let us jovial be as they,
> All on this holy holiday.

At Pinksterfest I go to Mr. Lattimer's booth decorated with pink azaleas. There are long lines outside his booth because his wife Dina, who works for Mr. Mancius, is famous for her gingerbread. Mr. Lattimer's brother Timothy entertains the crowd with his fancy foot tapping, head swaying, hip circling fandangos, so different from the sedate quadrilles taught at Mr. Merchant's dancing academy! Young Benjamin Lattimer swings a girl I do not recognize. Eight-year-old William dances with his sisters Betsy and Mary.

> Dancing true in gentle metre,
> Moving every limb and feature
> Or under shades they talk and laugh
> And the cheering nectar quaff.

At another booth there is singing.

> Handsome Phillis sings and shows
> Fine white teeth in ivory rows;
> And suffers him she fain would please,
> To give her now and then a squeeze.

The Negroes tell stories that poke fun at Albany's Burgomasters, Yankee Doodlers, French monsieurs, St. Patrick sons, Jack the Rover, and Joe the Politician. The highlight of Pinksterfest is the crowning of King Charley. He is resplendent in his hat of yellow lace, tan breeches, and a scarlet coat trimmed with gold.

> O could I loud as thunder sing,
> Thy fame should sound, great Charles, the king
> From Hudson's stream to Niger's wave,
> And rouse the friend of every slave.

They say King Charley is more than one hundred years old and descended from African royalty.

> Tho' for a scepter he was born
> Tho' from his father's kingdom torn,
> And doomed to be a slave; still he
> Retains his native majesty.

King Charley, the Lattimer family, Phillis, and all the colored people show us how to treasure every moment that will never come again.

Wednesday, June 9, 1813

During the Pinkster merriment there was a duel in Rensselaer between Captain Clark, the brother of James Clark in our church, and Lieutenant Bloomfield. Dueling is illegal in New York, but when hot weather heats men's blood and drinking and gambling are added to the mix, tempers burn out of control. Bloomfield was buried where he fell on the banks of the Hudson.

Thursday, June 10, 1813

Joseph Fry printed a sixty-page directory of the names and addresses of Albany men. It cost fifty cents. Ebenezer paid to add his name. It will be helpful to him in business.

Monday, June 14, 1813

Full moon, the strawberry moon

For those with provisions, this is the time to sell. The market is topsy-turvy. Prices for butter and other necessities go higher and higher while fine furniture and glass mirrors are sold for half their value, and there are few in line to buy them. War takes money out of the pockets of some and puts it in the pockets of others.

Ebenezer supervises my spending. Returning late from work, he goes over and over the accounts. There never seems to be enough to cover expenses. When he finally climbs into bed, he sleeps fitfully. He thrashes about, talks in his sleep, and wakes up exhausted.

Ebenezer's sister Esther Edwards introduced us to her neighbor Horace Goodrich. He will graduate from Union in August, and in September he will study law with Ebenezer and board in our home. It will help with finances.

Tuesday, June 15, 1813

Ebenezer has talked with several men about a subscription school for girls. I am not happy to hear some of their responses. Those who oppose educating girls beyond elementary reading, writing, and ciphering use Mrs. Russell's "threat to reproduction" argument, Mr. Groesbeeck's "waste of money" argument, and add another: the "inferiority of the fairer sex."

One of Ebenezer's associates held him captive with a lecture from Scripture. "God created the Universe in ascending order; fish in the sea, fowl in the air, cattle on the earth and Adam as lord of all. Recognizing Adam's need for a helpmate, He created Eve from one of Adam's ribs. Eve's disobedience to God and deception of Adam were the cause of their expulsion from the Garden of Eden. It is proof of the inferiority of women. The only salvation of women is through the labor of bearing children. The husband is the head of the wife. He should rule over her. He is her protector and provider. She should submit to him. Women should not have authority over men. They should not teach. They should learn in silence and be silent."

Ebenezer left the house for the evening and did not wait for my reaction or tell me how he responded to the gentleman. Women are to be silent? They should not teach? I am filled with the rage of all who feel diminished.

Wednesday, June 16, 1813

"Do not fret," Mrs. Ellison says, "the esteemed gentleman's knowledge of the Bible is limited. He probably thinks it was Jesus, not Moses, that was found in the bulrushes." Our walk to Wednesday's Church Society meeting was just long enough for her to give me a Bible lesson.

"The first creation story is in Genesis 1:27. It says man and woman were created at the same time. 'So God created man in his own image, in the image of God created he him; male and female created he them.' Men and women have equal dominion. The second creation story comes later in Genesis 2: 22. I do not know who added the story of Eve being an afterthought and formed from Adam's rib, but if God created woman after man, by the logic of ascending order, she should be Lord of all Creation. No. Man and woman are created equal. Their mind and free will are the gifts of God. The Garden of Eden story is about honoring the sovereignty of our Creator. Adam and Eve were instructed to not eat the fruit of the Tree of Life. By her disobedience, Eve taught us there are mysteries that should be known only to God."

Mrs. Ellison continued, "The gentleman with whom Ebenezer spoke knows how to select the Bible verses that suit him. Does he know in God's eyes, there is neither Jew nor Greek, neither bond nor free, neither male nor female? Does he know of the influential women of the early church, Lydia, Phoebe, and Priscilla? The gentleman artfully dodges the requirements of a good husband. He should not be a wine drinker, a striker, a brawler, greedy or covetous!"

Pausing before the rectory door, Mrs. Ellison admitted, "The man is right about one thing. I can attest to the enmity between women and those startling, sneaky, slippery creatures, snakes! Even the word sends a shiver up my spine."

I don't care for snakes either, but Lucretia loves them. The Russells' cat, Itchy, catches them in the fields behind our house. He is partial to the skinny green ones. He delivers them half dead to Lucretia who wants to nurse them back to health. Ebenezer will not allow it! Whenever we hear the high-pitched scream reserved only for snakes, we know Ebenezer has come upon a delivery. Ebenezer is deathly afraid of snakes, and he is a man. He won't admit it, but it is one reason he left farming. His older brother was killed after being thrown from a horse, startled by a snake.

After the meeting, Reverend Clowes pulled Mrs. Ellison and me aside. He is without a wife to talk over personal matters. He is upset and wants advice.

Recently Mayor Van Rensselaer delivered Reverend Clowes a collection of papers that included minutes from vestry meetings Reverend Clowes had not attended. Reading the minutes he discovered his salary is supplemented by rental income from church lands north of Maiden Lane. The rents have been increasing, so he feels he deserves an increase in his salary. He thinks the vestry is cheating him.

Mrs. Ellison and I warned him against making accusations. We urged him to get his emotions under control and obtain more information, especially before confronting Governor Tayler, who is one of the oldest vestrymen. He is a generous benefactor to the church and does not tolerate anyone questioning his decisions.

Reverend Clowes rejected our advice. He retrieved his hat and coat and left the church without a "thank you" or "good day."

Thursday, June 17, 1813

Ebenezer knows all about the controversy. Reverend Clowes talked to Matthew Gill, William Fowler, Edward Brown, and many other parishioners. The more people he talks to, the angrier he feels. The more he discusses the issue in public, the more this inflames Tayler, Philip Van Rensselaer, and the other vestrymen. They feel their integrity is being attacked.

He should have followed our advice to calm down and go directly to the vestry and make private inquiries. The small spark that burned in his heart might have been extinguished. Sharing it with others fanned the flame.

I understand Reverend Clowes' attempt to gain allies, but he is making matters worse by creating groups for and against him. The more people who become involved, the stronger the controversy becomes and the larger the opposing groups. Men work harder against their enemies than for their friends.

Wednesday, June 23, 1813

Mrs. Ellison and I brought Abigail to the meeting of the Church Ladies. She has settled into her new home and is happy with the move. She could not stop talking about Albany's wonderfully diverse population. "Everyone in Greenville looks and sounds alike, but here in Albany there are tall and short, stocky and thin, light and dark, and there are so many different languages spoken." She and John are outgoing. In the short time they have been in Albany, they have met more people than I have in five years.

She has found Albany to be "open-minded and accepting, tolerant, charitable, and very civic-minded." We were just turning onto State Street when Abigail revealed news I had not heard. She was talking so fast and what she said was so shocking, I wasn't sure I heard her correctly.

"It is wonderful. Albany will soon have a school for the colored children. Mrs. Mancius told me — that Mr. Mancius told her — their colored girl, Dina, told him — that her husband Mr. Lattimer is opening a school for the Negro boys and girls in Albany."

Without pausing for a breath, Abigail said what everyone knows about Benjamin Lattimer: "He is a licensed cartman. He lives over on Plain Street but he was born in Wethersfield, Connecticut. That's next door to Westbrook where John and I were born. Mr. Lattimer gained his freedom after serving as a soldier in the War of Independence. He has done very well in Albany. He has saved enough money to buy one of Mrs. Elizabeth Schuyler Hamilton's lots over on Malcolm Street. Mr. Lattimer plans to build a schoolhouse for the colored children. Imagine that! In Virginia it is against the law to teach black people to read."

Abigail continued, "Reverend Clowes agreed to tutor Maria and other girls in the parish. John and I have made several attempts to meet with him, but as you know, he is busy with many important projects. I am sure he will accommodate us towards the end of summer when things settle down."

At church, Abigail needed no introductions and immediately struck up a conversation with Mrs. Gill. What will Mrs. Gill think when she hears Betsy and Mary Lattimer will have a school before her daughters Martha and Margaret? Is it true Reverend Clowes will become a tutor? What happened to Miss Brenton? Abigail does not know everything that's happening in Albany. She does not know about the conflict concerning Reverend Clowes' salary.

Friday, June 26, 1813

Mr. Lattimer is planning a school to educate blacks, and this is the notice in The Argus:

"FOR SALE: A BLACK GIRL, about 20 years of age, who has two and a half years to serve."

What is it like to be bought and sold? What does it feel like to have your body owned by a man who decides what you eat, when you sleep, what your work will be, when, how long, and for whom you work? What does it feel like to know he will decide when and with whom you will bear a child?

She is a black girl about 20 years old. Does her mother know the date she was born? Did her mother sing to her and rock her to sleep? Did her father protect her? Does she know her father? Does she have brothers and sisters? Will she cry when she is sold and separated from her family? Has she sealed her heart against further pain?

The advertisement states she has two and a half years to serve. Then will she be free? Where will she go? How will she support herself? Some owners impose conditions on freed slaves. They force them to continue working for low wages or they charge a monthly fee to be paid as reimbursement for manumission. Sometimes they make the freed person sign an agreement to leave Albany. Most despicable, some men plot to have the freed slave kidnapped and sold down south. This is illegal, but laws do not apply to colored people.

What must it be like to have men physically examine you from head to toe and dispute your worth? The seller wants as much money as he can get. The buyer wants to pay as little as possible. What is the worth of a person?

New York has a law that all Negroes will be free by Independence Day 1827. At one time New York had the largest number of slaves of any northern state. When Aaron Burr was in the State Assembly, he felt emancipation should be immediate. Others thought it would create problems because freed blacks would not be equipped to care for themselves. This is also the plight of some women. Losing a father or husband, if they are not educated, they are helpless.

Some propose Negroes should return to Africa to be with their own people. Where in Africa would they go? If you asked Benjamin Lattimer where he came from, he would not know. They are like the Russells, the Roorbacks, the Scrymsers, Ebenezer, and me. Our families have lived here for generations.

My Great Uncle William freed his slaves more than fifty years ago. Inscribed on his headstone is what he believed to be the most important deed of his life:

> In memory of William Ely who died A.D. 1760. He was among the first who gave freedom to his slaves therein doing as he would be done by.

Those who think freeing colored people will disrupt the social order are the ones who are afraid of being "done by as they have been doing."

Friday, July 2, 1813

Four hundred soldiers crossed over the river from Greenbush and spent the night camped next to Capitol Park. Grateful citizens delivered them a meal of stew, pudding, and berries.

A lone bugler gave the wake up call this morning. Later there was the call to assemble and march. Under the command of Colonel Cutting, four hundred men, marching as one, headed to the western frontier. They are four hundred very young boys who leave mothers and sweethearts. Many will not return. Those who return will not be the boys who left.

Saturday, July 3, 1813

Lucretia, Hannah, Ebenezer, and even Samuel were up hours before the nine o'clock bell announcing Independence Day celebrations. Penny Postman Winne says it will be a sunny day.

> When the dew is on the grass
> Rain will never come to pass.

At ten o'clock militia regiments from Albany, Troy, and Schenectady were led by fife and drum into the city. All of Albany plus throngs of people from surrounding towns lined the streets. Stirred by the fanfare, small boys broke away from their mothers and marched alongside the soldiers to the Capitol. They looked very serious trying to keep in step and balance their mock guns. Everyone laughed at the small boys, but I felt sad. Why can't people march for peace?

The honor of delivering the opening and closing prayers alternates among the city's clergy. This year Reverend Clowes provided the blessing. The Republic of the United States does not have an official religion. Founding Fathers believed religion should be free from government control. On Independence Day, Episcopals, Presbyterians, Dutch Reformed, and Baptists stand together with Albany's landed gentry, merchants, country folk, cartmen, and coloreds. On Independence Day we are a perfect union of people who believe in liberty and justice.

There were speeches by Mayor Van Rensselaer and other city officials. As always, the audience heard exactly what they already value, and speakers were rewarded with foot stomping, whistles, and cheers.

Most stirring for me was Solomon Van Rensselaer's annual reading of the Declaration of Independence. Still limping from his wounds at Queenstown Heights, the Colonel climbed to the podium. Dressed in full military regalia, he waited for complete silence before beginning.

SOLOMON VAN RENSSELAER

> We hold these truths to be self-evident, that all men are created equal, that they are endowed by their Creator with certain unalienable Rights, that among these are Life, Liberty and the pursuit of Happiness.

In the afternoon, Ebenezer treated us to cider and gingerbread from Mr. Lattimer's booth. Later in the day, canons filled with gunpowder (but no canon balls) were fired at a fort constructed of tree branches. Men playing the role of American soldiers staged a mock attack and set the fort ablaze. The British retreated and the battle ended without casualties, which is why I prefer re-enactments. Everyone stood to sing *God Save America*.

> God Save America
> Free from tyrannic sway
> Till time shall cease.
> Hushed be the din of arms
> And all proud war's alarms
> Follow in all her charms
> Heaven born peace.

It was a good day. Ebenezer enjoyed visiting with friends. Samuel liked the military music and cider. Hannah liked the marching boys and gingerbread. Lucretia loved the booming cannons and fireworks. I liked the reading of the Declaration of Independence. For men and women, there is no life, liberty, or happiness without the freedom to live a life of purpose. Eudaemonia.

Long after Mr. Moore assured, "It's nine o'clock and all is well," I could hear the soft singing of men around a fire. The smell of wood smoke brought back a memory of the Fowler home struck by lightning, this time three years ago. Their house and the one next door burned to the ground. The family escaped in bare feet and Captain Roorback, Mr. Brown, Ebenezer, and Samuel helped rescue their precious piano with ivory keys. It suffered smoke damage, but Mr. Meacham was able to repair it.

While the piano was stored in our home, Mariam provided nightly entertainment. Even at thirteen, she could make the piano sing. Samuel stood close by to turn the pages of the sheet music and has been in love with her ever since.

Tuesday, July 6, 1813

Ebenezer is forty years old today. Two score years! He says he feels like an old man! His father, who died four years ago yesterday, lived three score years.

Thursday, July 8, 1813

Wooly sheep in the sky
Will bring raindrops by and by.

Along with this news, Penny Postman Winne delivered a letter from Litchfield. Lyman Beecher writes that Ebenezer's cousin Roxanna, delivered their eighth child on June 24. God willing, Henry Ward Beecher will not take after his father.

Lyman carries a heavy burden on his shoulder: the spiritual revival of his family, Litchfield, the state of Connecticut, and the entire republic. He wants no one to go to Hell while he is on watch! He believes the devil is always lurking to lure the unprepared into a life of sin. Man's only salvation is to prostrate himself before the Almighty, submit to the strict guidance of a man of God (such as himself), and beg for mercy. Ebenezer laughs at Lyman. "Sermons never stopped anyone from the pleasures of this world, only the full enjoyment of them!" Lyman is not foolish. He knows the power of fear.

It is a mysterious link that binds Lyman and the beautiful Roxanna. She brings sunshine to everyone around her, everyone except Lyman. He hangs as tight to the dark side as she does to the light. Roxanna is as elegant and refined as Lyman is rough. When she and Lyman lived in East Hampton, she taught French, English composition, drawing, painting, and embroidery. She only gave up teaching after the birth of Catharine, and when Lyman was called to the Congregational Church in Litchfield. He teaches Latin for Miss Pierce, and they board many of her pupils. Catharine attends the school. Harriet and Mary will be enrolled when they are older. If we wanted Lucretia to attend Litchfield Female Academy, she could live with the Beechers. It would be a wonderful opportunity for her, but I do not think our daughter would be happy in the Beecher household. I would not be.

Monday, July 12, 1813

I will never forget that hot, humid day nine years ago. Ebenezer and I had been married seven months. We had just left church when we heard the news. Alexander Hamilton was mortally wounded in a pistol duel with Aaron Burr.

The men were bitter political rivals, beginning with Burr's 1791 election to the Senate. It was the seat previously held by Hamilton's father-in-law Philip Schuyler. The enmity intensified during the 1800 presidential elections and deepened during Burr's campaign for Governor. Hamilton could not control his hatred of Burr and seized every opportunity to malign him. Men will fight to the death to preserve their honor. At the Hamilton-Burr duel, Hamilton lost his life. Both men lost their honor.

It is rumored the duel was caused by an incendiary remark made at the State Street home of John Tayler. Hamilton expressed a "despicable opinion" about Burr, intimating he was amoral. James Kent and Tayler's son-in-law Charles Cooper were part of the discussion. The remark may have referred to Burr's unusually close relationship with his daughter, Theodosia. Dr. Cooper passed on the comment in a letter to Philip Schuyler, and it was published in The Albany Register on April 24. I don't know if the actual letter was published or the comment.

People polish themselves by tarnishing others. The more negative the gossip, the more important and powerful they feel. People listen for the same reasons. They are happy to know a mighty person is flawed. Gossip is entertaining. It distracts people from their own problems.

Like a small ember in a hay-barn, slander can quickly burn out of control and destroy everything in the path. Hamilton should not have made comments about Burr's morality. People still talk about Hamilton's affair with Maria Reynolds. Furthermore, he knew the lethality of dueling. Three years earlier, Hamilton's son Philip was killed in a duel. Poor Mrs. Hamilton. She lived with questions about Alexander's fidelity and the senseless deaths of her son and her husband.

I disbelieve two-thirds of the rumors that circle the neighborhood and say nothing about the rest. I am careful what I say about others and very careful what I write in letters.

Tuesday, July 13, 1813

A full moon, the buck moon

We judge people with limited information. People condemn Aaron Burr, but Ebenezer and I can attest to his keen mind and great personal sorrows.

Aaron Burr's father was president of the College of New Jersey. His sister Sally married Burr's law teacher, Tapping Reeve. He was a frequent visitor in Tapping and Sally Burr Reeve's home when Ebenezer and I were students in Litchfield.

Some of the criticism of Aaron Burr relates to his views on the education of women. He taught his daughter Theodosia to think for herself. Most men believe women's legal rights and thinking should be covered by fathers and husbands. Burr wanted his daughter to reason as well as read and superintended a remarkable education for her. He hired tutors in French, Latin, and philosophy. He instructed her to write a journal to note daily occurrences, but more important, to reflect on their significance.

Aaron adored Theodosia. Some said their closeness was unnatural. Not only did he educate her as he would a son, he put her in the role of adult female companion after the untimely death of his wife and before Theodosia married Joseph Alston.

Aaron was not prosecuted for the death of Hamilton, but it destroyed his political career. Personal sorrows added to his despondency. After Theodosia married, she moved to South Carolina where her husband owned a large rice plantation on the Waccamaw River. It was a lonely life for Theodosia and she never regained her health after the birth of her son, Aaron Burr Alston. Last July, at the age of ten, Aaron Burr's only grandchild was struck down by a summer fever. Inconsolable, Theodosia planned a trip north to visit her father.

On New Year's Eve, Theodosia, her doctor, a cook, maid, and the captain of The Patriot, sailed down the Sampit River, past Georgetown and out Winyah Bay. The schooner rounded North Island, passed Pawley's Island and disappeared. Some say The Patriot was attacked by pirates and the passengers ordered to walk the plank. Others say the boat was torn apart in a storm off Nag's Head and all aboard drowned. One rumor says Theodosia was the lone survivor and lives alone in a cottage on the beach.

Aaron Burr lost both parents before he was two years old. He suffered the loss of a wife, his only sister, his only grandson, and finally his beloved daughter. How can a heart bear so much grief?

Thursday, July 15, 1813

St. Swithin's Day.

St. Swithin's Day dawned sunny and clear. Penny Postman Winne predicts there will be forty more days of good weather, because,

St. Swithin's Day if thou be fair
For forty days `twill rain na mair.

Monday, July 19, 1813

It is not going well for the soldiers in the western part of the state. The Albany Gazette printed a letter from Canandaigua. The British have burned barracks, stolen horses, and confiscated flour and salt supplies. They have wounded and killed our soldiers. The dead must be quickly retrieved to prevent Indians from taking their scalps. Our men are so hungry, they eat dead men's shoes. The list of deserters is long. There is a twenty dollar reward for Christian Sugars who deserted from the Navel fleet on Lake Champlain.

Thursday, July 22, 1813

Although Ebenezer does not have enough money for our household expenses, he is generous with others. There is a note of thanks in The Albany Gazette to the anonymous donor who left money at the Poor House. I would not be surprised if it was Ebenezer. Half the occupants of the Poor House are men suffering from "intemperance in the use of ardent spirits." The other half are unwed mothers and widows. The money will be used for children's books.

Monday, July 26, 1813

A warm, dark night

He who would scan the figured skies
Its' brightest gems to tell
Must first direct his mind's eye north
And learn the Bear's stars well.

A clear, moonless summer night is a night for stargazing. I show Lucretia and Hannah Ursa Major, the Great Bear in the northern sky. The long curve is the bear's tail. To me, it looks like a drinking gourd or a water dipper. Tonight the dipper is poised to scoop water from the Hudson for thirsty livestock. On autumn nights, the dipper's bowl turns up to catch falling leaves. In winter, the frozen handle hangs down like an icicle. When a spring thaw melts the ice, the dipper tilts to baptize newborn lambs.

Using the Big Dipper as a guide, I show the girls how to find heaven's other bright gems. Stars in the bowl of the dipper point the way to Regulus, in the constellation of Leo the Lion. Draw an arc from the end of the dipper's curved handle, and you "arc to Arcturus." Continue the arc and "speed on to Spica."

The jewel in the night sky is Polaris, the North Star. On land and sea, it is the guiding star for travelers because it never moves. I locate Polaris through the two guardian stars at the edge of the dipper's bowl. Lined up, the two stars point to Polaris.

Locate the North Star and you will never be lost. When I face the North Star and extend both arms out to my side, I tell the girls, "My left hand points west and my right hand points east to Hadley, my childhood home."

"And my home in Connecticut," Hannah said wistfully. I can tell she misses her family.

Two years ago Captain Roorback showed us Donati's Comet. It was so bright it cast shadows on the street.

"Some see it as a warning of impending doom and are afraid," Captain Roorback said. "I see it as a sign of change."

Ebenezer pointed out, "The comet's head and two tails are a trinity. Like our family, they appear to be separate, but are one. The comet inspires us to perform deeds that will radiate beyond our small house on Montgomery Street, even beyond Albany."

The Comet of 1811 still adorns my mind, but two years later, ten thousand concerns cast a shadow on the one bright deed that could make a difference in my life.

Tuesday, July 27, 1813

A new moon

This morning, Solomon Allen appeared at my door with a package. "Moses and I know of the deep respect our mother had for you. We discovered this shortly after she passed. Please forgive our delay in delivering it to you." Mr. Allen handed me the package, wished me good day, and left before I could properly thank him.

In my hand was a brown paper package tied tight with a double roll of jute. Inside was a collection of leather bound books; Paradise Lost, The Sonnets of John Donne, Two Gentlemen of Verona, and The Tempest. Enclosed with the books was a note and a second sealed envelope.

> *71 s. Market*
> *Albany, New York*
> *May 27, 1813*

Dear Betsey,

Please accept these volumes as a token of my appreciation for a friendship that nurtured me more than I expected this late in my life.

I dare to ask you to fulfill a last request. I am confident when the time is opportune, Mr. Foot will prepare subscription papers for a school for Lucretia, my granddaughters Rebecca, Sarah, and Ruth, and other Albany girls. When the time comes, I am bold to ask you to deliver this note to Moses and Solomon along with the enclosed financial support. I want to be assured my granddaughters will be among the first to march in procession to a school for female scholars.

Be patient. At the proper time, I know there will be an academy for girls. Esto perpetua.

Fondly,
Judith Allen

She instructs me to make her wishes known to her sons and deliver the financial support when a subscription document is prepared. Does she really believe Ebenezer will draft it? Does she believe others will sign? I will honor her request. I will lock away the note and envelope of financial support until it is time to deliver it to her sons.

Later in the morning, there was another delivery. Penny Postman Winne brought two letters from Connecticut. One was for Hannah.

The other was for me from Miss Pierce.

South Street
Litchfield, Connecticut
July 12, 1813

Dear Betsey,

Thank you for your lovely correspondence of July 9. We are all thankful Henry Ward Beecher arrived safely to his earthly home, but I fear this birth has weakened Roxanna. I was especially pleased to hear news of your students. Did I tell you in my previous letter how proud I am of your cousin Caroline Ely who has become a teacher? I can assure you all the Ely girls are safe. The British campaign has not extended to the Connecticut River.

I enjoyed your account of Independence Day in Albany. For the Daughters of the Revolutionary War, the battle for independence has just begun. We are free only if the mind is free. Developing the mind does not weaken the female body, it makes it stronger. The reverse is true as well.

Girls must be educated in the same academic subjects as their brothers. The first objective of education is to strengthen memory through knowledge about the facts of our world. The second is to develop the ability to reason through philosophy, science, and math. The highest goal of education is to nurture the imagination through literature and the arts. It is our creativity that elevates us above God's other creatures.

The English language is stocked with a rich choice of words and we use only a sample. Good literature expands our vocabulary. I understand your concern about the expense of buying the great works of Pope, Milton and Shakespeare, but you need only purchase one of each and solicit books from the libraries of your neighbors.

If possible obtain the writings of the Irish writer Maria Edgeworth. She is best known for her novels like Castle Rankrent, but I recommend Letters for Literary Ladies. She affirms it is because of women's inferior education they are judged intellectually inferior. It was Miss Edgeworth's good fortune to have a father who supervised her education and set a high standard. Mothers have the hidden power in the home. It is essential to gain the support of both parents in the education of daughters.

I doubt anyone in Albany knows of the British writer Mary Wollstonecraft. She asserts that, just as men have declared independence from the Divine Right of Kings, women must be freed from the dominance of fathers, husbands and sons. This is accomplished through education.

All who dream have fear, but dreams are stronger than fears. Persisting despite our fears gives us courage. On the other hand, it is wise to be patient. If you advance too quickly you will muster an organized group in opposition. All will unfold when the time is right.

Semper et in aeternum, your dear instructress,
Sarah Pierce

Union College commencement exercises are tomorrow. Ebenezer, Samuel, Lucretia, and I will travel by coach to Schenectady. I can only think about Mrs. Allen's gift and Miss Pierce's letter.

Friday, July 30, 1813

On July 28, Dr. Eliphalet Nott conferred degrees on Horace Goodrich and his friend Lebbeus Booth. The music was splendid but the student speeches dragged on. Samuel counted fourteen! There was no compassion for the guests, especially the frail elderly fanning and fainting in the heat. The students probably felt they had suffered through four years listening to lectures and wanted to reciprocate.

We were proud of Horace who delivered the Uranean Society oration. Lebbeus Booth delivered the oration of the rival Cliosophie Society. Lucretia was immediately smitten with Lebbeus. During his speech, she whispered she thought he was the most handsome man she had ever seen. "He is a Greek god. He is Adonis come to life."

I was surprised to hear her carry on about the young man. He looked pale and plain to me. She is growing into a young lady faster than I realized. Ebenezer did not notice her infatuation. He was more interested in the fact Aaron Burr founded the Cliosophie Society at the College of New Jersey.

All were relieved when Dr. Nott urged the new graduates to endure the pain of parting (the students laughed), bid a fond farewell to their Alma Mater (the students hooted), and step into the light to serve their land and Lord (there was respectful applause). The new graduates led the recessional followed by the faculty, trustees, regents, and President Nott.

Lucretia is disappointed to learn Lebbeus will serve the Lord at divinity school in New Jersey. Horace will do his service studying law with Ebenezer. Beginning the first of September, he will board with our family, and I will have one more person to serve.

Thursday, August 5, 1813
Very hot

Thursday, August 12, 1813
A full moon, the corn moon

Sunday, August 15, 1813

Two hundred British Soldiers marched through Albany and are camping tonight in Greenbush. Ebenezer says they are not a threat, but I will be glad when they move on.

Monday, August 16, 1813

Fears and dreams live together. On the other side of every fear is a dream. I am sure Uncle John Ely and cousin Worthington had fear fighting in the War of Independence, but their dream of freedom was stronger. Fighting gave them courage.

After the war, Worthington and his wife Prudence moved south of Albany to Coeymans. He could not earn a living in the isolated village and he never regained his youthful vigor. When Worthington was dying, he sent his daughter to summon her Uncle Edward who had deeds that would be assets for the family. Sixteen-year-old Charlotte had her father's courage.

Prudence packed food for the two day ride to Goshen, and Worthington gave her just enough money for three night's lodging. He did not want to tempt highway robbers and fortunately there were not as many bandits on the road as there are today. Charlotte rode the ninety miles alone, retrieved the papers from her uncle, and returned to Coeymans. Sadly, it was too late to say goodbye to her father. Worthington had passed, but his wife and children would be financially secure.

Would I have the courage to make the trip? I believe love for my father would be greater than fear for my life. Men view women and girls as weaker, in need of protection, except when needed for an urgent and dangerous mission. New Yorkers know the story of Sybil Ludington of Carmel. Also sixteen, she rode forty miles through the night to rally her father's regiment. As a result, they successfully forced the approaching British back to their ships in Long Island Sound.

Tuesday, August 24, 1813

St. Bartholomew's Day

St. Bartholomew's is a dark day in history for the Ely family, and for all Protestants who trace their ancestry to sixteenth century France. On August 24, 1572, Catholics massacred thousands of Huguenots. According to family lore, the Elys fled to England with only one possession, a silver cup. The Legend of the Silver Cup persists. It is a tradition in the Ely family to name the first daughter Lucretia and present her a silver cup.

THE LUCRETIA CUP
COLLECTION OF
SUSAN B. STRANGE

My mother, Lucretia Ely Colt, received a silver cup at birth and gave it to her first daughter, Lucretia. Unfortunately, she died at the age of four. The next daughter she named Lucretia died before her second birthday. A third daughter named Lucretia survived and was given the cup. When we visit Aunt Lucretia in Hadley, our Lucretia wants to see the cup and hear the story. She hopes her aunt will not have any daughters. On our last visit I was mortified when she asked, "Aunt Lucretia, when you die, can I have the silver cup?"

My cousin in Sand Lake, Lucretia Ely Gregory, named her daughter Lucretia. I do not know if she has a silver cup.

Monday, August 30, 1813

My energy and creativity returns with the cooler days of September.

Horace Goodrich moved into our home on Saturday. Today, he begins as Ebenezer's law clerk.

Wednesday, September 1, 1813

My birthday

Mother says I was born thirty-nine years ago today. Sometimes I feel twenty-nine. Mostly I feel forty-nine!

Before I was born my parents moved from Lyme, Connecticut, to Hadley, Massachusetts. My father was a blacksmith, known for his scythes, axes, and fine tools. He was a storyteller, and everyone loved him. There was one story I begged to hear over and over, especially on my birthday. Father told me I was a lucky girl because he was almost not born, and if he had not been born, I would not be born. He thought that was funny. Lucretia thinks it is so romantic.

"Once upon a time," my father would begin, "in the little town of Lyme, there lived a beautiful maiden named Miriam. Soon after her birth, she and her parents moved to Turks Head in the West Indies. Sadly, her parents died when she was a young girl. Poor and alone, Miriam returned to Lyme and supported herself through her needlework. Miriam's charms attracted the attention of all the young men of Lyme, especially your Grandfather Benjamin. He fell hopelessly in love with her. It was hopeless because his father opposed the marriage. Since Miriam had no dowry, a union with one of the Griswald or Ely girls would be more advantageous. Heartbroken, Benjamin ran away to Philadelphia. He had not been there long when he met an important gentleman from Lyme." Here, father would wink at mother and chuckle, "It was one of the fancy Ely relatives on your mother's side of the family. Mr. Ely was traveling on business to the City of Brotherly Love, heard Benjamin's sad story, and promised to intervene. He persuaded Benjamin to return to Lyme, reconciled father and son, and gained approval for the union of Benjamin and Miriam. They married and lived happily ever after." Father would proudly say he was their fourth son, one of the six children "who were almost not born."

The family story gives all the credit to the important selectman. I think it reveals more about the character of my great-grandfather. He looked into the eyes of Benjamin and Miriam and saw the love between them. He recognized Miriam's riches were not in earthly treasures but in the purity of her soul. Great-grandfather had the courage to make a wise decision and bless the couple.

The last time I heard this story I was six years old. Father died two days before I turned seven.

Thursday, September 9, 1813

In these tumultuous times, President Madison calls for the country to unite in support of our military forces. This second Thursday in September has been designated as a Day of Public Humiliation and Prayer. At St. Peter's I will pray for our soldiers and their families. Then I will pray for success in our country's battle for freedom. Then I will pray for my own.

Before we left for church, Penny Postman Winne delivered the sad news that Ebenezer's uncle died in Cheshire on August 30. Reverend John Foot was a man of God, a scholar, and a teacher. His oldest daughter was certified by Yale's President Stiles as fully qualified, except for her sex, to be accepted into Yale's freshman class. Because of Uncle John's high standards, Ebenezer was well prepared for Tapping Reeve's Law School.

May Uncle John rest in peace.

Friday, September 10, 1813

A full moon, the harvest moon

Autumn is one long chore preparing for winter, but it is my favorite season. The maples are still green, but will soon blaze red and orange. Then the leaves will turn brown, fall to the ground, and blow away. The trees will be bare. What will the winter bring?

As the seasons change, so does my life. What can I change and what is outside my control? Ebenezer says God's gift to man is the ability to create his own destiny. Does he believe this is true for women?

As the oldest son, Ebenezer was expected to take over the family farm. Farming is a great life if it is by choice. Ebenezer's choice was to become a lawyer. Was it our destiny to meet in Litchfield, fall in love and marry? If my father had lived a long life, would I have studied to become a teacher? Would my life be different if I had stayed at Miss Pierce's school as her assistant? What is Lucretia's destiny? Will God spare her from the premature loss of a father? Between birth and death, how much of our destiny do we control?

Monday, September 13, 1813

Should we know the future? There are many who want answers and visit Madame Doortje on Pine Street. She is descended from a long line of women in Albany who practice the dark art of fortune telling. Women visit her to find the lost dessert spoon. The young suitor wants to know if his heart's desire will change her "no" to "yes." The merchant inquires about the prosperity of his business. Before trusting in Madame Doortje, seekers ask questions to test her knowledge about their private life.

Samuel dismisses her as a quack. "She has enough brass in her to make a kettle!" He claims Madame Doortje sends spies to Market Street to eavesdrop. He consulted her and did not like what she said about his "uncertain financial future."

For a fee, her customers receive common sense advice and think she is brilliant. She sends the housewife to the sweetmeat pot to find the lost spoon. The suitor is told he will receive a favorable answer after completing studies at Harvard, Yale, or Brown. The merchant hears he will prosper if he pays attention to his debtors and creditors.

Lucretia endlessly asks, "Who will I marry?" Samuel teases her that he is a soothsayer and can predict the future. To my dismay, Samuel turns over a glass, waves his hands over it and chants three times.

"What will the future bring? What will the future bring? What will the future bring?" After gazing into the glass for several minutes, he repeats the question and provides the answer. "The future will be just like the past, only longer."

Lucretia is not amused.

I would like to know the future, but will not trust in Madame Doortje. Samuel is right. My future will be just like the past unless I do something different.

Monday, September 20, 1813

Captain Roorback had long promised to take us on a boat to see the falcons that nest high in the cliffs overlooking the river. Saturday was sunny with calm winds, perfect for the outing. Mrs. Roorback, Orville, and Fanny had already settled themselves in the boat when Ebenezer, Lucretia, Hannah, and I climbed aboard. Captain Roorback fired up the engine, blew the whistle, cast off the dock lines, and steered the boat south. For one precious afternoon we left our ordinary life behind.

Along the way, I pointed out riverbank plants: wood ferns, goldenrod, wild clematis, carrot, purple asters, and brown milk pods with silky clusters.

"Kak, kak, kak," we heard before spotting the raptors camouflaged in the rocky cliffs. Their beauty is not from coloring but from design. With long tail feathers, they are built for speed. Captain Roorback lowered the anchor and stopped the engine so we could watch the birds of prey. The peregrine falcon waits for small birds to cross the river and swoops when the prey is most vulnerable, mid-river. He never misses.

Mrs. Roorback and I thought the children would be horrified, but they were fascinated and asked many questions.

On the return trip, I quizzed Orville, Fanny, Lucretia, and Hannah to see which plants they could identify. The excitement, warmth of the day, and rocking of the boat quickly put Orville and Lucretia to sleep. Hannah and Fanny were wide awake. Hannah named all the plants correctly. Fanny remembered all except for the clematis, which she mistakenly called clementine. Captain Roorback was amazed at his daughter's memory.

It was a day filled with the beauty of nature.

> I want to live
> As the river flows
> Surprises at every turn.

Wednesday, September 22, 1813

It is hard to imagine our small American naval force could stand up to the British Navy. Ten days ago, after the enemy sank his ship, Oliver Perry rowed through gunfire to take command of the USS Niagara, waving his battle flag, "Don't Give Up the Ship." He routed the British and sent the message to General William Henry Harrison: "We have met the enemy and they are ours; two ships, two brigs, one schooner, and one sloop."

He is the hero of Lake Erie.

Monday, September 27, 1813

Saturday's good weather brought Mr. and Mrs. Dibble to Albany to stock up on supplies for the winter. It was a heartwarming reunion for Samuel.

The December before Samuel was to graduate, Ebenezer told him he was ready to study law with James Thompson of Milton. The truth was Ebenezer did not have the money for Samuel's final term. The Dibbles, a kind farming family, offered him room and board even though Samuel had only the few dollars Dr. Nott had given him.

The Dibbles were reluctant to stop for a visit, fearing Samuel might think they'd come to collect the debt. They had started toward Milton, but listened to their heart and turned back. They wanted to see the young man they had grown to love like a son.

I had just taken cornbread with a lovely brown crust from the oven and urged the Dibbles to stay for tea. They shared news from Milton, and Samuel proudly told them he had been admitted to the bar and would soon be able to repay them. The Dibbles are not concerned about the money.

Ebenezer affirmed, "The sacred rule in the Foot family is better to go to bed supperless than to rise in debt."

Tuesday, September 28, 1813

Joseph Russell was re-elected to the Common Council.

Wednesday, September 29, 1813

Michaelmas.

Today marks the beginning of longer nights. It is the feast of the Archangel Michael, protector against the dark. A frost has taken the purple aster. The last flower in the seasonal parade is the Michaelmas daisy. "Don't eat the blackberries after Michaelmas," Mother warned us. "See the tiny droplets on the berries? That is Satan's spit."

Sister Lucretia and I ate the berries anyway. As far as I know, we suffered no harm. They did taste bitter.

Friday, October 1, 1813

Commercial traffic on the river has increased. There are now two hundred and six sloops traveling between Albany and New York harbor.

Monday, October 4, 1813

The Hudson is second in beauty only to the Connecticut River. Both have two faces; life giving and life taking. The Albany Gazette reports an accident involving a father and two sons who went fishing.

The younger boy lost his footing and was swooped up by the river. His older brother attempted a rescue but was dragged away by the current. The father tried to retrieve them. It was foolish, but any bystander would have made the same effort. None knew how to swim. All three drowned.

Tuesday, October 5, 1813

Sometimes we hang to life by a thread, other times by an iron chain. We never know which it is.

On a fine autumn afternoon, a father and his sons go to the river to take fish. At the end of the day, the river takes them. On the other hand, my great-grandfather William survived in a raging sea for three days after his ship sank in a storm. William's father, Richard Ely, managed a shipping company in Plymouth, England. His boats sailed the circuit from Madeira to Cape Verde to Barbados. It is uncertain whether he left a comfortable life in England to escape anti-Puritanism or because of the death of his wife and two children, but in 1661 Richard immigrated to Boston. Through marriage to a wealthy widow Richard acquired considerable land holdings in Lyme, Connecticut. The story is that once Richard was settled he sent for his son, working for an uncle in the West Indies.

On the voyage home, a storm tore the boat apart, sending all but William to a watery grave. William lashed himself to the yardarm and rode the waves for three days and three nights. Exhausted and near death, there was a miracle. A Spanish galleon rescued him and brought him to his father's home on the Connecticut River. The reunion for William and Richard was emotional. In gratitude for this Divine Intervention, father and son pledged to dedicate their lives to good works. Ora et Labora is the Ely family motto. We survive through prayer and hard work, plus a strong iron chain known only to God.

When the wind shifted to the Northwest last night, it blew so hard our windows rattled. I thought about my great-grandfather and what it must have been like bobbing alone in an angry ocean for three days and nights. Was he afraid or thinking only of survival?

"It was hope that kept him alive," Ebenezer said. "Like a man losing at cards, he always believes the next game will give him a winning hand."

Ebenezer's explanation was perplexing. In a life or death situation there is only one thought: survival.

Saturday, October 9, 1813

A full moon, the hunter's moon

There is an apple bee at Gansevoort's orchard tonight.

Sunday, October 10, 1813

Turning apples into applesauce, apple butter, apple cider, apple vinegar, applejack, and apple brandy (the list goes on and on) is a big job. It starts with peeling and coring the apple. Around the edge of Mr. Gansevoort's barn were bushels of apples. In the middle of the barn was a curious contraption.

"This here thing will take the skin off an apple in one swipe," Mr. Gansevoort announced to the gathering of neighbors. With flair, he held up a polished red apple in one hand and pointed to the menacing gadget with the other. It was fitted with razor-sharp blades, a spike, clamps, and a hand crank. His pride in the invention was obvious, and he scanned the crowd to see which brave soul would volunteer to try it out. "Step right up, friends. Who will be the first to test his skill?" Twirling once around, almost losing his balance, he assured the gathering, "We'll have all these apples into the barrel in no time."

Young boys jumped at the challenge and formed a line. Hannah pushed in front. The old folks shook their heads, booed, and said, "What will they think up next!" Sitting in small groups with good old-fashioned, just-sharpened knives, they kept a close eye on those who came forward. In spite of their skepticism, the old folks were soon drawn into the hooting and hollering, cheers, jeers, ceremonious bowing, clapping, and laughter. One person impales an apple onto the spike and tightens the grip around the fruit. The other person cranks a handle which rotates a blade that peels off the skin in one long ribbon.

Young girls gathered the peeled apple skins to toss over their left shoulder. The way it lands reveals the initial of the boy she will marry. Samuel told Mariam Fowler she had tossed an "S." For Hannah, he thought her apple peel fell in the shape of a question mark. She laughed. For Lucretia, he was certain her peel formed the letter "L." She pouted.

Once the apples were peeled and in the barrel, Mr. Gansevoort lit a bonfire. Couples entertained themselves roasting nuts to foretell their compatibility and future happiness. Two nuts are placed on a shovel and held over the fire to see whether the nuts roast quietly, dance gaily, or crash into each other and explode. Some couples kept at it till the fire died down and they received a favorable prophecy.

Mrs. Gansevoort set out platters of sliced apple and cheese. Mr. Russell tuned up his fiddle for dancing. It was a mild evening under the full hunter's moon. With the approach of colder nights, Samuel says we hunt for love.

> The cold and frosty weather
> Brings Jack and Jill close together.

He danced with Mariam all evening.

Lucretia, who loves to dance, moped because of Samuel's prediction. On the way home she could not hold back her tears. "The "L" is for Lucretia," she sobbed. "It means I will not marry. I will be a spinster."

"Not necessarily," Samuel teased, "there's Leonard, Lawrence, Ludwig, and Lewis." Under his breath, he added, "Lucifer." To cheer her, we all thought of "L" names; Lancelot, Lyman, Lionel, and Lemuel.

This morning she is sniffling and coughing. I think she is getting a cold.

Monday, October 11, 1813

The Russells will have a new church on Chapel Street between Maiden Lane and Pine Street. Church trustees, members of the Albany clergy, and parishioners laid the cornerstone today.

On top of the sixty-eight-foot steeple will be a magnificent weathervane. After many meetings and much discussion, Mrs. Russell says, the weathervane has been chosen. It will be a fish and a pumpkin.

The fish, an acronym for Jesus Christ, will not be the Hudson River sturgeon. It will be the Massachusetts cod. It will distinguish the Presbyterian parishioners from the Albany Hollanders. A globe testifies to the worldwide power of the Gospel. As a pumpkin, it represents the bounty of New England and the growing presence of New Englanders in Albany.

Tuesday, October 12, 1813

Lucretia caught a heavy cold at the apple bee. She has a fever and cough. I do not believe it is serious, but I will keep her quiet and away from Hannah, Julia, and Elizabeth. No lessons this week.

Thursday, October 14, 1813

Lucretia is still sick. Ebenezer thinks she will get better with rest. Her forehead feels hotter than yesterday and her cough is getting worse. We moved her to the front room and I spent the night bathing her forehead with a cool cloth, encouraging her to take small sips of tea and humming, hush-a-bye, don't you cry. I sing to calm her and to dispel my own dreadful thoughts. I should never have given my daughter that ill-fated name. My two older sisters named Lucretia died before the age of four. Mother Nature persists in looking for ways to send us to death's door. I persist in trying to prevent her.

Friday, October 15, 1813

When Lucretia coughs, her face turns red and she stops breathing. Each time I think it is her last breath. I close my eyes and plead, "Please God." She gasps, takes in a short breath, and the coughing starts again. I have never seen Ebenezer so upset. He sits next to her bed and holds her hand. Over and over he recites "The Lord is my shepherd." He has canceled his business appointments to keep watch. Cousin John says it is whooping cough.

Mrs. Ellison made an elixir of rum and turpentine to rub on Lucretia's chest twice a day.

Sunday, October 17, 1813

Mrs. Ellison's poultice, Ebenezer's watch, and my prayers have succeeded. Lucretia is weak, but the fever is down and she is not coughing. Thank God. One benefit of the ordeal is she has forgotten Samuel's prophecy about her future husband. Today, we kept the Sabbath at home.

Friday, October 22, 1813

There was an early, heavy snow. Penny Postman Winne says it was worse in the western part of the state. "Three feet of snow fell in Lewis County. Roads were not passable until farmers brought out cattle to plow. Do you remember I told you last summer that a hot first week in August means a winter with heavy snow?"

Mention guns, fast horses, midnight bandits, his missing teeth, or snow, and Penny Postman Winne will tell the tale of how he captured the Pye robber. Today it was the snow that triggered the story. He has told it so many times I know every word by heart.

"You think this snow is bad. You should have seen the snow the December night four days before Christmas, back in '08. A burglar busted into John Pye's tavern out on the Albany-Troy Road. It was late. Mr. Pye and the missus were sound asleep. The highwayman woke them and demanded all the money they had locked behind the bar. Mr. Pye fumbled for the key and got a bullet in his chest. Mrs. Pye was not about to give away one cent of their hard earned money. She grabbed a gun and shot the burglar in the head. You wouldn't believe it. Wounded and bleeding, the crook escaped on horseback.

As Captain of the Watch, it was my duty to apprehend the bandit. Me and my posse followed the trail of blood to Columbia Street, over North Market, and down to Quay Street. Believe it or not, the man's horse leapt twenty feet into the air, onto the ice, and across the river to Greenbush where he fell into a swamp and floundered. My man had no choice but to dismount and run, with me running right behind. I captured him single handed, but lost a few teeth in the scuffle. You probably always wondered what happened to them. In the dead of night, I marched that man through the streets of Albany straight to Mr. Steel's jail. I must say I attracted a large audience. Believe it or not, some foolish women were pleading for me to have pity on the poor man.

The poor man died in jail and there was a tug of war over who would get to dissect that poor man's body. Albany and Troy both wanted him. Troy won and I know for a fact, the skeleton is now in the possession of one of that city's most eminent physicians. I wont tell you which one. I can tell you Mr. Pye survived his wound and only recently passed on. The missus married the Inn's bartender, Mr. William Nutt. By the looks of things she will out live him even though he is forty-nine years younger than she is.

What happened to the horse? My God, I never saw a horse run so fast. *Donder and blitzen.* Thunder and lightning. He ran like the devil was chasing him. No one ever saw him again."

Mr. Winne's story amuses me every time I hear it. I wait until he has moved on before I burst out laughing.

Saturday, October 23, 1813

For the second time, a fire destroyed the Caldwell's tobacco plant. Mr. James Caldwell moved to Lake George after the first fire and Thomas Boyd took over the management. At one time they were one of the area's largest tobacco producers. The snuff they manufacture is of exceptional quality. Thankfully, no one perished in the fire, but there are many workers without a job. Mr. Joseph Caldwell is Orville Roorback's teacher.

Monday, October 25, 1813

The tobacco plant fire created excitement for the cartman, Mr. Dalton, and it solved a mystery about his horse, Jack. Men who are honest in all other matters make an exception when it comes to horse trading. The buyer is sometimes surprised to learn his horse's history. This is what happened to Mr. Dalton. He bought Jack from a man who bought him from the firehouse.

Firehouse horses are fast and smart. Each one is stabled in front of a pump wagon. A harness hangs overhead ready to drop into place at the sound of the fire bell. Once harnessed and hitched to the pump wagon, the horse races up and down hills and through narrow alleys directly to the fire. Occasionally the horse's idea of the most direct route differs from the driver's. The horse always wins.

After a firehouse horse slows down, he is sold. When Mr. Dalton bought Jack, he was amazed how quickly Jack learned the cartman's route. When Mr. Dalton loaded crates on the docks and made deliveries to Market, State, or Pearl, Jack never needed to be hitched to a post. He would wait patiently for Mr. Dalton to climb back into the cart before moving on to the next stop.

Friday was different. Mr. Dalton and Jack were on Quay Street when the fire bell sounded. Jack's ears perked up. He took off at a gallop and headed straight for the tobacco plant. Once there, Jack was confused to discover the other horses already lined up and firemen pumping water.

When Mr. Dalton found him, he reassured Jack he had always done a fine job as a firehouse horse, but that was in the past. His new job was just as important as the old.

Did Jack agree?

Tuesday, October 26, 1813

Mr. Goodrich is a quiet man. He rarely joins our conversations at supper, eats very little, and retires early to read in his room. This evening he said he paid ten dollars to join Mr. John Cook's new reading room and circulating library. If you only join the reading room, it is six dollars.

Ebenezer wants to pay only for the reading room, but unaccompanied ladies are not permitted in the reading room. Ebenezer promises to join both when his financial affairs are in order. I look forward to a circulating library to secure books for Hannah, Lucretia, and myself.

The money Mr. Goodrich contributes to our household helps, but I have not heard anything from Ebenezer about his progress as a law clerk. Samuel is frank. He admires Mr. Goodrich's intellect, but questions his future as a counsellor. Mr. Goodrich is not aggressive like Ebenezer, or smart with money like Samuel.

Recently, Samuel took over the financial management of the law office. Overhearing conversations with Ebenezer, I detect there is a problem. According to Samuel, there is no lack of clients, but it is not reflected in their ledger. He says something is wrong. Ebenezer dismisses his concerns.

Wednesday, October 27, 1813

This evening Samuel's conversation about finances was with me. After much pacing back and forth, clearing of the throat, and false starts, he dove in.

"Betsey, there is something I have to tell you." The manner in which he said this frightened me.

"Betsey, Ebenezer has accrued some large debts." He hesitated for a moment then continued. "The debts are greater than…." I held tight to the arm of my chair, took a deep breath, and asked for the details. "The debts are greater than fifteen hundred dollars." Fifteen hundred dollars! The news is worse than I imagined. What he said next was even worse.

"Betsey, I need to tell you, Ebenezer has succumbed to the vice that ensnares many prominent gentlemen."

Oh, no. Not Ebenezer. I wanted to cover my ears.

"Betsey, Ebenezer's nightly business is with other groups of men who…" I shut my eyes. He hesitated then continued, "men who gamble at cards." My heart stopped.

"He gambles not for financial gain. There is none. He gambles for entertainment. I have investigated the problem and know the identity of several of his creditors. Betsey, I do not need to tell you, if Ebenezer continues to acquire losses, it will lead to his financial ruin, yours, and mine."

I hear my mother say,

> For every evil under the sun
> There be a remedy or there be none.
> If there be one, try and find it.
> If there be none, never mind it.

Simple but useless advice. There is no good remedy for this evil. It is not possible to "never mind it." The evil that has ensnared Ebenezer affects our whole family. With large unpaid debts, Ebenezer could be sent to jail. We could lose our home.

When Ebenezer and I first talked about the late nights, we agreed it was for the welfare of the family. It would be temporary. Ebenezer would soon get ahead and not need the extra work. That was a long time ago. Lately I have not talked with Ebenezer about this or anything else of significance. He returns from work, eats quickly, then leaves again and does not return until late. He interprets what I say as interference with his position as head of the family. Samuel says it is the same with him. When Ebenezer asks Samuel for money, he feels it is his duty as a brother to honor the request. The problem is the requests are coming closer together, and the amount of money is increasing.

We are like that family who went fishing. A boy falls into the river and cannot swim. Father and brother attempt a rescue, but are unsuccessful. All three drown.

Friday, October 29, 1813

This morning I did not help Ebenezer search for the hat and muffler he'd carelessly cast off last night. He left home angry and without them. One minute, I too, am angry. The next minute I am frightened.

Samuel says he has failed every effort to keep Ebenezer from the gaming table. He fears Ebenezer will tarnish his reputation and questions if he can continue as his law partner. He has decided to visit his mother, sister, and brother-in-law in Ballston Spa. It is possible he could work in Isaac's law office and live with the Edwards family. Samuel assures me he will weigh the decision carefully. "An hour of reflection is better than a year of repentance."

Even though I understand Samuel's need to sever relations with Ebenezer, I think only about how this will affect me. Ebenezer and Samuel have exchanged positions. The responsible one is leaving and my husband plays the role of a carefree bachelor.

Saturday, October 30, 1813

October draws to a close. There is a stillness in the air this morning. Samuel is in Ballston Spa. Ebenezer, Mr. Goodrich, and the girls are still sleeping. I watch for the sun to rise above the Greenbush hills. It seems to take longer than usual, but finally appears. With the light of day, I notice most trees have lost their leaves. I listen for the one bird that stirs others to begin the morning cantata. I hear nothing.

Tomorrow is All Hallow's Eve, the night when witches, goblins, and demons cross from "the other side" and cause mischief. Lucretia does not like All Hallow's Eve. She fears those who have departed will drag her into the grave.

We decorate our home with fallen leaves to show our trust in the cycles of nature. We carve a face on a pumpkin and put a candle inside. Demons and devils shun the light.

At this time of year there is a thin veil between our world and the next. We can hear the voices of loved ones who have passed.

I hear my father say, "Keep the faith. Keep the faith."

Sunday, October 31, 1813

The Sabbath

Ebenezer, Lucretia, Hannah, and I attended church but left abruptly.

I cannot fault Hannah and Lucretia because it has also happened to me. It's the kind of thing that occurs only in church or some other somber setting. Trying to stop it only makes it worse. A hasty exit is the only solution.

Just as Reverend Clowes climbed to the pulpit. I heard Hannah whisper something to Lucretia. When I leaned over to scold her, she was staring wide eyed at a spot just above Reverend Clowes' head. All color had drained from her face. Next to her, Lucretia was trying to stifle a giggle. Hannah was holding her stomach. She and Lucretia were trying so hard to keep from laughing out loud they were shaking. Mrs. Gill turned around and glared. Recognizing an embarrassing outburst was imminent, I took each one by the arm and ushered them quickly down a side aisle and out to the street. I hoped people might think it was a coughing spell.

On the street, Hannah, cried, "I saw it clear as day! I saw him. I saw the Ghost of Lord Howe. He had long white hair that flowed behind him. He floated over Reverend Clowes head and disappeared through the glass window."

She looked around as if she expected Lord Howe's ghost to follow her and jumped when the side door of the church creaked open then shut. Ebenezer had followed us, worried Lucretia had suffered a relapse of the whooping cough. This set off another spell of nervous laughter for Lucretia. It was contagious. Hannah and I started laughing and soon Ebenezer joined in, not knowing why. We laughed all the way back to Montgomery Street. It took forever for us to stop laughing long enough to explain to Ebenezer and then Mr. Goodrich what Hannah thinks she saw.

Ebenezer, Lucretia, and I saw nothing but Hannah says she clearly saw the Ghost of Lord Howe. He had long white hair that reached to the middle of his back.

Mr. Goodrich was amused. "It is possible," he said. "It is well known that Lord Howe cut his hair short before beginning the march to Ticonderoga. He was killed at Trout Brook before reaching the fort. Hair continues to grow after death."

Lord Howe was an English nobleman, an officer in the British Army, and a vestryman of St. Peter's Church. Captain Philip Schuyler was with him when he was mortally wounded and brought the body back to Albany. He is buried under the church chancel.

Privately, Mr. Goodrich confided there are others who also have seen Lord Howe's ghost.

Monday, November 1, 1813

All Saint's Day

The winds have shifted to the North. The temperature dropped and the sky is gray. The almanac page turns to November, the dreary month.

Ebenezer went to work at the usual time, returned for a silent midday meal, and was out again till late. Samuel returned from Ballston Spa on the afternoon coach. There is more bad news. Ebenezer has used Samuel's name to endorse several gambling loans. The man I thought I knew has stolen from us and lied.

"How will this work out?" I asked Samuel.

"It will all work out," Samuel reassured me repeatedly. Repeatedly I asked how.

"It is a mystery," he finally admitted, "but it will all work out."

Samuel usually retires after me and sometimes after Ebenezer returns home. Last night he bid me an early good night.

"At Union I learned sleep has the power to solve the most complex problems."

I sat before a dying fire, alone, and cold. Finally I too took a candle and went to bed. I was still awake when I heard Ebenezer's heavy footsteps on the stairs. When he heaved himself into bed I did not speak. Only when I heard his sleep sounds did I succumb to my own fitful sleep.

Tuesday, November 2, 1813

Samuel has decided not to leave Albany. He feels it is his duty to rescue Ebenezer and protect Lucretia and me. There is only one solution. If Ebenezer will not stay away from his gambling associates, and if Samuel and I cannot keep him away from them, he has only one choice. He must keep the gamblers away from Ebenezer. He has an opportunity to drive a wedge between Ebenezer and one of his biggest partners, a gentleman from New York. The man will be in Albany later this week. When he arrives, it is his custom to contact Ebenezer to arrange a card game. Samuel will contact the gentleman first.

The risk is great because it may cause Ebenezer to do something desperate, but there is no other choice.

Keep the faith. It will all work out. Keep the faith. It will all work out. I say the words over and over. Keep the faith it will all work out.

Friday, November 5, 1813

Guy Fawkes Day

Remember, remember
The Fifth of November
The Gunpowder Treason and plot.
I know of no reason why Gunpowder Treason
Should ever be forgot.

Guy Fawkes, Guy Fawkes,
`Twas his intent
To blow up the King and the Parliament.

Three score barrels of powder below
Poor old England to overthrow.
By God's providence he was catch'd,
With a dark lantern and burning match.

Ebenezer returned home early looking disheveled. He would not say what was wrong. He went straight to bed without eating. Did Samuel carry out his plan?

Later, Samuel explained. "When Mr. "X" comes to Albany, he goes to Mr. M'Donald's retreat for bathing and hair-dressing. When I heard he had arrived I delivered a letter to him which stated I would take measures against him if he permitted Ebenezer to accrue further debts. I warned Mr. "X" that future loans would not be repaid."

When Ebenezer learned about the letter, he was furious. "What do you mean by writing such a note to my friend? Do you intend to pursue all my friends in this way?"

Samuel said there was a stormy outburst between the two but he stood up to his older and much taller brother. "Friends? It is not your friends I pursue, but your enemies."

Flooded with anger, Ebenezer was speechless.

"He recognized my resolve. I believe if Ebenezer was not financially dependent on me, he might have told me to pack my belongings and leave. Betsey, if it were not for you and Lucretia, I might have done just that."

Saturday, November 6, 1813

This morning Ebenezer woke early. He packed a small travel case and said he'd been called out of town. He did not say where he was going or how long he would be away. Samuel's guess is that for the second time in a week, his mother, Esther, and Isaac will receive a visit. Mr. "X"? He returned to New York.

Over and over I rehearse what I will say to Ebenezer when and if he returns. My thoughts become tangled. I lose the logic of my lines and start over.

My mother was born today seventy-one years ago. How did she ride life's ups and downs?

Monday, November 8, 1813

For three nights I lay in bed storm-tossed and sleepless. For three days I tried to concentrate on my chores. I felt as jittery as a maid with a snake loose in the cellar.

When Ebenezer returned, would things be better or worse? Not knowing, I felt helpless. Keep the faith. It will all work out. I said the words to convince myself.

When Ebenezer returned early this morning, it was like seeing a ghost. He said the trip was productive. He did not mention the Edwards, Mr. "X", or the row with Samuel.

There were so many feelings swirling around me, I didn't know which one to latch on to. I felt confused. I was relieved, but also angry. Ebenezer didn't notice. His mind was on the day's festivities to honor Oliver Perry who is passing through Albany on his return to Rhode Island.

Citizens and local military commands will meet Perry at Douw's Tavern on the Western Turnpike and escort him to Albany. A salute will be fired and Capitol bells will ring for one hour. Mayor Van Rensselaer will present Commodore Perry with an engraved sword and a gold box containing the keys to the city.

Ebenezer accepted Cousin John and Abigail's invitation to join them tomorrow evening at the gala planned to honor our "Hero of Lake Erie."

Wednesday, November 10, 1813

A full moon, the frost moon

THE EAGLE TAVERN

November's full frost moon was the perfect backdrop for Oliver Perry's reception at the Eagle Tavern. Draped across the front of the tavern was a banner bearing Perry's famous words: "We have met the enemy, and they are ours."

In attendance were Mayor Van Rensselaer, Judge Kent and his wife, the Russells, the Henrys, the Fowlers, the Van Vechtens, Ten Eycks, Marvins, Gills, Goulds, and numerous other Albany citizens. All were dressed in evening finery. All, including Ebenezer and I, were in high spirits.

Commodore Perry is a handsome young man. He appeared to enjoy the attention he received from the ladies at the reception, but I know he is looking forward to returning to his wife Elizabeth Champlin in Kingstown.

The belle of the ball was Maria Gansevoort. Since her father's death last year, her brother has been entrusted with securing a suitable husband: one who could strengthen family ties (and property). A proper match would be to another Dutch patrician. General Peter Gansevoort would not want his daughter falling into the hands of a Yankee or, heaven forbid, a foreigner! Maria attended Mr. Merchant's Dancing Academy and studies piano with Mr. Goldberg. She is a pious woman who reads Scripture in English and Dutch.

ALLAN MELVIL

Maria looked beautiful in a flowing shell pink gown, cut low. At her throat was a string of matched pearls. Her hair, the color of polished chestnuts, was arranged in loose curls pinned in place with ivory combs. Many young officers sought Maria's attention. However, she had eyes only for the dashing Allan Melvill, dressed and coiffed in the latest French style. He is not the kind of man her father would choose, but she seems enamored.

It was an evening of gaiety, reminding me why I married Ebenezer despite my family's concerns. We danced till late in the evening and did not return to Montgomery Street until after ten o'clock.

This morning I received an invitation addressed to Mr. and Mrs. Ebenezer Foot, Esq. Judge and Mrs. James Kent request the pleasure of our company for tea at their home on Saturday next. Last evening they had engaged Ebenezer and myself in a pleasant conversation.

I'm excited, but nervous. What will I wear?

Friday, November 12, 1813

What happened when Ebenezer was away? He seems a changed man. For the third evening in a row, he and Samuel are playing chess. Neither one speaks. Samuel fingers one game piece then another, deliberating his next move. Ebenezer lifts his head, leans back with his arms crossed and smiles. It is too early to tell if Ebenezer is winning. It is too early to tell if Samuel's intervention succeeded.

> Keep the faith.
> It will all work out.

Monday, November 15, 1813

Tea at the home of Judge and Mrs. Kent was elegant. We arrived at the door of their beautiful home at 21 Columbia Street just as the sun was setting.

After taking our coats, the Kent's manservant Jack led us down a paneled hall, past the Ezra Ames portraits of Mrs. Kent and the Judge, and into their large dining room. Ten matching mahogany chairs surrounded a long table. On the snowy white linen cloth were crystal goblets, blue and white china, transparent teacups, and two silver candelabra with six tapers. At one end of the room was a Dutch cabinet. Along the side wall were two inlaid card tables. In the fireplace was a pyramid of blazing birch logs laid on brass andirons. The fire and candles reflecting in the room's window glass, mirrors, and table crystal made the room sparkle.

Mr. and Mrs. Henry were seated. The Van Vechtens, who arrived after us, waited in the hall with Judge and Mrs. Kent to greet Mr. and Mrs. Ten Eyck, rounding the corner of North Market onto Columbia. Once all the guests had arrived, Judge Kent escorted Mrs. Kent to her seat at one end of the table and took his position at the other.

Mrs. Kent poured tea for each guest, adding sugars, lemon or cream as requested. A servant carried a cup to each guest, starting with Mrs. Henry, the most elderly lady present, then to the other ladies by seniority, and finally the gentlemen in the same order. Each of us had a saucer into which we poured the tea for cooling. I prayed I would not spill tea or knock over the delicate cup. Two other servants passed bread, butter, meat, toast, cheese, preserves, and fruitcake. I made careful note of the seating assignments and exact placement of the dishes so I could later make a map of the table.

Mr. Van Vechten engaged me in a conversation about the romantic poetry of William Wordsworth. He laughed about the "mad, bad, and dangerous" Lord Byron. He turned to me and recited,

> And on that cheek, and o'er that brow,
> So soft, so calm, yet eloquent,
> The smiles that win, the tints that glow,
> But tell of days in goodness spent,
> A mind at peace with all below,
> A heart whose love is innocent!

Everyone laughed. My cheeks turned pink.

After tea, the men retired to the library and Mrs. Kent entertained the ladies in the withdrawing room. Ebenezer says men have been discussing the same three topics since the beginning of time: politics, money, and the current scoundrel of the day. He confirmed later the men's conversation was about Mr. Madison's war, the outrageous increase in the price of wheat, and the scandalous behavior of a local bank official.

Women have been talking of their children since the beginning of time. Mrs. Van Vechten and Mrs. Henry commented on the remarkable progress of over four hundred children at Mr. Dale's Lancaster School. With more enthusiasm they turned the topic to their own sons Jacob and John, Jr. Both will attend The Albany Academy. Mrs. Ten Eyck said nothing about her daughter Betsey. Mrs. Kent did not mention Mary.

Toward the end of the evening, Mrs. Kent asked me to call her Betsy and inquired how I was adjusting to Albany. I wanted to tell her that, after six years, Albany is adjusting to me but I am not adjusting to

Albany. I felt I could be more frank if we were having a private tête-à-tête. I simply replied I was looking for a proper school for Lucretia. The ladies smiled but said nothing because at that moment the gentlemen entered the room and the female conversation halted.

At the sound of the nine o'clock bell we said our thank-yous and farewells. As Ebenezer and I were leaving, Betsy took my hand and asked me to call on her after Thanksgiving. She said she would enjoy talking further with me. I am surprised. What would we talk about?

Saturday, November 20, 1813

Bless the sage who invented Thanksgiving and placed it in the bleak month of November. Thanksgiving turns us inward to our fire and family. It cheers body and soul.

Mother is joining us for Thanksgiving this year. She thinks it is humorous to visit her daughter. "When children grow up," she says, "they fall from the tree and blow away. How often do you see the tree follow the scattered leaves?"

Even before the Thanksgiving proclamation was read, wagons began rolling in from surrounding towns loaded with turkeys, chickens, and ducklings. Now they are flying out of the markets and into homes on Columbia, Montgomery, and Water Streets.

Last night Ebenezer said he had a plan. "On Thanksgiving Day, I will sell for thirteen cents the turkey we bought this week for ten. Don't worry, we will still have our turkey dinner. The day after Thanksgiving, I will buy a turkey for eight cents. How much will that put us ahead?" he quizzed, laughing to himself.

Only Hannah was amused and calculated the number. Lucretia's mouth dropped open in horror. Mr. Goodrich shook his head and frowned. Samuel and I locked eyes, making a silent agreement to safeguard our turkey. Except for Ebenezer's chuckling, there was silence before Mother stood and directed Hannah to clear the dishes.

When I heard Lucretia's bedtime prayers, I knew she was worried about our Thanksgiving dinner. I told her what I hoped was true. Her father was only teasing.

Wednesday, November 24, 1813

In the pie closet are apple, mince, squash, and cranberry pies. Mother and I will make a Marlborough pudding.

MARLBOROUGH PUDDING

Mix 12 spoons of stewed apples, 12 of sherry, 12 of sugar, 12 of creamed butter and 12 well beaten eggs, a little cream, lemon juice if available, and a pinch of nutmeg. Pour into a pastry lined baking dish. Bake in a hot oven until it is firmly set, about 1¼ hour.

This afternoon I will bring a chicken pie, a squash pie, and a package of Hyson-Souchong tea to the Widow Henry on South Pearl.

The poor of Albany are too proud to beg. Not in Hadley. Children go door to door with a pillowcase asking, "Please can you share something for our family's Thanksgiving?" I remember Mother would fill the bottom of the pillowcase with rice and tie it with twine to make a second layer for the flour. The flour layer would also be tied off. At the top, she stuffed apples and raisins. It wouldn't be Thanksgiving without raisins. Pressing and shaking her offerings to squeeze in more, mother said, "Always give in good measure, pressed down, shaken together, running over."

She never guessed sister Lucretia and I would dress in raggedy clothes and beg from neighbors. In this disguise I am ashamed to say we got back more than we gave.

Thursday, November 25, 1813

Thanksgiving Day

There is no frugality of food on our table or gratitude in our hearts. The turkey is roasting in a hot oven. A large table is set in the front room. John, Abigail, Maria, Edwin, and Adelaide will join us for the feast. We are well and fortunate to be together. After dinner, there will be games of hide the slipper and blind man's bluff. Ebenezer will tell family stories.

Thanksgiving is a time for family. Tomorrow is the ordination of Reverend Clowes.

Saturday, November 27, 1813

Young people are not often interested in history. Having so little past of their own, they cannot imagine ever having any. The exception is family history. Gathered around the fire on Thanksgiving, Ebenezer enthralled Lucretia, Hannah, and the three Ely children with stories of Nathaniel Foote. He emigrated from Colchester, England, almost two hundred years ago. Ebenezer's side of the family dropped the "e" on the Foot name.

"Uncas, a friendly Mohican sachem, invited great-great-great-great-grandfather Nathaniel and nine other men to settle in Wethersfield. It was called Dancing Place or Place of Games. It took courage and hard work for the Ten Adventurers, as they were called, because back in 1634, Wethersfield was a wilderness. They had no livestock, no agriculture, no church, and no schools. They had no roof but the heavens and no bed but the forest floor. There were no comforts of any kind except family. Furthermore, they lived in constant fear of the Pequot Indians who tried to drive out the white settlers. Three years after Nathaniel and his family arrived in Wethersfield, a terrible thing happened."

To build the tension of the story, Ebenezer stood up and acted out the next part. "A band of Pequot warriors paddled up the Connecticut River and hid in the forest to spy on the settlers. After dark they made a surprise attack on the village, massacring six men and three women."

Ebenezer crouched down to imitate the Indians and leapt toward the girls with an imaginary tomahawk in his hand. "Two young girls were kidnapped and carried off to the Pequot's campgrounds in Mystic." Here he grabbed Lucretia and little Adelaide and galloped around the room. Their kicking and squealing was just the effect Ebenezer wanted. "The girls would be raised as Indian maidens and married to Indian braves. Fortunately, they were rescued and returned to Wethersfield where they lived happily ever after. Great-great-great-great-grandfather Nathaniel owned over four hundred acres and became one of the wealthiest men in town."

I believed it was a mistake to tell this story to the children right before bed, but Lucretia thought it would be fun to live in a tepee and become an Indian princess. "My Indian name is Light From Above. I will marry an Indian prince named Light Horse."

Monday, November 29, 1813

Betsy Kent sent an invitation for tea. Why does she want a special visit with me? We are so different. She is elegant and dignified. What will we talk about? Do we have anything real to discuss? A conversation about the weather, even if drawn out beyond the day's situation to yesterday's conditions and tomorrow's forecast, would be concluded in five minutes. Her refreshments will occupy us for a while. "What fine tea. The almond toast is delicious."

Should I ask her opinion of Mr. Bernard's theater? Is it proper to inquire about the books she is reading? Dare I ask her thoughts about The Albany Academy? Should I ask how Mary is progressing with Mrs. Thompson? When there is a lapse in the conversation she will offer more tea. Would it be rude to decline? How many cups of tea are sufficient before I can leave? What will I do if I need to use the necessary room? Who determines when the visit is over? Do I need to return her hospitality? She has the manners and decorum that would dignify a duchess and I have no one to guide me in social matters.

Wednesday, December 1, 1813

Ten years ago Ebenezer and I promised to love, comfort, honor, obey, and keep each other through sickness and health as long as we both shall live. We were married a few days past the full moon at my mother's house in Hadley when the family gathered for Thanksgiving.

"Your mother is the reason I married you," Ebenezer told me. His mother had advised him "Marry a woman with a good mother who does not meddle with the concerns of her neighbors and who, along with a proper degree of industry and economy, possesses a love of reading and a desire of knowledge."

I think women should follow the same advice; marry a man with a good mother who loves learning. Ebenezer's mother gave him her blessing to pursue an education even though he was needed to help with the farm. She told Ebenezer she was happy I was more than a "pot wrestler!" Is this how she viewed herself? My brothers and sisters feared I was too serious to be married, and Ebenezer not serious enough. Mother's silence at our wedding was disturbing. I attributed it to my move to New York.

Women walk a narrow line in courtship matters. They must not be too flirtatious or they will risk being considered forward. If they are too reticent, they are passed over. Before entering into a courtship, a lady needs to be sure of the gentleman's character. There is no room for a mistake because once the relationship has begun, it is difficult (if not impossible) for the woman to extricate herself. She will be viewed as fickle. Even worse is the potential for being jilted. She will be blamed.

Choosing a husband is like buying fabric. From a distance the material may look attractive, but it is important to thoroughly inspect the quality of the goods and not appear too eager. I recommend visiting trustworthy shopkeepers. Be sure of the price, learn the origin of the material, and watch closely as it is measured. Once cut, the material cannot be returned.

Samuel's advice about marriage is the same as Benjamin Franklin's:

Keep your eyes wide open before marriage, and half-shut afterwards.

Since his out of town business trip, Ebenezer has been home every night. He reads to us from one of Mr. North's books or plays chess with Samuel.

I resolve to be a good partner to Ebenezer, but by keeping my eyes wide open.

Friday, December 3, 1813

The problem with my worrying is, I am usually wrong about which ones to latch on to. Most things I worry about never happen. My tea with Betsy Kent was nothing like I imagined. Did we converse about the weather, Thanksgiving, tea and toast, or children? No. Did she share the hidden spaces of her heart, the places rarely shared with others? To my great surprise, yes.

"My dear Betsey," she began, "can I be candid with you?" Before I could reply, she continued. "I believe I have a confidential friend in you and Ebenezer. James and I both feel we must share with you and your husband, a matter we believe is of mutual concern."

I hesitated, and she continued. "First, I must tell you that, throughout our marriage, the Judge has had one weakness. His love …" Here she paused. I wanted to halt the conversation. Intimacies shared too soon are risky. Before I had a chance to stop her she finished the sentence. "… his love of books." I relaxed. "His love of books is admirable, but it has led to an extravagance that occasionally leads to a problem with our finances. As happens with so many things, however, his love of books and extravagance on a library turned out to be an unexpected blessing for me and possibly you."

JAMES KENT (1763-1847), CHIEF JUSTICE
NEW YORK SUPREME COURT, PAINTING BY EZRA AMES.
COURTESY, ARCHIVES AND COLLECTIONS OF THE ALBANY ACADEMIES

Betsy still did not wait for my response. "Let me tell you about a book I discovered one afternoon when he was away: A Vindication of the Rights of Women. It is written by an extraordinary British writer, Mary Wollstonecraft. Truthfully, I do not know when or how the book came into my husband's possession."

I couldn't believe my ears. A book written by a woman? About women's rights? It suddenly struck me this was the book Miss Pierce recommended.

"Yes, I can see your shock," Betsy said. "I also was shocked. So bold. Written right on the spine of the book. Rights of Women. Women are told they do not need rights. Their rights are covered by fathers and husbands. Mary Wollstonecraft asserts that males and females are spiritually and intellectually equal. They both have God-given rights to life, liberty, and the pursuit of happiness."

She was giving the speech I could never have given to her.

"Betsey, you and I know Albany girls must have a school. I am grateful for the elementary education Mrs. Thompson has provided Mary. Now I believe she needs to be educated like her brother. Mrs. Thompson agrees. She has not taken any new students the past six months. She will keep her current students for as long as we wish. When a new school is ready, she promises to provide books for a modest library. We have gained tentative financial support from Mr. Henry, who has three daughters, and Mr. Ten Eyck and Mr. Van Vechten, who each have one. Mrs. Thompson believes Mr. Hutton will also support a girls' school.

Please share what I have said with Mr. Foot. Through his professional associations he is in an excellent position to solicit subscribers. We need to persuade others but we must proceed with caution and not create a strong opposition. As women, we must be inconspicuous. We exert our influence within the home. We know men do not succeed without the influence of the women closest to them, first their mothers, then their wives."

I assured her Mr. Foot would do all within his power to advance the idea of female education in Albany. We then turned our conversation to the heavy snow in November and our hopes for a mild winter. We promised to meet again in the New Year.

At the door, Betsy put her hand on my arm, turned away abruptly, and went back down the hall. When I saw her enter Judge Kent's library, I understood. She returned with Mary Wollstonecraft's book.

"Betsey, please share this with Mr. Foot. James and I would be honored to trust it with you for as long as you need." She drew me toward her and placed her face next to mine.

I have no idea how I descended the front steps without falling. How did I find my way home? I only remember carrying the book carefully, in two hands, aloft, a procession of one.

That evening Ebenezer and Samuel did not play chess. There were no stories from Aesop. I did not write letters. My husband and I retired early to our bedchamber. Ebenezer heard about my tea with Mrs. Kent and promised to read the book.

Saturday, December 5, 1813

Ebenezer has given Mary Wollstonecraft's book a close reading. He paid special attention to Judge Kent's notes in the margins. He agrees with him that although some of Wollstonecraft's ideas about marital relations are radical, she presents a well-deliberated argument for the rights of women regarding education.

I believed he was ready to "Be Bold and Begin." I was mistaken. Ebenezer has a realistic understanding of the challenges involved in garnering support. His explanation, though tedious, helped me understand why not to plunge forward.

"There is a diversity of opinion about female education. We need to be aware of all points of view. There are strong supporters for educating girls. Some are outspoken and some are silent. On the other side, there are those who want to preserve traditional roles. Many ladies and gentlemen enjoy the benefits, the stability, the safety, and security of separate spheres for men and women. They oppose change. They see only the disruption change brings and none of the rewards.

In both groups are individuals driven by strong emotion. They are angry either about what is being denied them, or fear what they might lose. Men rally against a cause with more passion than for a cause. Fear is a powerful tool, and this is the tool they choose."

How many times have I heard it is women who are controlled by their emotions?

Ebenezer's strategy is to reach the ones who will be supportive when they are informed. They need to know what will be taught and by whom, the tuition, what kind of school building is planned, and where it will be. Some will be influenced by the status of other subscribers. All need to be persuaded of the advantages of female education and the risks to our society of the status quo.

With the support of Mr. Van Vechten, Mr. Ten Eyck, Mr. Henry, the Kents, Cousin John and Ebenezer, we have eight students. According to Ebenezer, "We need ten. Twenty would be better."

I wanted to add the three Allen girls, but Mrs. Allen's instructions were specific; deliver the note to Moses and Solomon when Mr. Foot has prepared the subscription paper.

"Fifteen girls would be sufficient," Ebenezer said. "I know Mr. Fowler approves. I will speak to Mr. Gill, Mr. Brown, and the men at St. Peter's. Reverend Clowes is not gaining support for the tutoring group he's been talking about since spring."

Monday, December 6, 1813

St. Nicholas Day

Dutch children love St. Nicholas. Fanny Roorback showed Lucretia a picture of a kindly man with twinkly eyes and rosy cheeks. The scarlet cape and shepherd's crook he wears is because a long, long time ago he was a bishop. He rides a white horse and carries a huge pack filled with gifts for good children."

The night before St. Nicholas Day, Fanny and Orville fill a wooden shoe with straw and carrots for St. Nicholas's horse. Mrs. Roorback uses a cookie press, a koeplanken, to bake special St. Nicholas spice cookies. Children leave a note.

> St. Nicholas my good friend
> I have served you always.
> If you give me something now
> I will love you all my life.

The next morning, Fanny and Orville find their shoes filled with nuts and an orange. If they have been bad, the shoe is filled with coal.

Lucretia wants to put out a shoe to see if Saint Nicholas will leave her something. Ebenezer says no. "Good behavior is its own reward. Do you love St. Nicholas only if he gives you a treat?"

Samuel dismisses Ebenezer. "It sounds harmless to me. We need fun this dark time of year. It's like fishing. Drop a hook and line and see what you catch."

Fanny scolds Samuel. "The gifts of St. Nicholas are to remind us Christmas is about service and generosity."

St. Nicholas lived more than fifteen hundred years ago. The power of good deeds is strong.

Tuesday, December 7, 1813
The full moon before Yule

Wednesday, December 8, 1813
Society of Church Ladies meeting

In a hushed voice, as if it was confidential, Mrs. Brown told me her husband talked with Mr. Foot after church. She did not elaborate but I think it is a good sign. Not a good sign is what I overheard Mrs. Gill tell Mrs. Henry. "The Marvins plan to send Emma and Louisa to Miss Pierce in Litchfield. That's the school Mary Clark attends. Mr. Marvin wants us to send Martha and Margaret. That way we could share the cost of coach travel. It is three dollars and twenty-five cents one way. It would be a wonderful opportunity for our girls but I don't know if I could send them so far away."

My stomach flipped.

When I told Ebenezer about the ladies' conversation, he confirmed Mr. Brown will withdraw Annabella from Miss Brenton's when the new school is ready. He is sure neither Mr. Gill nor Mr. Marvin will send their children away while the girls are so young. He has not been able to talk with Mr. Fowler, but is certain he will lend his support.

The Kents (one), Henrys (three), Van Vechtens (one), Ten Eycks (one), Elys (one), Lucretia, and now Annabella Brown makes nine. Mariam Fowler is ten. Mrs. Allen's granddaughters add up to thirteen.

Thursday, December 9, 1813
Lucretia's birthday

Nine years old on the ninth. Lucretia's feet have not touched the ground since she opened the gift from her father: a rose gold bracelet made by Mr. Boyd. It is the first present he has ever given her. There is a delicate chain woven from Lucretia's hair. The octagonal clasp is set with a dark stone. She dances around the front room, holding her wrist high, admiring her reflection in the glass window.

"Now that Lucretia is turning into a young lady, she needs to be adorned like a young lady." Since her recovery from the whooping cough Ebenezer has been spoiling Lucretia. I do not intervene. I know of a more precious adornment she will soon receive.

Thursday, December 16, 1813

There was a terrible accident at the Watervliet arsenal. Cartridges exploded trapping workmen and twenty children inside. Three children were killed instantly. It is a mystery why some are given so few years and others many. In The Gazette is a story about Jacob Bellijeaux, a tailor from New Canaan. He was born in 1697 which means he is one hundred sixteen! Someone verified his age from his original apprentice papers.

The truth is, it is not the number of years we are given, but what we do with the years we receive.

Friday, December 17, 1813
Samuel's birthday

Samuel is twenty-three. Except for being a prisoner to the weed, from which he is trying to break free, he is a credit to the Foot family.

When his father became mentally and physically exhausted by the farm, it was Samuel Mrs. Foot relied on. When he turned fourteen, Ebenezer believed Samuel should begin a classical education. Mrs. Foot recognized Samuel's need for more supervision than she could provide. She knew he deserved to further his studies like his two older brothers. Her decision to release him is testimony to the high value the Foot family places on education.

Through Ebenezer's generosity Samuel attended the grammar school at Union, then the College. He left before finishing the last term and began a law clerkship with Judge Thompson in Milton. Each week Samuel is setting aside a portion of his earnings to repay Ebenezer.

At Union, Samuel learned to read Latin. After supper he often entertains us with a story from Mr. North's Fabulae Aesopi. Samuel knows I am impatient for an academy for girls. He knows I want to add Latin to the curriculum. Tonight, the fable is about patience and greed.

One sunny morning, a housewife gathers a large basket of newly ripened filberts, brings them to her pantry, and stores them in a pitcher. A few days later, she is hungry and remembers the delicious nuts. She puts her hand in the pitcher and grasps as many as her hand will hold. With her fist so full, she cannot withdraw her hand past the neck of the pitcher. The wise husband offers the solution. "Do not be greedy, my good wife. If you take a smaller handful, you will succeed." The moral is do not take too many filberts at once.

Although it was another foolish housewife and wise husband story, I understand it is wise not to attempt too much at one time. Lucretia will have a school. Perhaps my great, great granddaughters will study Latin.

Saturday, December 18, 1813

The Scovilles want Hannah to return to Connecticut for a visit at Christmas. They sent the fare for a coach, and she leaves Monday morning at eight. I will miss her, but Christmas is the time for families to be together, warm their toes before a blazing Yule log, drink a cup of wassail, and eat roast spare rib with Yorkshire pudding.

Tuesday, December 21, 1813

The night of the winter solstice is the longest of the year. The sun dips low behind the back garden and has disappeared by supper. The river is closed to navigation. Ebenezer promises he will not cross until the ice is thicker. He teases:

Strong beer, stout cider, and a good fire
Are things this season doth require.

Captain Roorback's almanac confirms December 25 is Christmas. Mr. Goodrich says December is too cold to have "shepherds abiding in the fields keeping watch over their flock by night." Samuel agrees. "If Jesus wanted us to know the exact day of his birth, he would have told us."

Some Protestants disdain celebrating Christmas. I believe in keeping Christmas. Lucretia and I will gather princess pine to decorate the doors of St. Peter's.

Friday, December 24, 1813

Christmas Eve

Te Deum Laudamus. We praise thee, O God.

The doors and windows of our church are dressed with evergreens. The smell of fresh pine lifts the spirit. The sanctuary is illuminated with candles.

For New England Congregationalists, Christmas is a somber day. They are horrified at the glory of our service. They criticize the singing, chanting, standing up, and kneeling down in the English Church.

It is true. Christmas can be irreverent. Revelry in cities like Boston, New York, and Philadelphia is primarily about the bottle and bowl. We have lost the true meaning of wassail. It used to be an opportunity to open our homes and share with the poor. It has become a chance for bands of rowdies to break into rich men's homes and make demands.

Good master and good mistress
As you sit beside the fire
Pray think of us poor children
Who wander in the mire.
Love and Joy come to you
And to you your wassail, too,
And God bless you, and send you
A Happy New Year,
And God send you a Happy New Year.

Saturday, December 25, 1813

Adeste Fidelis. Glory be to God on high; and on earth, peace to all people of good will.

On Christmas Day businesses are closed, though some only draw the shutters tight to appear closed. Lift the latch and you'll be welcomed inside for business as usual.

Our family believes in keeping Christmas, not with rowdy revels, drinking, and gambling, but with love of family, gratitude for our blessings, and charity to those less fortunate.

Thursday, December 30, 1813

I expected the letter from the Scovilles would bring greetings and best wishes for the year ahead and information about her return to Albany. I was wrong. Hannah has decided to remain with her family. I thought she was happy in our home. Mr. Scoville believes Hannah will benefit from further tutoring in mathematics. He has engaged a recent graduate of Yale College.

Over and over I read,

Mrs Scoville and I are grateful for your influence on Hannah. We expected she would gain housekeeping skills. We did not expect she would become interested in furthering her education. Her dream is to become a teacher like you. One never knows what the future will bring.

Thank you for accepting Hannah into your family. She has wonderful memories of her time with you, Mr. Foot, Samuel, and her

Albany sister, Lucretia. We send kind regards and pray you will be blessed in the new year. John Scoville, Watertown, Connecticut

I am happy Hannah will pursue an education. It means a brighter future for her. Mr. Scoville's kind words help. Nevertheless, I am sad. One person's steps forward means loved ones are left behind.

Friday, December 31, 1813

A gibbous waxing moon

Hold a mirror to the moon on the evening before the New Year. The number of moons reflected reveals the number of blessings for the year ahead. I see one nearly full moon. It looms large and clear in the western sky.

I face the first day of a new year with a grateful heart. We have an abundance of hickory logs, a well-stocked root cellar, a cheerful and healthy family, and the prophecy of the moon. 1814 will be an important year for me, a turning point in my life.

Saturday, January 1, 1814

On First Day, Montgomery Street is busy as midsummer. Bundled against the cold, the neighbors tip their hats, curtsy, and greet each other with "Happy New Year" and "Wes Hail: Good Health to You and Your Family."

The Children sing:

We are not daily beggars
That beg from door to door,
But we are neighbors' children
Whom you have seen before.

Adults reply:

Love and joy come to you,
And to you your wassail, too,
And God bless you, and send you

A Happy New Year
And God send you a Happy New Year.

On First Day, we open our home to neighbors. The Gould family, Mr. Backus, Mr. Mancius, Teunis Van Vechten, Roorbacks, Browns including the older Mrs. Brown, Mrs. Ellison and her boarder Mr. Haney, the whole Russell household, the Scrymsers and even the old curmudgeon, Mr. Groesbeeck, honored us by stopping in for a cup from our wassail bowl. I could not buy cardamom this year, but the wassail was spicy enough. One change I made to the recipe was to separate the eggs. First I beat the yolks, then the whites and slowly stirred them into the hot ale.

WASSAIL RECIPE

2 qt. ale, 4/5 qt. dry sherry, 2 cups sugar, 3 whole cloves, 3 whole allspice, 3 cardamom seeds coarsely broken, 1 cinnamon stick, broken, 1 teaspoon ground ginger, 1 teaspoon ground nutmeg, 6 eggs, separated, 2 red apples, sliced to float on top.

There was no shortage of love and joy around our wassail bowl. Mr. Russell took me aside to thank me for helping Julia. "I have great admiration for you, Mrs. Foot. I wish Julia's two older sisters had a similar opportunity."

In front of Mr. Russell, Mr. Gould, Captain Roorback, and several others, Mr. Scrymser bragged about his granddaughter Katrina's progress in arithmetic. Chuckling to himself, he lifted his third cup of wassail to toast me. "Katrina has changed the way we keep our accounts thanks to you, Mrs. Foot-and thanks to me who planted the idea in her father's head."

Such a bold compliment! I was amazed at the confidence of my response. "Thank you for your kind words, Mr. Scrymser. Katrina is gifted in mathematics. It is my pleasure to observe her gaining mastery in the subject. She will advance further." More amazing was his agreement. Tapping his cane forcefully to draw in a larger audience, Mr. Scrymser said, "Yes, our girl will go further."

Lately, Old Mrs. Brown is never far from Mr. Scrymser's side. She is in love. She touches the old man's hand, gazes into his eyes, agrees with his every word, and he thrives on the attention. Mrs. Brown adds, "Yes, yes and I am so proud of my own beautiful and smart granddaughter." Mr. Scrymser is hard of hearing, and people scatter when Mrs. Brown starts talking, so I don't think anyone but me heard what she said next. "Annabella is one of a select group of girls who have been chosen to enroll in a special school for girls in Albany."

Mrs. Brown's comment was disturbing. Our school will not be selective. Our mission is democratic.

"Don't worry," Ebenezer reassured me later. "No one listens to her, plus when she hears the latest news, that is all she will talk about." I had not noticed Ebenezer's shift in mood. He just learned two young lads fell through the ice on the river. It took more than an hour to retrieve the boys, but they could not be revived. One was the carpenter's son, young John Meads. The other boy was his cousin William.

My happy First Day closed abruptly. How helpless I feel. As much as we warn young people of the dangers of thin ice, they still amuse themselves skating on the river. I pray for the souls of the two boys and solace for their parents, sisters, and friends.

Sunday, January 2, 1814

There was a pall over the Second Presbyterian Church during funeral services for John and William Meads. When the ground thaws in the spring they will be buried in the Presbyterian section of the cemetery.

At St. Peter's Church, the first Sunday after Christmas, there were prayers for those who grieve and prayers for those in need of renewed spirit. Mariam told Samuel she will soon be enrolling in an academy for girls. Ebenezer confirmed Mr. Fowler will subscribe now for Mariam and for the twins Louisa and Sarah when they are older. Mr. Fowler's business associate is also interested. "Mr. Knower is another of the New England men in Albany who place a high value on education. He is a generous benefactor to many civic causes in Albany, including an aid society for widows and orphans. Mr. Knower provided burial funds for John and William Meads."

Ebenezer forgot Mrs. Knower was my guest for tea last April. He has no recollection of me describing Mrs. Knower's disturbing visit to Mrs. Nugent.

Monday, January 3, 1814

Girls will not be chosen, as Mrs. Brown boasts. Our school will enroll girls without regard to the social standing, political leaning, or church affiliation of their father. We welcome any girl whose father wants and can afford an academy education. Our goal is to unite not divide.

Our school will not be a seminary. Our family left behind the Church of Connecticut where it belongs: under every white steeple, at the edge of every green, in every town and small village in the state where liberty and justice exist for all as long as you are a member of the Congregational Church. Even after the Declaration of Independence in 1776, Connecticut retained their 1662 Charter. The state maintains the right to collect taxes to pay the salary of Congregational ministers. Elected officials are from the pillars of the church. Church members only do business with other church members. Separation of church and state is not an honored tradition in Connecticut. In Connecticut, Congregationalists are The Chosen. Episcopals, Baptists, Methodists, and Quakers are not The Chosen.

No. Our school will not be a seminary.

Thursday, January 6, 1814

A full moon, the wolf moon   Epiphany

The Ely family and the Foots celebrated Twelfth Night at the Gregorys in Sand Lake. Cousin John is good with horses and reserved a sleigh from Robison and Vanderbilt. Early this morning we departed from Montgomery Street in style. Our sleigh was freshly painted in colors of the newest fashion, twilight blue with black and gold decorative scrolls. The interior was painted a fiery vermillion. Tucked under pelts of gray wolf, and thanks to the warming effect of the vermillion, we were toasty warm.

Nothing lifts the spirits like gliding over fresh snow in an open sleigh. The sky was cerulean, a color seen only on a winter morning without clouds. The air smelled sweet as just baked johnnycake. I relaxed once we crossed the river and were headed east along the country cart road lined with white fences. Under a crystal canopy of hemlock, I felt like one of the three kings from the Orient. It is unusually quiet after a heavy snow, but the steady rhythm of harness bells stirred us into choruses of My Country `Tis of Thee and Yankee Doodle. We announced our approach to the Gregory house with the old favorite, Comin' thro' the Rye.

Cousin Lucretia welcomed us with cups of warm toddy. There were toasts to all at least once, sometimes twice. She served a spicy sausage pie from pork that had been given to Dr. Gregory. To commemorate Three Kings Day, she baked a vanilla gateau de rois. The lucky one who finds a bean hidden in the cake is crowned king or queen. Our Lucretia found the bean and will wear the crown.

Cousin Lucretia's daughter Lucretia did not find the bean and pierced our ears with a tantrum. It stopped when her mother promised to bake a second cake specially for her. Ebenezer, Cousin John, and I planned to solicit a subscription to our school from Dr. Gregory. Their daughter could board with one of us. Without even discussing the matter, we knew it would not be a good idea.

The best part of a party is when the dishes are cleared and the cloth is removed. The guests are well fed and relaxed. Restless youngsters are excused from the table to play games. The host and hostess are satisfied all has gone well. Everyone is aglow.

After the children tired of their games, they begged for a story from Uncle John. He obliged them with tales of his father, Colonel Doctor John Ely, a hero in the Revolutionary War. Before departing, Cousin Lucretia played the new parlor piano Dr. Gregory bought from Mr. Meacham. She and Dr. Gregory entertained us with a duet, Sweet is the Vale. He brought us to tears with a heart wrenching rendition of Highland Mary, and they sent us on our way with Meet Me by Midnight. The song was a perfect choice for our ride home under the full wolf moon. Guided by Polaris and protected by the great hunter, Orion, we neither saw nor heard a single wolf. We out-howled them with our Yankee Doodling and arrived home before Mr. Moore announced, "Twelve o'clock and all is well."

A Yankee boy is trim and tall,
And never over fat, sir;
At dance, or frolic, hop and ball,
As nimble as a rat, sir.

His door is always open found,
His cider of the best, sir;
His board with pumpkin pie is crown'd,
And welcome ev'ry guest, sir.

His country is his pride and boast,
He'll ever prove true blue, sir;
When call'd upon to give his toast,
'Tis Yankee doodle, doo, sir!

Lucretia put the Epiphany bean under her pillow and says she will sleep with it every night for one whole year.

No need for a candle tonight. I write by the light of the moon reflecting on snow.

Friday, January 7, 1814

We have lived on Montgomery Street six years, and yesterday was the first time I was invited inside the Gould home. Mrs. Gould asked to return my hospitality of last April. I am becoming quite the hoddy doddy. Betsy Kent invited me for the third time to her home next week.

After the required pleasantries, Mrs. Gould came to the point of her invitation. "Mr. Gould has built a flourishing hardware business in Albany. It is unfortunate our prosperity is because of Mr. Madison's war. We always expected Charles would be the beneficiary of Gould's Hardware. Alas his heart is elsewhere."

Mrs. Gould inhaled deeply, lowered her head, and sighed. Then she sat tall, smiled, and told me she and Mr. Gould are pleased Charles is interested in the field of medicine. "We will support his education to become a doctor." I returned a supportive smile, and she continued. "Mrs. Foot, Mr. Gould was surprised to hear you have been helping Katrina Scrymser with her arithmetic and she has made great progress. My husband believes our daughter Eliza has the mind for numbers, goodness knows I don't. He feels she would benefit from tutoring. She might be an asset to Gould's Hardware, at least until she is married. We would never send our daughter away, as the Marvins are contemplating, nor do we think it proper to engage a male tutor. Mrs. Foot, are you aware of a suitable female teacher for our daughter?"

Was she asking to engage me? I was uncertain. Somehow I found the courage to reply, "No, I am not aware of a suitable female teacher, but I believe it is time for Albany girls to have an academy, like the one being planned for Charles." Mrs. Gould didn't think that was what her husband had in mind, but said she would discuss it with him.

This matter concluded, we turned our conversation to the controversy about building a bridge across the river. It would boost business in Albany, but Troy merchants oppose the idea. They fear it will interfere with river traffic. The Dutch oppose any change that dips into their pocket. They look down on the liberal ideas of the growing number of men from New England. Mrs. Gould's solution is simple. "If the Dutch don't like the way things are changing in Albany, they should go back to where they came from!"

I hope to elevate girls above this level of problem solving.

Saturday, January 8, 1814

War creates many changes. Charles Gould wants to become a doctor. Eliza's father wants her to help in the hardware business.

After hearing about the heroism of her great uncle, Lucretia wants to become a doctor. She wants to attend Yale College. She wants to do something important so her descendants will remember her.

From the beach in Westbrook, we could see the hospital on Duck Island where Uncle John treated smallpox patients. At the beginning of the War of Independence he left the comforts of home, the attentions of his wife (one of the celebrated beauties of Connecticut), and his small hospital. He organized, equipped, and commanded a military unit. In the Battle of Long Island, the British burned his hospital and took him prisoner. His son Worthington made a daring rescue attempt, but Uncle John would not abandon his comrades. He remained as their physician for three more years until he was released on Christmas Day in 1780.

After the war, Uncle John rebuilt his hospital on Duck Island and developed a way to prevent small pox by injecting individuals with a small amount of the disease. This doesn't make sense to me but he was successful. Through word of mouth and advertisements in The Hartford Courant, he had many grateful patients.

Uncle John paid a high price for liberty. He gave generously to his country and fellow soldiers and was not repaid. I don't think he ever recovered physically or financially.

Should I tell Lucretia Yale College does not admit women and women cannot be doctors? Ebenezer struggles to secure subscribers for an academy for girls because some people do not believe in educating daughters.

What will I say to her? I will remind her of the Ely family motto, Ora et Labora. With prayer and work, anything is possible.

Tuesday, January 11, 1814

It has been snowing for three days, but nothing could keep me from my engagement with Betsy Kent. Head bent, skirt hiked up, I plowed through and arrived at 21 Columbia Street without mishap.

More difficult was to be patient through tea table talk. "Two sugars and cream please. Thank you. Yes, we had a happy Christmas. Yes, it was terrible news about the Meads boys. Yes, it is generous of the Common Council to send one thousand dollars to the farmers in western New York. They have been devastated by the war. Yes, I agree. There will eventually be a bridge across the Hudson River. You can't stop progress."

Finally, we arrived at the important topic. I confirmed Mr. Foot supports an academy for girls and has pledges from Dr. Ely, Mr. Brown, Mr. Fowler, and Mr. Knower. This week he will meet with our neighbor Mr. Russell who has three daughters and Mr. Gould who has one.

Betsy had her own good news. "As I informed you before Christmas, the Van Vechtens, Ten Eycks, and Henrys are supportive. With Margaret Hutton and our daughter Mary, that adds up to seven students. At the Dutch Church, Mr. Ten Eyck has persuaded Captain Roorback, and Mr. Van Vechten has persuaded Mr. Bleecker. He is one of the wealthiest men in Albany!"

Betsy continued, "Mr. Marvin at our church plans to send Emma and Louisa to Miss Sarah Pierce in Litchfield, but the girls are young. Perhaps they will change their mind and support a school in Albany."

I wanted to share my opinion that if the Marvins subscribe, the Gills also will. I wanted to tell her about Mrs. Allen's three grandchildren. I was adding up the total when she mentioned Mr. Henry and a vacant lot on Montgomery Street.

"Yes, it is true," Betsy said, responding to the questioning look on my face. "More than a year ago Mr. Henry represented Mr. John Lansing, Jr., in the matter of the Montgomery Street property abandoned by Thomas Anderson. The man has not responded to published notices about the issue, and Mr. Henry believes the property can be acquired. This would be the perfect location for the school. It would not be difficult to erect a suitable building."

When Betsy and I parted, she hugged me and said, "We are ready. It is time for Mr. Foot to prepare the subscription paper."

Thursday, January 13, 1814

According to Ebenezer, we are not ready. "Men will want to know the character and credentials of the teacher, the location of the school, and the tuition."

"And, we should give the school a name," John added.

I expected the name would be The Albany Academy. Since that is not possible, I suggested Albany Female Academy.

"It sounds too bold," objected Abigail.

John agrees with Abigail. If we want to appeal to a broad base of men, we need a less controversial name.

"A school name in good time," Ebenezer asserted. "First we should appoint a teacher. A lady teacher does not have the proper credentials, but we need to be sensitive to the concerns of fathers about trusting a male teacher with girls."

Overhearing the conversation, Mr. Goodrich suggested we seek the advice of Dr. Nott at Union College. John travels to Schenectady next week and will consult him.

Friday, January 14, 1814

Old Mr. Scrymser is hard of hearing, so how did he know of the discussion inside our house, four doors away? Katrina delivered this note from her grandfather.

Mrs. Foot, stop at my house this afternoon. James Scrymser, Sr.

"Stop at my house" meant exactly what it said. Though we were in the midst of a blizzard, he remained at the open door while I stood outside like a beggar, blown about on the front stoop.

"Mrs. Foot, I want the Scrymser name at the top of the school list. Bring that paper of your husband's to me. I'll see my son signs up Katrina."

I nearly fell backward off his slippery steps. Before he closed the door, I assured him the Scrymser name would be at the top of the list.

Saturday, January 15, 1814

Sunny

State Street is usually a racket of buyers and sellers. Folks from the country peddle turkeys, deer, and firewood. City folk are always haggling over price. During last week's blizzard, the street was quiet. When the snow finally stopped and the sun appeared, there was a total shift in the atmosphere. Tomorrow, men can dig out from the snow and return to business as usual. Today should be a day to play. Grown men, including Samuel, reverted to boys, bombing each other with snowballs and sliding recklessly down State Street.

Coasters collected in front of St. Peter's. At the sound of a whistle, they pushed off and flew down the hill at top speed. The goal is to dodge or dislodge other sledders and be the first to the bottom of the hill. Any obstacle sends the sledder and the obstacle flying. The somersaults and roll-overs are comical. Yips and yelps could be heard up and down the street. On the sidelines, spectators cheered for their favorites.

There will be plenty of work days ahead. Today was a day to celebrate snow. I have a special name for this silver letter holiday. Snow Day. It is a gift from Mother Nature. It is always a surprise, always appreciated.

Monday, January 17, 1814

So much can change in one year. It seems like yesterday Mr. North taught us about living a life of purpose. When I close my eyes I see Lucretia, Hannah, and I linked in our "eudaemonia" dance. I miss Hannah every day, but I know she is using the gift with her name. She is living a life of purpose.

I miss Mr. North. He would have made a great teacher, but God had other plans.

Friday, January 21, 1814

The new moon

John returned from the visit to Dr. Nott with this advice:

"Your teacher should not be an old man, lest the girls play the fool with him, or a very young man, lest he should run away with one of your daughters. There are many recent graduates of Harvard, Yale, and Brown who would be qualified to teach the girls. I can personally testify to the character and scholarship of Union College graduates." John hesitated before sharing Dr. Nott's specific recommendation. "You will not find a better man for the position than Horace Goodrich."

Horace Goodrich? It is true he is a scholar in Greek and Latin, the arts and sciences. He was a respected tutor at Union College and the top orator in the class of 1813. I have grown fond of Mr. Goodrich. He is not, as some believe, cold or aloof. He prefers to spend time in study and reflection. He thinks before he speaks and deliberates before he acts. He enjoys serving others and is loyal, but independent. Most important, he is a man of integrity.

John is ready to accept Dr. Nott's recommendation. Is Ebenezer? What about Mr. Goodrich's plan to become a lawyer? Ebenezer's quick response stunned me.

"Goodrich is an excellent choice! He can continue to read law with me and be our headmaster. At the school, he will be in an excellent position to bring me new business."

As expected, Goodrich said he would take the weekend to consider the proposal.

Monday, January 24, 1814

Two steps forward!

Mr. Goodrich has accepted the position and both Mr. Thomas Russell and his son Joseph will subscribe; four Russell girls. The Russells will speak to Mr. Center and other members of the Second Presbyterian Church. They believe the response will be positive.

"It is about time," Mrs. Russell said when she brought Julia for her lesson. She now claims, "A school for our girls is something I have wanted for many, many years. Finally Mr. Russell relents! Mary and Isabelle will have the same opportunity as Julia. Also, Joseph's daughter Abigail."

Tuesday, January 25, 1814

One step back!

We will not have the support of one neighbor. I do not carry the burden of judging men's souls for eternity, but I can point to the earthly evils of intemperance. When our neighbor imbibes, he beats his wife. When he returns from work, she cowers like a dog. Each beating is worse than the one before and she believes she must submit. I fear he will do irreparable harm. I want to help, but do not know how. None of the constables will interfere in a family matter. Most of them also drink too much and beat their wives.

Some men stand upright by clinging to the pillars of the church and marching in battalion. When they step off the path of righteousness, they have no individual strength. The Ely's expression is "petit coucher," meaning the man is a bit tipsy, but can get himself to bed. A "grand coucher" describes our neighbor. He needs help.

Some stray off the path with the change of seasons. They view it as a way to "clear out the cobwebs." Their wives know, like the weather, things change. The wind softens. The sun comes out. The men recover their senses and they step back in line. Our neighbor's problem is not seasonal. He has fallen so far down there is little chance for recovery. I am afraid his family will soon need help from Mr. Knower's aid society.

Reverend Clowes quotes the Bible. "Wives are to submit themselves to their husbands. The husband is the head of the wife as Christ is the head of man and God is the head of Christ." I say husbands should love their wives as Christ loves the Church and as God loves Christ. Beating is not love.

According to Samuel, it is all the fault of women.

Women make men love,
Love makes them sad;
Sadness makes them drink,
And drinking makes them mad.

Samuel Alfred Foot! Women are not the problem. It is not love that is the problem. It is immoderation. I ask Samuel if he blames women for his immoderate use of tobacco.

He always has an answer. "My dear Betsey, we only become old and wise like you by being young and foolish like me."

Friday, January 28, 1814

Ebenezer is optimistic success will be achieved one person at a time. "Remember Mr. Aesop's crow dying of thirst. He has a pitcher half filled with water, but he cannot get his head in far enough to drink. If he tips the pitcher, it could topple over and shatter on the stones. The clever crow sees that stones are the solution. Dropping one stone at a time into the pitcher, the crow brings the water level high enough to quench his thirst."

We now have more than twenty students. Does Mr. Aesop have a fable about counting your chicks before they are out of the shell?

BETSEY COLT FOOT (1774-1847). PAINTING ATTRIBUTED TO EZRA AMES.
GIFT OF SARAH ELIZABETH ARNOLD IN MEMORY OF HER MOTHER
MARTHA BOOTH SEELYE, GRANDDAUGHTER OF BETSEY FOOT.
COURTESY, ARCHIVES AND COLLECTIONS OF THE ALBANY ACADEMIES.

LUCRETIA FOOT, JUNE 1807, UNSIGNED PAINTING,
COURTESY OF SUSAN B. STRANGE.

SAMPLER OF LUCRETIA FOOT, TROY 1811. GIFT OF SUSAN B. STRANGE.
COURTESY, ARCHIVES AND COLLECTIONS OF THE ALBANY ACADEMIES.

CUPOLA, FISH AND PUMPKIN WEATHERVANE, PHOTOGRAPH
BY ALFRED K. SABISCH, COURTESY, ARCHIVES AND COLLECTIONS OF
THE ALBANY ACADEMIES.

NORTH PEARL STREET, NORTH OF MAIDEN LANE, ALBANY 1805.
JAMES EIGHTS, 1850. FISH AND PUMPKIN WEATHERVANE
VISIBLE ON SECOND PRESBYTERIAN CHURCH.

EAST SIDE OF MARKET STREET FROM MAIDEN LANE SOUTH,
ALBANY, 1805, JAMES EIGHTS (1798-1882). WATERCOLOR ON PAPER.
COURTESY, ALBANY INSTITUTE OF HISTORY AND ART.

We the Subscribers agree to send to Union School in Montgomery Street under the tuition of Mr. Horace Goodrich the number of female scholars affixed to our names for the space of one year from the first day of May next, and we also agree to pay to Ebenezer Foot, Twenty four Dollars, for each Scholar in four equal quarterly payments, the first payment to be on the first day of August next ——

February 24th 1814

SUBSCRIPTION DOCUMENT, FEBRUARY 24, 1814.
COURTESY, ARCHIVES AND COLLECTIONS OF THE ALBANY ACADEMIES.

UNION SCHOOL ON MONTGOMERY STREET. WATERCOLOR BY WILLIAM MORGAN,
COURTESY, ARCHIVES AND COLLECTIONS OF THE ALBANY ACADEMIES.

CENTENNIAL GRADUATION PROCESSION OF ALBANY ACADEMY FOR GIRLS, 1914.
COURTESY, ARCHIVES AND COLLECTIONS OF THE ALBANY ACADEMIES.

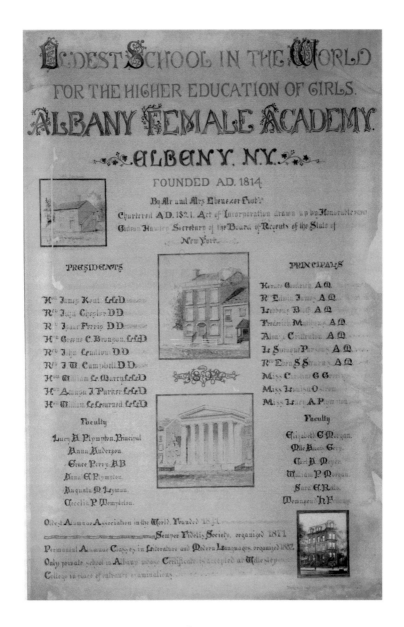

COLUMBIAN EXPOSITION WORLD'S FAIR, CHICAGO, 1893. CALLIGRAPHY
AND ART WORK BY WILLIAM MORGAN. COURTESY, ARCHIVES AND
COLLECTIONS OF THE ALBANY ACADEMIES.

Tuesday, February 1, 1814

Judge Kent contacted Mr. Stewart at the Presbyterian Church. He is an unassuming man. When Mr. Stewart speaks, people listen. He persuaded Mr. Marvin to change his mind about sending Emma and Louisa to Litchfield. Mr. Ten Eyck assured Ebenezer that Captain Roorback will be a subscriber. Cousin John says the same about Dr. Stearns. Ebenezer can find neither one at home.

Wednesday, February 2, 1814

The Church Ladies made final preparations for tomorrow's installation of Reverend Clowes as Rector.

Mrs. Gill sought me out to say Mr. Gill wants Martha and Margaret enrolled in "that school." It is time for me to visit Moses and Solomon Allen.

Saturday, February 5, 1814

A full moon, the snow moon

From the street, I could see Solomon Allen alone at his desk. He assured me he was pleased for the interruption. He offered a chair and asked his girl Phyllis to serve coffee.

I expressed my appreciation of his mother's gift of books. Paradise Lost has convinced me of the unrelenting cleverness of Satan.

Solomon smiled when I took the two envelopes from my pocket. He recognized the handwriting. "Moses and I have been expecting you, Mrs. Foot. We trust Mother asked you to grant a request just as she made final requests of us."

After Solomon read the note from his mother, he drew it to his heart and bowed his head. I feared I had made a terrible mistake. Perhaps I'd been wrong about Solomon and Moses and they had no intention of doing as their mother asked. Would the brothers view this as female interference and reject the request? I sat tall, took a deep breath, and held it long enough to tell myself, "Be strong. Be of good courage. Be not afraid." Exhaling slowly, I added, "Keep the faith. Keep the faith. Keep the faith."

After a moment of silence, Solomon broke the seal of the second envelope. He unrolled the bills and counted seventy-two dollars. I tremble to think there was so much money in our home.

"So, mother and father will have their way at last. What they could not accomplish on earth, they will achieve from beyond. It is incredible they set aside this large amount, but I know of their prudence and forethought. Our family prospered because of their wise decisions. These are the qualities mother admired in you, Mrs. Foot. Moses is out of town until Monday. When he returns, I will inform him of Mother's bequest for Ruth, Rebecca, and Sarah. Please give us the honor of being among the first to sign Mr. Foot's subscription paper."

This was not as I had imagined. I could think of nothing to say.

After Phyllis cleared away the coffee tray, Solomon confided his mother left money and instructions for her manumission. "We are teaching her to read, write, and count. Miss Phyllis Jackson is a fast learner and plans to become a teacher in Mr. Lattimer's school for the colored children."

I am amazed but not surprised.

My feet did not touch the ground on the way back to Montgomery Street. Now I can share the news with Ebenezer. We are ready to prepare the subscription document.

Monday, February 7, 1814

I knew Mr. Fowler was in the front room before I heard his voice. Wherever he goes he carries with him the rich aroma of Moroccan leather from his factory on Ferry Street.

When we first moved to Albany, the Fowler family lived two doors away. After the fire destroyed their home and they moved to South Market, our families remained close. Samuel is smitten with young Mariam Fowler. When he is financially secure and she is older, I predict he will marry her.

William Fowler and Ebenezer are like brothers. Although neither had the privilege of a classical education, both are endowed with a keen mind and warm heart. From the top rungs of society, including the New York fur trader Mr. John Astor, down to our impoverished soldiers and their families, people respect Mr. Fowler's business judgment and community spirit. His visit today was to help Ebenezer and cousin John with the wording of the subscription document. He wants it simple, without too many "whereas and wherefores." When I entered the front room, the three were discussing tuition and fees.

The tuition at Litchfield Female Academy is five dollars with added charges for books, supplies, language courses, music, dancing, and the ornamental subjects. Miss Brenton charges ten dollars per quarter for the advanced classes. For elementary reading, writing, and plain sewing, the fee is three dollars. French, vocal, and instrumental music are each an additional charge of three dollars per quarter. Mrs. Wilson charges by the hour.

Since there will be no ornamental subjects at our school, there will be no additional fees. To keep it simple and affordable, the men set tuition at six dollars per quarter for all levels. Mr. Fowler's draft:

"We, the undersigned, engage Mr. Horace Goodrich to provide instruction in reading, writing, grammar, arithmetic, and geography. For each student we enroll, we will pay six dollars per quarter."

John said the document needs to specify the date for the first quarter. I added we should specify the school will be for female students.

The second draft:

"By the signing of this paper, we appoint Mr. Horace Goodrich to superintend a female education for the number of students following our name. Tuition will be six dollars per student per quarter. The first quarter will begin on May 1, 1814."

Ebenezer made a good suggestion. He recommends we state the annual fee to be paid in quarterly installments. To show confidence and trust, no payment would be collected until the beginning of the second quarter. John questioned the wisdom of offering a service before payment.

"Dr. Ely," Mr. Fowler quipped. "No offense to you, Mrs. Foot, but we all know your esteemed husband's strategy. Get 'a foot' in the door and the rest of the body will follow." After much laughter, it was settled. Money for the first quarter will be collected August 1, and deposited in Mechanics and Farmers Bank.

Still to be decided is a name for the school and location.

Thursday, February 10, 1814

We did not want to rent rooms. We wanted a school building that is light and airy in the summer and easy to heat in the winter. Today, on William Fowler's fortieth birthday, Ebenezer gave him the good news. Mr. Henry obtained title to the Montgomery Street property between Orange and Columbia. Until two years ago, Thomas and Elizabeth Anderson lived there with their daughter Sophia, but they abandoned the property. They said they were moving to Ohio and would never be back. I hope they are faring better there than they did in Albany. The house will be torn down and replaced with a proper but modest school building.

Monday, February 14, 1814

Each day we add a block to our foundation. We have a name. It will not be The Albany Academy as I wished or my second choice, Albany Female Academy, but the name will have more dignity and meaning than other proposals: the Albany School for Girls or the Montgomery Street School or the Montgomery School for Girls. The hero of the Battle of Quebec would not inspire our daughters.

I dreamt Academy would be part of our name, but understand the need to appeal to a diverse group for support. For now, our school will be The Union School. It reflects our democratic mission. The girls will be a union of female scholars.

Sunday, February 20, 1814

The new moon

The power of the new moon is strong. What is planted at the time of the new moon will flourish. The subscription paper is prepared.

After Ebenezer makes the final revisions, John will sign and Ebenezer will bring it to Solomon and Moses Allen, Mr. Scrymser and the others. We have crossed The Rubicon. There is no turning back.

Thursday, February 24, 1814

"We, the subscribers, agree to send to Union School in Montgomery Street, under the tuition of Mr. Horace Goodrich, the number of female scholars affixed to our names for the space of one year from the first day of May next; and we also agree to pay to Ebenezer Foot Twenty-four Dollars for each scholar, in four equal quarterly payments, the first payment to be on the first day of August next. February 24, 1814."

The ink from Ebenezer's pen was still wet on the document when Ebenezer, John, and I stood back to admire it. Ebenezer took my hand and pointed to the flourish he had given the first word: WE. "This includes you, Betsey. You have been our guiding light." There was a moment of silence before he entered the date and marked rows and columns for the orderly placement of signatures and numbers.

Cousin John wrote his name in the first column and the number 1 in the second.

Friday, February 25, 1814

A new baby

We had just finished the evening meal on yesterday's historic day when Mr. Allen Brown rapped on the door. "Hurry," he said. "Gather the women. Her time has come."

I did not expect the call for a few more weeks but immediately collected Mrs. Ellison and followed Mr. Brown to his brother Edward's house on Hudson. Lucinda Brown was in the middle stage of labor.

Bringing a child into the world is not one of nature's gentle rhythms. Birthing a baby is hard especially during the dark hours meant for sleep. Hazards loom over the joyous expectation of new life.

Mrs. Ellison took charge. She directed Mr. Brown to build up a fire, heat water, and bring fresh linens while I hustled the children back to bed. Throughout the night Mrs. Ellison and I took turns encouraging Mrs. Brown, calming her fears, and trying to make her more comfortable. When Mrs. Ellison saw she was ready, she sent Mr. Brown to fetch Dr. Stearns. He arrived just in time for the easy part of the delivery and took all the credit.

Jane Eliza Brown came into the world at the golden hour of dawn. "It looks like you have another scholar for your school, Mrs. Foot," said Dr. Stearns holding aloft the robust infant and presenting her to Mrs. Brown.

Jane Eliza is a happy surprise the Browns did not expect in their middle years. Mr. Brown is grateful his daughter is healthy and his wife survived the ordeal, but he could not hide his disappointment. He had wanted a son.

I left Mrs. Ellison with the job of bathing and dressing Jane Eliza, changing Mrs. Brown's bed shift and tidying up the room. I will return with a plum cake to serve friends who call. Now that mother and baby are safe and well, we are free to bring caps, shirts, and gowns for the infant. It is a great accomplishment to bring mother and child to the other side of confinement. After one month's rest and recuperation, Mrs. Brown will be strong and useful again.

Saturday, February 26, 1814

Mr. Russell is a member of Albany's Common Council, a trustee at the Second Presbyterian Church, a benefactor of the Green Street Theater, and always generous to the poor. I was not aware how strongly he supported female education. Some say what they don't believe and are easily swayed. Others do not think about what they say, then retreat and apologize. Mr. Russell is a skilled fiddler, and he understands the power of timing. He shares his thoughts when the time is right. Beneath the signature of Moses Allen and James Scrymser is, T & J Russell, 4. He subscribes for his own three daughters and the daughter of his son Joseph.

When the weather moderates, Mr. Jonathan Brooks and his son will start building the schoolhouse. Mr. Russell promises to paint the building inside and out in any color the ladies choose.

Monday, February 28, 1814

When Ebenezer was at Brown's store on Hudson, he met Mr. and Mrs. Stewart who were there to congratulate the new father. This was fortunate because Ebenezer obtained signatures from both men. Elizabeth Stewart has had several different teachers since leaving Mrs. Nugent's Seminary. None have been satisfactory.

Wednesday, March 1, 1814

The wind roars like a lion

March came in like a lion and brought a small member of the cat family to our door. Mr. Kitty called unannounced early this morning and invited himself in. All black with a white bib, he looked like he was dressed in formal attire. After sniffing every corner of the hall, front room, kitchen and pantry, he installed himself next to the stove and signaled he was ready for breakfast. He did not pounce on the saucer Lucretia placed before him or gulp the cream I poured, but displayed the polished manners of one accustomed to fine dining. Mr. Kitty did not lick the saucer clean. He turned away before he was finished and found a private corner for grooming. This completed, he searched for a place to settle. He rejected a pile of sewing filled with pins and needles and chose my knitting basket filled with soft balls of wool. After making three circles, he curled up and lowered his eyelids, indifferent to the excitement his appearance had created.

"A black cat living in the house means the young ladies will have many suitors," exclaimed Lucretia, stroking Mr. Kitty. He purred in agreement.

Ebenezer was not pleased. "Cats do not belong in a house. They should live either in a barn or in a cold cellar and catch mice."

"My dear brother," said Samuel, bowing before Mr. Kitty, "don't you know if a cat comes to your door, he brings prosperity?"

Ebenezer was not persuaded. "Cats, especially black ones, are bad luck."

Mr. Kitty lifted one eyelid in disgust, rearranged himself and resumed his meditation.

I confirmed if a black cat has some white hair, it is good luck. "Anyway," I teased Ebenezer, "you can always cancel bad luck by turning around clockwise three times and making the sign of the cross."

Recognizing he was outnumbered, Ebenezer raised his hands in surrender, turned around once, and announced, "I withdraw from the field, but if I find that cat has a taste for snakes, he is out the door!"

"Hail to Le Petit Caporal," Mr. Goodrich declared. Samuel, Lucretia, and I raised a cheer and saluted Mr. Kitty, who henceforth would be called Napoleon. The Little Commander acknowledged us by nodding then lowering his eyes. He had been assured of victory before he selected our door.

Thursday, March 3, 1814

Mrs. Gill informed me at the Ladies Church Society meeting that Mr. Foot could find Mr. Gill at his place of business on Thursday, March 3 at 3 o'clock in the afternoon.

"It is pronounced Gill as in 'grand', not Jill as in 'junior'." Mr. Gill is precise about his impeccable appearance as well as his wife's and his daughter's. The addition of an elliptical window in the gable of his Federal style home on South Market, the fresh paint on the coat of arms over the door of his mercantile business at 37 State, and his status on the vestry at Saint Peter's Church all point to his deep personal pride. He makes it known, "The roots of the Gill family tree are deep."

After ceremoniously placing his signature under that of Gilbert Stewart, he informed Ebenezer, "You will find the Gill name recorded in the eleventh century King's Book, the Domesday Book. The English Conqueror granted William Gill land in Yorkshire in gratitude for his heroic military service at the Battle of Hastings."

He added, "Mrs. Gill and I are patrons of the arts in Albany. We have donated money to the New York State Museum to display Mr. Trowbridge's collection of natural world artifacts. It is also the mission of Mrs. Gill and myself to advance the cause of female education in Albany. I will encourage my good friend Ezra Ames to follow our example. He is just now finishing portraits for the Gill family."

The next signer, Mr. Uriah Marvin, is also attentive to his standing in the community. Since his past is murky, his eye is on the future. He sees what others do not and makes business decisions that assure generous rewards. Like Mr. Gill, he sealed his signature with three loops of the pen, added the number 2 in the next column, and dismissed Ebenezer without further conversation.

That evening, Ebenezer and I admired both signatures and agreed there was no need to tell either gentleman that Ebenezer's ancestor is also in the Domesday Book, but not as a landowner. Goduin Fot was an under-tenant of a tenant of a landowner. It is good to live in a democracy where one's present endeavors count more than one's past.

Friday, March 4, 1814

"Mr. Russell told me you would be at home," announced Mr. Gould when I answered the door late this afternoon. "If Mr. Foot is available, I would like to add the Gould name to the subscription list. I led Mr. Gould into the front room where we are keeping the document, becoming more precious every day. When he saw there were eight signatures ahead of him and that his name would be under that of Matthew Gill and Uriah Marvin, he cleared his throat. "It was my intention to meet with you earlier in the week, but business interfered." He measured out two spaces for his name, penned his signature and shook Ebenezer's hand. "Mr. Foot, I have great respect for your efforts on behalf of our daughters. Please visit Gould's Hardware for any supplies you need to build the school. You have my assurance we will be generous."

Saturday, March 5, 1814

Solomon Allen delivered the message that he could be found at his establishment today. Mr. Fowler brought the paper to him to sign and added his own signature. Solomon Allen's signature is one of the smallest on the page and is followed by four dots. He said, "my father, my mother, my daughter Ruth, and myself."

Sunday, March 6, 1814

A full moon, the sap moon

Even though the maple trees appear lifeless, sap is flowing. Tiny brown buds promise there will soon be leaves.

Reverend Clowes gave parishioners his blessing to attend the Dutch Church today. The great orator, Reverend Dr. Nott, preached an ecumenical sermon to benefit The Humane Society. He raised four hundred and seventy-eight dollars. The Elys, the Henrys, Ebenezer, Samuel, and I represented St. Peter's. Dr. Stearns, the Kents, and the Knowers represented the First Presbyterian Church and the Russell family visited from the Second Presbyterian Church.

The Bleecker, Ten Eyck, Van Vechten, and Roorback families sat in their reserved pews looking stiff and pious. I hardly recognized Captain Roorback who is usually ruddy and boisterous, full of jests and jokes spiced with colorful language. He means no harm, but he makes me blush. He would be fined in the "Holy State of Connecticut," where taking the Lord's name in vain is not only a sin; it is against the law. There was a student at Tapping Reeve's Law School who peppered his conversations with a heavy dose of profanity. He was a New Yorker and did not care about the laws of Connecticut. One of Litchfield's magistrates, overhearing him, fined him one dollar. The New Yorker replied he cared not "a ----!" and was fined a second dollar. This resulted in more swearing and more fines until there was a total of fifteen dollars due.

"Here's your-----money!" he exclaimed slapping twenty-dollars in the magistrate's hand.

"Now it is a total of sixteen dollars," the magistrate calculated and handed him back four dollars. "Keep the change," our friend insisted. "It entitles me to four more violations."

Privately, he told Ebenezer he thought he was overcharged for his freedom of speech, but thereafter he was more careful about his language.

Captain Roorback disappeared after church, but Mr. Bleecker, Mr. Van Vechten, Mr. Knower, Mr. Ten Eyck, and Judge Kent all set a date and time to meet Ebenezer to sign the subscription document.

Tuesday, March 8, 1814

We are free of snow, but now we have wind. There are two days of calm, then the winds build and blow from a different direction. If it isn't the wind, it is the rain. The Hudson River is a channel for melting snow. In the rush of water is an assortment of tree trunks, barn boards, old boats, carriages, and occasionally dead cows and horses.

Rain revives the War of the Gutters. The Dutch object to the new ordinances banning water spouts that drain sheets of rain off the roof and into the street, turning them into rivers. It made sense with the canals of Amsterdam. It does not work in Albany.

Penny Postman Winne always sees the bright side.

March winds and April showers bring May flowers.

Thursday, March 10, 1814

There are still no signatures from Isaac Hutton or Dr. Stearns, but yesterday a neighbor of Dr. Stearns' stopped Ebenezer and said, "I want to enroll my girl, Emily." The Reid family are members of the Presbyterian Church, but have kept to themselves since their recent move to Albany.

After his name and under the number 1 in the second column, Mr. Reid added four dots and whispered "Father, Son and Holy Ghost."

Mr. Reid told Ebenezer, "My Missus and girl would like to meet Mrs. Foot." He wrote out his address and said, "She'd be welcome to stop by anytime."

Saturday, March 12, 1814

I surprise myself traveling into unfamiliar neighborhoods and making calls on women I do not yet know. The Reid's house is next to

Dr. Stearns, north of the Market House, beyond the Elys and Gills, but before the Ten Eycks. There are some Federal style homes on Market Street, but most are tall, narrow Dutch houses crowded together. The Reid's two-story clapboard house stands out because it is not brick. There is a warehouse above. Mr. Reid imports wools and plaids from Scotland.

Ten-year-old Emily looks more like a girl of eight. She sat at the edge of the kitchen, sketching while Mrs. Reid prepared a simple tea with biscuits. They seem content in their sparsely furnished home. Mrs. Reid and Emily are both tiny and speak with a dialect, difficult at times to understand.

When Mrs. Reid presented Emily, she tousled her curly, red hair. "No mistakin' my girl fer a Reid. Her hair is jest like her fayther's and her fayther's faythers. The Reids cum straight down frum John the Red who lived in Englan' back in the ten hoondreds." I did not ask if John the Red was in the Domesday Book.

"We moved to Albany from Newcastle, that's way up in the noorth of Englan' near't the border of Scotland."

I almost blurted, "Yes, I know Newcastle. Our late rector is from Newcastle. His widow is my neighbor. Did you know the Ellison family in Newcastle?"

Dear Lord! What if Mrs. Reid knew the Mrs. Ellison left behind? Fortunately, Mrs. Reid continued. "Many yures ago my husband's uncle started a business right here in Albany. Fer many yures he's been wantin' us to join him. After he pass't, his widow sent us money fer the trip, and so here we are."

Mrs. Reid doesn't speak, she sings. I was surprised how frequently she drew Emily into our conversation. "I take my girl dun ta Montgom'ry evr'y day. She knows they'll do away with that falling down house and put up a luvly wee cottage fer her and t'other girls."

Emily brought over an almanac. Leaning close into me, she counted fifty more days until May first. I didn't realize it was so close.

On opening day Mrs. Reid wants the girls to wear matching white dresses and march to the school in a procession. Emily showed me a drawing of the dress her mother designed.

I was surprised it was so beautiful. Mrs. Reid misinterpreted my raised eyebrows. "Ooooh," she apologized covering her mouth. "Is it too daring? I don't mean to be unkind about the Dutch, Mrs. Foot, but those big skirts, coats, and trousers they wear are from the same pattin' they brought over, two hundred years ago, fittin' fer their broad frames, but not fer our wee girls settin' out in the world."

Mrs. Reid showed me a bolt of gauzy material in ivory, a roll of pink satin ribbon and strips of white lace. "There's enough here fer yer girl and mine, Mrs. Foot! T'will be my way of thankin' ya."

I was touched by the offer, but can not accept her generosity. I thanked Mrs. Reid and started to say I would show the drawing to the other women when I heard Emily at the front window calling, "Fayther, Fayther."

Mr. Reid has a boyish face. He is shorter than I with a girth half mine! "Pleased ta see ya, Mrs. Foot, and pleased ta tell ya I have just cum from Quay Street." He wasn't just pleased, he was bursting to tell me he "told Mr. Center and Mr. Davis to add their names to the school list."

"Listen here," Mrs. Reid said before I left. "Mr. Reid and I can supply all the material fer the girls' dresses. 'Course I'll need some help with the cutting, piecing, and sewing."

Thursday, March 17, 1814

Mrs. Gill and Mrs. Henry approved the idea of dressing the girls alike. Mrs. Gill thought Mrs. Reid should make the neckline higher and more round than square. Mrs. Henry insisted Mrs. Reid be paid for the material. Adelaide Ely and Margaret Fowler will help with the cutting and piecing.

Friday, March 18, 1814

Mr. Gill, Mr. Knower, and Judge Kent have all talked with Ezra Ames. He is interested in subscribing, but does not commit.

Mr. Ames' paintings of Judge Kent and Benjamin Knower are masterpieces and I expect the Gill portrait will be as well. All of Albany's important citizens commission him for a portrait. Betsy Kent tells me his painting of Simeon De Witt, Surveyor General of New York, is impressive. He stands in front of a Doric column with his hand resting on a map. There is a world globe and telescope in the background. De Witt gave many New York towns Greek or Roman names; Troy, Utica, Syracuse, Ithaca. In Albany, he named the north/south streets after birds; Eagle, Hawk, Swan, Dove, Lark, and Robin. The east/west streets he named after animals; Elk and Beaver. Recently, Deer was changed to State Street. Fox was changed to Sheridan, and Lion became Washington.

Many believe Lucretia's portrait was painted by Ezra Ames because of the pastoral background, the detail of her dress, and the artist's ability to capture her personality. Betsy Kent urges Ebenezer and I to engage him for a portrait. Ebenezer says he is too busy. The truth is the fifty dollar fee is too high. "For a dollar and an hour of my time, Mr. Wood on Beaver Street will make a silhouette. That's good enough to preserve my likeness for posterity."

SILHOUETTE OF EBENEZER FOOT (1773-1814).
GIFT OF MRS. WILLIAM H. ARNOLD. COURTESY,
ARCHIVES AND COLLECTIONS OF THE ALBANY ACADEMIES.

Saturday, March 19, 1814

Cousin John visited this morning. Pacing back and forth and wringing his hands, he apologized for burdening me with a disturbing event he witnessed at the Cantonment barracks across the river. He said, "I can usually carry the weight of my position as physician to the soldiers. This incident, I cannot release. I've suffered through two weeks of night terrors." He begged to share the story and gain relief.

During war, newspapers are filled with the names of deserters. Currently there is a twenty dollar reward for Christian Sugars who deserted from the naval forces on Lake Champlain. John wanted to tell me about one of the ten men at Cantonment accused of desertion. After a court-martial, the frightened men lined up to hear the verdict; desertion or away without leave. Nine were determined to be away without leave. One man's verdict was desertion. The sentence would be death by an eight-man firing squad. When the young man heard his fate, he gasped for breath, turned red, and collapsed. It looked like he was having a seizure. After reviving the man, John heard the story of a young husband and father forced to leave his family without support. Twice he made the twenty mile journey home to bring food to his wife and three babies. On the third visit, he was arrested, hastily tried, and declared a deserter. He pleaded for mercy, claiming he planned to return to camp after he'd taken care of his family.

The Camp Commander ordered the entire regiment to witness the execution. The convicted man was led to the fatal spot by fife and drum playing a funeral dirge. It was quick. The young man's life was extinguished in seconds by eight bullets. After John pronounced the man dead, the fife and drum corps played Yankee Doodle for a sprightly march back to camp. The Commander invited officers to his headquarters for gin and water.

I had never seen a man cry, except for my brothers when father died. They wept. John sobbed. He feels relieved and now the story is forever in my head. I think about the terror of that young man's final moments. I think about his family left behind. John will not say who they are, or where they live, or even if they know what happened. How long will they wait for him? Will they think he was killed in battle? Will they be informed of the truth? How does it feel to know your husband or father was executed because he wanted to take care of you?

A family is held together by a single link. One man's disease, disability, desertion, or death can break the whole chain.

Monday, March 21, 1814
A new moon and the first day of spring

"With a hey, and a ho, and a hey noni no, in the spring time, the only pretty ring time, when birds do sing, hey ding a ding, ding; sweet lovers love the spring."

Handing me a letter from Mrs. Wilson, Penny Postman Winne did a jig and gave an extended trill to "sweet lovers." Reading Mrs. Wilson's note confirmed my suspicion Mr. Winne had already read the contents.

My dear Mrs. Foot, please accept my heartfelt congratulations on the success of your efforts to create a school for Lucretia. I would like to offer the collection of books I found helpful through many years of teaching. I would also be honored to have you accept the beautiful globe you admired last March. Mr. Joseph Caldwell and I are to be married in one month's time. We are moving to the village of Caldwell where his brother relocated two years ago.

Sincerely yours,
Martha Wilson

Fanny Roorback's teacher will marry Orville's teacher and they will leave Albany. When and how did this happen?

March 22, 1814

"Mr. Caldwell believes the mountain air and clean waters of Lake George will be good for us both," Mrs. Wilson blushed. She no longer coughs.

"Mr. Lattimer chose books for his school. Please make arrangements for him to deliver the globe and the books he doesn't want."

She must have seen me glance at the newly polished chronometer. Smiling, she said, "I would give you Father's chronometer, but Mr. Caldwell fancies it. It will be my wedding gift to him."

What a difference a year makes.

Monday, March 28, 1814

March came in like a lion and is going out like a lamb. Napoleon, Le Petit Caporal, commands our household from my knitting basket. He continues to bring us good fortune and not a single snake. All is well.

Mr. Isaac Hutton penned his signature, neat as the engraving on his silver. Mr. Reid was correct about Asa Center's interest in subscribing, and Mr. Center reports his partner Mr. Davis will enroll Sarah when he returns from Boston. Dr. Stearns and Captain Roorback are busy and never at home. Twenty names are sufficient.

The document was complete, or so we thought. Mr. and Mrs. Clark returned from their business in London and were at church on Sunday for the first time since Thanksgiving. With uncharacteristic emotion they thanked us for our prayers while they were away. They said they were especially grateful for prayers during the return voyage. "We thought we would never again see the beautiful city of Albany, our dear friends at St. Peter's, or our precious daughter."

Mr. Clark explained. "The first week out of Southampton was smooth sailing. Suddenly the wind shifted, blew hard, and the sky turned dark. We never imagined the ocean could become so mean, so powerful, so terrifying, so fast. The waves were as tall as St. Peter's bell tower. Each wave pushed the boat to the top of a wave where we teetered for several seconds then plunged straight down into a black hole. We did not know if the boat would land right side up. I held my breath each time, thinking it was the last. In the trough between the waves, the boat rocked side to side. Her timbers groaned and shivered. We thought she would break apart. We bucked waves like this, up and down, side to side for three days. More than once, Mrs. Clark and I and the other passengers were flung from one side of the boat to the other. It was only by the grace of God, no one was swept overboard."

"For three days, we lived between this world and the next," Mrs. Clark said. "Singing hymns kept us strong."

> A mighty fortress is our God,
> A bulwark never failing.

"We sang every hymn in the hymnal twice. We sang Advent, Christmas, Easter, Saints' Days, National, and General Hymns. When the seas settled into long swells, we sang hymns of Thanksgiving. Finally Captain Moffett and a strong southerly wind brought us past Governors Island into New York Harbor and up the East River. When we saw the steeple of Trinity Church in Manhattan, we knelt on the deck and sang."

> Lord of all, to thee we raise,
> This our hymn of grateful praise.

After a moment of silence, Mr. Clark announced, "I have decided Mary will leave Litchfield at the end of the spring term. The Lord has provided her a good school in Albany. We will not be separated again."

We embraced the Clarks with tears of joy.

What will Miss Pierce think when she hears Mary will be one of our first students?

Wednesday, March 30, 1814

John's godson, our nephew was married last evening to Margaret Lee of Saybrook. It was a simple ceremony at John Ely, Jr.'s State Street home. The bride's father and mother, her brother Samuel, and sisters Elizabeth and Lucia, traveled to Albany from Connecticut. Margaret wore a dove gray silk gown in the Grecian style. On her head she wore a turban decorated with a white ostrich plume. At her throat was a delicate coral necklace, a gift from her father.

The couple sat on chairs in front of Reverend Bradford. When he signaled, the guests stood for the joining of hands. Filled with faith in their future, John and Margaret pledged to be loyal through sickness and health. Their vows stir me to recall my own. I pray it will be a long and happy journey for John and Margaret before they part at death. I pray this for Ebenezer and myself.

Following the vows, there was a sup-per of cold meat, cheese, and pastries. After the usual toasting, Mr. Russell played the fiddle and we danced into the night.

Ebenezer had never heard the story of the bride's father, Captain Ezra Lee. During the summer of 1776, British ships blocked New York Harbor. Lee's neighbor in Saybrook was David Bushnell who in-vented a boat that could be maneuvered undetected, underwater to attack the Brit-ish fleet from below. Captain Lee success-

DAVID BUSHNELL'S TURTLE

fully navigated The Turtle, as it was named, to a position under the HMS Eagle. He was unable to screw the bomb into her hull so he set it off in the harbor.

The strange looking boat was stored in the Bushnell's barn. My cous-ins and I played in it as children. I never understood how Captain Lee could keep the boat underwater and still breathe. Imagine a submergible boat that doesn't sink! How did Mr. Bushnell dream up the idea? How did he persuade General Washington to fund the crazy invention? How did Mr. Lee have the courage to drive it? I'd be afraid of drowning.

Friday, April 1, 1814

April first is the day for mischief, tricks, and surprises. My child-hood prank was to sugarcoat a radish and tell my friends it was candy. They didn't think it was as funny as I did.

Uncle John told about a joke his medical students played on the local Westbrook boys. One Sunday, the boys dislodged the medical students from their customary pew in the Congregational Church. The students were mad and plotted revenge.

The following week, the village "dandies" again took the seats they had usurped from the students. In an instant, the boys jumped up scratching and screaming about a terrible itch on their posteriors. Dr. Ely was called to diagnose the problem. The pew had been dusted with cow itch! The boys learned a lesson they will never forget:

> Give and it shall be given unto you.
> For with the same measure that ye mete withal
> it shall be measured to you again.

Today's April first joke is on Captain Roorback. Beneath John Stearns' name, Mr. Ten Eyck forged Roorback's signature! It wasn't really a trick. Captain Roorback gave his permission because he is so frequently out of town and not available to sign it himself.

SUBSCRIPTION DOCUMENT

Holy Week, April 3-10

It is Holy Week. This year my head, heart, and hands are filled with plans for the opening of the Union School, less than one month away.

Monday, April 4, 1814

A full moon, the grass moon

Under the full moon and watchful eyes of Constable Worthington and Mr. Fry, families stood round a bonfire that consumed the house abandoned by the Anderson's. It is the lot where the Fowlers' house was destroyed by fire four years ago.

"The school will be like the phoenix rising from ashes," Mr. Fowler said graciously, "but please forgive our family for not attending."

Thursday, April 7, 1814

Now that the lot is cleared, Peter and Jonathan Brooks will deliver lumber and begin building. They promise it will be ready for the girls on May 1. Mr. Meads is building benches and desks in memory of the boys who drowned. "We must think of the future," he said. "When Charlotte and Louisa are old enough for school, they will have a fine classroom."

William Gillespie is building an oak lectern for the headmaster. John and Samuel Norton are building the fireplace and chimney. Mr. Haney is fencing in the backyard "to keep the little chicks safe from harm!" Mr. Russell will paint the school in yellow, my favorite color. The door and shutters will be green and the trim, lead white.

Mrs. Reid finished cutting the pattern for the girls' dresses. Mrs. Knower and Mrs. Fowler are helping with sewing and fittings. Adelaide Ely is adding lace to the petticoats. Mrs. Russell made sashes of pink ribbon. Mrs. Clark will make crowns with the flowers that are blooming on May 1. Mrs. Marvin and Mrs. Gill are in charge of refreshments for a reception following the opening day ceremony.

Sunday, April 10, 1814
Easter

Monday, April 11, 1814
Easter Monday

German families tell their children an Easter rabbit lays special eggs, the symbol of new life. I tell Lucretia the rabbit doesn't lay eggs, she only delivers them. Easter Monday there is an egg roll down State Street hill. Eggs are more plentiful this time of year, but to me it seems a waste of good eggs. In Hadley we played the game of Touch with six eggs: four colored, one white, and one gold. Children have a wand and are blindfolded. Each one takes turns pointing to an egg and chants,

Peggy, Patrick, Mike, and Meg,
See me touch my Easter egg;
Green and red and black and blue,
Count for six, five, four, and two.
If I touch an egg of white,
A forfeit then will be your right;

If I touch an egg of gold,
It is mine to have and hold.

Even when I won the golden egg, I didn't like to see the other children cry. I prefer games where everyone wins.

Tuesday, April 12, 1814

One of life's great pleasures is to sit in a dark theater free to laugh without restraint. It is comical how accurately our friends and neighbors were portrayed in last evening's comedy at the Green Street Theater, Rule a Wife and Have a Wife. It was amusing to watch the characters on stage struggle to liberate themselves from problems of their own creation. The best part is the whole mess is cleaned up by the third act.

The antics of Mr. Robertson and Mrs. Young provided an entertaining evening. I knew Mr. Young was a great comedian, but I did not know his wife was as well. Mr. Robertson is superb in every role he plays.

The biggest laugh is the title of the play. If a woman wrote the play, the title would be, To Keep a Husband, Rule a Husband.

Thursday, April 14, 1814

A letter from Miss Pierce.

South Street
Litchfield, Connecticut
April 2, 1814

Dearest Betsey,

I am glad to learn you have received the gift of a globe for your school. Geography will teach the girls about the natural world and be grateful for the superior resources of our United States, New England, and especially Connecticut, though I am sure you can find examples of God's handiwork in New York.

As the girls mature, Mr. Goodrich should make the girls aware of their good fortune to live in a country that values liberty, equality, and learning. We should always be thankful we do not live amongst the savages of the non-Christian world, where women eat and sleep with the beasts of burden or even worse are bought and sold like property.

My nephew John Pierce Brace, a recent graduate of Williams College, is now my assistant. He will instruct our girls in the higher branches of mathematics. Progressing beyond lady mathematics strengthens the power of reasoning and will result in greater independence for girls. John will also teach logic and moral philosophy using his two college texts: Hedge's Elements of Logic and Paley's The Principles of Moral and Political Philosophy. I recommend them to Mr. Goodrich to cap the education of the older students. Mr. Brace plans to develop a course on Natural Philosophy. It will cover mechanics, hydrostatics, pneumatics, meteorology, electricity, and magnetism.

Please forgive me. I do not follow my own advice. Change must be gradual. Pioneers of female education walk a narrow line. To gain financial support, first offer what society believes are the proper academic subjects for women. Wait until the school is more established before introducing the advanced courses.

As the warmer days of spring unfold, the girls will enjoy gathering, pressing, and classifying herbs and flowers and learn of their medicinal and economical uses.

I was relieved to hear of the Clarks' safe return to Albany. I will expedite Mary's transfer to The Union School where I am assured she will thrive. I well understand your feelings about the departure of Hannah. We never know where life's journey will take us. I have assured the Scovilles I would be pleased to accept her as one of my older students.

Give as much care to the final steps as to the first. One often falls approaching the door.

Semper et aeternum, I am your dear instructress,
Sarah Pierce

Friday, April 15, 1814

Mr. Haney is finished fencing in a yard behind the school, and sent me to John Spenser on Hardware Row for gate hinges. Their new clerk, Erastus Corning, recently moved to Albany from Troy, but is from a farm family in Connecticut. As he says, "Either you make it on a farm or the farm breaks you. The smart ones like me, leave before that happens."

He feels like a foreigner in Albany's Dutch city. We laughed at the way they call a stream a kill. A lake is a pond and the town square is a park. Front steps are stoops. Boats are sloops. The female cat is a puss.

"You must admit," Erastus conceded, "the Dutch are smart when it comes to business. I've learned more from them than either of my fancy Yale tutors. Don't misunderstand what I am saying about education, Mrs. Foot," he added, "I know about your efforts to provide a school for the young women of Albany. Women elevate and adorn the lives of men and children. They deserve to elevate and ornament their own mind as well. My good friend William Marcy is sweet on Cornelia Knower who will be one of your students."

After I paid for the hinges, Erastus walked me to the door. I was shocked to see he is crippled, but using crutches doesn't seem to bother him or anyone else. He is a charming and intelligent young man. If my instincts are correct, Mr. Erastus Corning is on a straight road to fame and fortune. He is a clerk now, but I wouldn't be surprised if he soon owns the store. His eye is on the future.

Mr. Spenser's eye is more on the past. He made sure to tell young Erastus that I was the wife of the eminent, Ebenezer Foot, Esq., who was involved in the famous Battle on State Street. It was a few years ago, but Albany still talks about it. Yes, Ebenezer was in the middle of the fray, but as counsellor not combatant. As with all battles, it started when a tiny spark landed on something flammable. The fire was fanned and fed and eventually there was a blaze several blocks long.

Mr. Spenser would not let me leave until he had told Erastus every detail of the Battle on State Street.

"It began on April 21, 1807. It was one of those days showing the quiet side of April. Even the river was still. Albany was enjoying a warmer than usual spring. Housewives were inside cooking kraut and had opened the top half of the door to bring in fresh air. Husbands sat outside smoking. It was just before the election and Solomon Van Rensselaer was taking his customary walk down State Street, but his mood did not match the sweetness of the day. Van Rensselaer was broiling about his opponents, the Anti-Federalists. When he met their principal spokesman, Elisha Jenkins, he struck him with his cane and knocked him into the street. Van Rensselaer thought that was the end of it. It wasn't. Later in the day, Governor Tayler sought revenge. Van Rensselaer attempted to fight back, but was soon outnumbered. Frances Bloodgood attacked Van Rensselaer from behind, seriously injuring him. Governor Tayler's son-in-law, Dr. Charles Cooper tried to intervene, as did Mrs. Cooper, but both were unsuccessful. A crowd gathered and joined in the fight. By the end of the day, half the men in Albany were involved. Those not on the street, were on rooftops cheering for one side or the other."

Everyone knows the outcome. At the trial Ebenezer represented Jenkins, Tayler, Cooper, and Bloodgood. Abraham Van Vechten represented General Van Rensselaer. Arbiters made the following judgment:

-Jenkins was awarded $2500 from Van Rensselaer who had made the first attack.

-Van Rensselaer was awarded $300 from Tayler, $500 from Cooper, and $3,700 from Bloodgood because he inflicted the most serious wounds.

How did the battle start? When did it end? Who won? The battle started long before it began and continues today. Seven years later, some families refuse to trade with each other, do not speak, and sit on opposite sides of church. People, like Mr. Spenser, keep the story alive

Saturday, April 16, 1814

Ebenezer did his best for the men he represented, but we both believe Aaron Burr averted a similar battle with greater wit and wisdom.

His opponent was one of the leading lawyers and thinkers of the day, our good friend, the honorable Judge James Kent. Kent is usually in control of his emotions, but his hatred for Burr was deep. Meeting Burr on Nassau Street in Manhattan, he felt compelled to share his feelings. Shaking his cane in Burr's face, he exclaimed, "You are a scoundrel, sir! A scoundrel!"

Burr removed his tall hat, bowed deeply, and replied, "The opinions of the learned Chancellor are always entitled to the highest consideration." What could Kent do or say in response? I wish I had been there.

Wounding with cane, tongue, or pen, the results are the same: physical and/or emotional injury. Both perpetrator and victim suffer. To resist the provocations of others, one must strengthen the mind as well as the body.

A wise man hath more ballast than sail.

I do not know how Aaron Burr could be drawn into the duel with Hamilton.

Wednesday, April 20, 1814

The new moon

There is bad news from the Ely family in Lyme! On April 8, British warships anchored outside Fort Saybrook at the mouth of the Connecticut River. At the dark hour before dawn, they sent 136 men in 6 rowing boats up the river to Pettipaug. Unsuspecting town folk were still asleep when the British stormed ashore.

The order was to destroy everything and capture the fleet, but there was a miracle. A local merchant greeted the British Commander with the secret Masonic handshake. Through mutual agreement there was no resistance, no torching of the beautiful villagle, and no casualties. However, the British captured two privateers, confiscated the town's store of rope, and helped themselves to rum from the Griswald Inn-one hundred thousand dollars worth! When the British returned to their boats, there was a second miracle. They were grounded by a low tide which made them an easy target for militia dispatched from Killingworth. Two British sailors were killed, and the stolen privateers destroyed before the tide turned and the boats sailed away.

Tuesday, April 26, 1814

This week we are putting the finishing touches on details for the Union School's opening ceremony. Mrs. Reid has scheduled the final fittings. Fortunately, there were panels on the dresses so the hems could be let down. Betsey Ten Eyck and Sally Stearns grew two inches in one month.

Mrs. Gill announced she ordered Mr. Benne's special confections made with Slaugher's chocolate.

Sunday, May 1, 1814

Opening Day

I awakened to the sound of rain on the roof. Penny Postman Winne says,

If it rains before seven,
It will clear by eleven.

Mother Nature believes Montgomery Street needs a good wash-down. I hope she is finished before our opening day procession. No matter, "In rain or shine, we will walk a steady line."

The rain stopped by midmorning. Montgomery Street was scrubbed clean and the trees' baby green leaves sparkled.

1814 UNION SCHOOL, DRAWING BY MARY KENT,
COURTESY OF ARCHIVES AND COLLECTIONS
OF THE ALBANY ACADEMIES.

On a May afternoon with the aroma of violet and sweet lilies filling the air, mothers and daughters gathered at Montgomery and Steuben. Each mother presented to her daughter, a crown of flowers. Dressed alike in their white gossamer dresses, the girls fluttered like a flock of pearly angels. When Mr. Hochstrasser played the first notes of Mozart's flute concerto in G major, Lucretia and I began the procession to the school. Along the way, family and friends applauded. I felt like Minerva bringing neophytes to the Temple of Learning.

Reverend Neill, Judge Kent, Ebenezer, and Mr. Goodrich greeted each mother and daughter as they passed. Each of us curtsied to the distinguished gentlemen.

Following Scripture, prayers, and words of inspiration, the door to the new school opened and the girls rushed in, oohing and ahhing over the cloakroom with 36 hooks and cubbies, a large center fireplace, Mr. Gillespie's oak lectern, and shelves filled with book donations from Mrs. Wilson and Mr. Backus. Next to Mrs. Wilson's globe was a gift from old Mr. Scrymser: a wooden frame with rows of small colored balls on wires. According to his note, "The abacus will help the girls with counting."

Desks and benches had been moved to the edges of the room. Mrs. Marvin served assorted tea cakes. Mrs. Gill poured glasses of sweet lemon with fresh mint and handed out one piece of Mr. Benne's confection to each guest. In the garden, Mr. Russell played the fiddle for singing and dancing. Esto perpetua, we chanted. Esto perpetua. Loyal and long will be our song.

Tonight, I tuck away every detail of a perfect day into a chest of treasures; memories that can never be stolen. Our girls have been elevated to a world more richly adorned than I imagined.

May 1, 1814, fathers, mothers, brothers and sisters, the sun, trees, and flowers all pulsed as One Perfect Union.

Monday, May 2, 1814

No organized procession to the school today. The girls from Market and Hudson Streets were at the school before Lucretia and I arrived. The Russell sisters were just behind us. Mrs. Gould emerged from her front door with a tight grip on Eliza. Katrina Scrymser led her mother. Fathers and brothers waved from open doorways. Betsy Kent turned the corner onto Montgomery Street with Mary, Margaret Hutton, and the three Henry girls in tow. It was touching to see Miss Thompson accompany her former students. She wanted to wish them well. One lone boy, head down, walked slowly toward his tutor at 39 Montgomery.

Waiting outside the school, some girls stood blank-faced, eyes straight ahead. Some hid in their mother's skirts. Others, like Lucretia found a friend to play pat-a-cake.

At the 8 o'clock bell Mr. Goodrich opened the school door. Some bolted ahead, some entered cautiously, and some needed prodding. Mr. Goodrich greeted each girl by name. After a hullabaloo of farewells and last minute motherly advice ("Be a good girl." "Mind your manners." "Do what Mr. Goodrich tells you."), Mr. Goodrich closed the door.

I had dreamed about this day for so long. I expected to feel a sense of accomplishment. I expected this to be one of the happiest days of my life. For nine years and five months, I alone have watched over Lucretia. Will Mr. Goodrich recognize how special she is? Will he do a good job? Will she be safe? Have I made a terrible mistake? Betsy Kent, Abigail Ely, and I stood together in silence. I wondered if they had the same thoughts and questions.

The other mothers seemed not to notice the wave of sadness that washed over me. Mrs. Gould and Mrs. Scrymser hurried off in opposite directions to some important errand. Abigail, Miss Thompson, and Betsy Kent joined a circle of friends to chat. I bid the group a polite good-bye and returned to an empty home. I had the sacred space I had yearned for. The silence was deafening.

Tuesday, May 3, 1814

36 Montgomery comes alive earlier and earlier each day. Mr. Goodrich is out the door before the sun rises. Lucretia wakes before me and dresses herself. Ebenezer and Samuel are preoccupied with the details of the day ahead and eager to get started. I face the 10,000 duties of my daily dogtrot and cannot get started.

Wednesday, May 4, 1814

Full moon, the flower moon

My throat is sore. The Church Ladies will meet without me today. Mrs. Ellison says Reverend Clowes is still upset about his salary. Nothing has been resolved with the vestry. The conflict is dividing the church.

Friday, May 6, 1814

At the end of the first week of school, Mr. Goodrich doesn't share much. Lucretia gives all the details.

"Maria Ely reads to the younger girls, and Elizabeth Bleecker is teaching them to write a simple sentence, and Katrina Scrymser is good at ciphering, and Emily Reid showed us how to sew a copy book, but I already know. Sally Stearns cries a lot and misses her mother, and so does Ruth Allen. Mary Clark learned everything about geography with Miss Pierce and she thinks our school is boring. Cornelia Knower is scolded for talking too much, and Fanny Roorback likes recess the best, and some of the girls are mean, but I think it's 'cause they are afraid, and I talk to them and they are really nice. Margaret Gill sits under the bench all day, but Mr. Goodrich says it is okay because she will come out eventually. The Marvin girls think they know all the answers, but they don't. Elizabeth Stewart knows all the answers, but she doesn't say so."

After five days Lucretia acts like she has been at the Union School for years.

Monday, May 9, 1814

Instead of starting a new week going round the mulberry bush, I joined Mrs. Roorback to visit the steamboat docked along Quay Street. She wants me to meet Captain Bunker and take a tour before the boat departs for New York. The Fulton was scheduled to navigate between New York and New Haven, but that would be dangerous. Long Island Sound is overrun with British ships.

At the dock, I was relieved when Mr. Brinckerhoff detained me from boarding the boat. I was afraid the 327-ton boat could blow up with me in it. Mr. Brinckerhoff would like to enroll Maria for the term beginning August 1.

Tuesday, May 10, 1814

"What did you learn in school?" I ask Lucretia every day. Today she learned May 10 is the traditional day to plant corn. Mr. Goodrich used the farmer's rhyme to teach the older girls about arithmetic.

> One for the bug,
> One for the crow,
> One to rot,
> And two to grow.

Lucretia explained, "We had to calculate the number of kernels the farmer must plant to harvest two ears of corn. Katrina Scrymser blurted out the answer, but Mr. Goodrich said Katrina did not follow directions. We were supposed to figure the answer by ourselves, and she ruined it."

The farmer's advice could be applied to the Union School. We have thirty-two students, each paying $24. The total should be $768.00 for the year. If, like the corn kernels, the yield is two-fifths, next May there could be only twelve point eight students and an income of $307.20. To keep the school alive, we need to interest many new families.

Thursday, May 12, 1814

Fathers control finances in the family, but mothers have the power of persuasion. To keep a steady enrollment, Betsy Kent, Abigail Ely, and I decided to organize the mothers of the Union School students. Abigail likes my idea of calling ourselves the Union School Mothers' Association. Betsy Kent agrees it sounds more serious, more important. The Association's newly elected officers are Abigail Ely, president. Betsy Kent, membership, Betsey Foot, secretary. Our primary mission is to maintain student enrollment and persuade others of the benefits of educating girls.

To build friendships among the mothers, we will hold a monthly tea. I will send invitations and be responsible for future communications. Once the group is established the Association will offer events of broad appeal. Mr. Goodrich will tell us how we can help him at the school. Women know how to manage details.

Tuesday, May 17, 1814

Lucretia doesn't know how it happened, but she broke the clasp on the bracelet her father gave her only six months ago. Mr. Boyd repaired it without charge. "It is the least I can do for you and Mr. Foot," he said. "The parents of Albany girls are grateful for your school. Mrs. Boyd and I will enroll Margaret and Jane Ann when they are older."

Soon we will have a new problem. The school is too small for the number of students now enrolled. We need to build an addition.

Thursday, May 19, 1814

The new moon

While running errands on Pearl Street, I met Mrs. Betsey Schuyler Hamilton at Webster's Corner. She looked elegant in a fern green gown with a shawl the color of morning glories. On her head she wore a shell pink turban with one long green plume.

She inquired about the Union School. "It is remarkable Albany now has a proper school for girls and there will soon be one for the colored children. Mr. Lattimer bought one of my lots on Plain Street and is building a school."

After I left Mrs. Hamilton, I glanced back at her. She was watching the traffic as if she planned to cross. A well-dressed elderly gentleman approached her, tipped his hat, halted traffic, offered his arm, and guided her safely to the opposite corner. Deposited on the other side, she smiled. The gentleman tipped his hat again and continued on his business. When he was out of sight, Mrs. Hamilton returned unescorted to Webster's Corner. A coach pulled up, her coachman helped her aboard, and they drove away.

I laughed to myself all day and fell asleep with a smile.

Tuesday, May 24, 1814

Today in The Albany Argus:

"WANTED HOUSE CAT, at 2 shillings per skin, for those of good quality. John Bryan."

Napoleon has wanderlust. He prefers Albany after dark and did not appear for breakfast this morning. This is not the first time he failed to return after a night on the prowl.

I fear the worst. Napoleon has the skin of good quality Mr. Bryan seeks, and the streets at night are populated with those who could use 2 shillings.

Samuel adds to my fear. "If Mr. Bryan doesn't get Napoleon, Old Dunderbeck will." He chants,

> Oh Dunderbeck
> Oh Dunderbeck
> How could you be so mean
> As ever to invent such a terrible machine?
> For dogs and cats and long tail rats will never more be seen.
> They're all ground up for sausage meat
> In Dunderbeck's machine.

He laughs and warns me not to worry. "A cat has nine lives. For three he plays, for three he strays, and for three he stays. Napoleon is looking for a Josephine. He'll come back after he has found her and when he is hungry."

Wednesday, May 25, 1814

Napoleon returned with his skin intact, but smelling of fish.

Sunday, May 29, 1814

Pentecost

On Pentecost, fifty days after Passover, Jews celebrate Shavuot, the Feast of Harvest. For Christians, Pentecost celebrates The Holy Spirit.

When the twelve apostles gathered for Shavuot, they experienced a strange phenomenon. A ball of fire appeared before them. It divided into twelve flaming tongues. Each apostle began speaking in a different and unknown language miraculously understood by all because it was the language of spirit. Easter had been the resurrection of the body. The gift of the Holy Spirit was given at Pentecost. In Christian churches Pentecost is known as Whitsunday or Wisdom Sunday. At St. Peter's, it is also White Sunday. Dressed in white christening dresses, infants and new converts are baptized. Leah, a black woman, has been a member of our church for nine years. This Pentecost, she and her little girl will be baptized.

Monday, May 30, 1814

Pinkster

At Pinkster, it is the Negroes who teach us about freedom.

Men from every grade you'll see
From lowest born to high degree.
Indians from the west will come,
And people from the rising sun.
Tho' lordlings proud may domineer,
And at our humble revels jeer
Tho' torn from friends beyond the waves
Tho' fate has doom'd us to be slaves
Yet on this day, let's taste and see
How sweet a thing is Liberty.

King Charley appears younger this year than last. He understands that when the mind is free, the soul is free.

You'll know him by his Pinkster clothes
You'll know him by his pleasant face
And by his hat of yellow lace.
You'll know him by his princely air,
And his politeness to the fair:
And when you know him, then you'll see
A slave whose soul was always free.

Lucretia and my circle of friends is wider than it was last year at Pinksterfest. She has her classmates and I have an association with their mothers. Mrs. Kane approached me at Mr. Lattimer's booth.

Taking both my hands in hers, she told me she and her husband will forever be in debt to Ebenezer. "Mr. Foot recently represented us in a legal matter that threatened to destroy our family. Mr. Foot restored our freedom."

I knew nothing of this and did not know how to reply, but she continued, "Mr. Kane and I have heard many good things about your school. Julia will be enrolled in August."

Thursday, June 2, 1814

A full moon, the strawberry moon

Penny Postman Winne says his favorite time of year is June,

The month of leaves and roses,
When pleasant sights salute the eyes,
And pleasant scents the noses!

"My favorite day in June is the fifth, the day I was born," he says, "many, many years ago."

Mr. Winne always asks about the girls' new school. "If I had a daughter, I would enroll her! I don't know why Mr. Smith sends his daughter to that fancy school in Litchfield when there is a perfectly good school here in Albany. Mrs. Smith cries every time I bring her a letter. I know for a fact Abigail wants to come home. My brother plans to send his daughter Maria to Litchfield when she turns ten, but I hope he changes his mind. My other brother has more sense. He says he plans to enroll Cornelia in the Union School."

Saturday, June 4, 1814

"It is only a milk jug," I consoled Lucretia while mopping up the spilled milk and tossing the broken pieces into the refuse.

"No more cream for my porridge!" she wailed. For me the loss is not milk. It is the loss of the pitcher Miss Pierce gave me when I left Litchfield. Her father was a potter who made many pitchers, but this was Miss Pierce's favorite and one I had frequently admired. Like me, she lost her father as a young girl.

I am grateful to have one beautiful daughter who now has a school. A milk pitcher is easily replaced. One thing is certain, I will not return to Mr. Jesse Everett's. Last week Lucretia and I had a most unpleasant experience there.

The store is packed with earthenware, woodenware, children's toys, and a collection of strange contraptions. Mr. Everett told Lucretia she looked sickly and persuaded her to rest on a wooden straight chair at the back of the store. While I continued to shop, he attached cuffs with wires to her ankles and wrists and put a cap with wires on her head. He started to attach the wires to posts on a box under the chair when she screamed, "STOP." She bolted out of the chair and tore off the paraphernalia he'd attached. Her face was white as a cold, frost moon.

Mr. Everett was surprised. "What? You are refusing my healing?"

Grasping Lucretia's damp hand, I led her out of the store. Mr. Everett followed close behind. "Mrs. Foot, Lucretia has an imbalance of positive and negative energy. It is easily corrected with an electrical charge. I have had one hundred twenty cures over the past year. I cure rheumatism, numbness, sprains, nervous afflictions, swellings, night-mares, and all kinds of pain."

I feared he would chase us down Market Street, but we escaped into the crowd of shoppers. Turning onto Steuben Street, Lucretia and I burst into tears of laughter.

Later I thought, there might be merit to his treatment. All inventions seem crazy at first. In the future there may be doctors who use electricity to treat the heart, the lungs, the skin, and even the mind. And, there could be doctors who treat just one part of the body. Mr. Skinner on Beaver Street specializes in teeth and gums. He advertises he studied with Ruspini of London, and LeMaire of Paris.

In spite of skeptics, I'm sure Mr. Everett will persist with his elec-trical thingamajig. First he needs to cure his own lunacy and Mrs. Ev-erett's nerves. She is jumpy as a long-tailed cat in a room full of rocking chairs! For a new milk pitcher, I will go either to Mr. Daniels on north Market or Paul Cushman on Washington Street.

Tuesday, June 7, 1814

Paul Cushman's store bombards the nose with the aroma of damp clay. He has shelves and shelves of earthenware on display. One that caught my eyes is a butter urn, decorated with a sturgeon suckling a cow! The joke is there are so many sturgeons in the Hudson River, they are dubbed Albany Beef. If I churned my own butter, I would buy that urn and have something to laugh about every day.

The plain milk jug I bought will take the place of the one Miss Pierce gave me, but it will never replace it.

Monday, June 13, 1814

At the June 10 Church Vestry meeting Reverend Clowes' salary was clarified. It was explained to him that income from church property lands is already included in the rector's salary. He is not satisfied. Land values in Albany are increasing, so he feels his salary should also be increased. Mr. Willett persuades Clowes not to pursue the issue. Time will tell if Clowes takes his advice.

Money given to him at Christmas was also discussed. The Christmas before last, the vestry gave Reverend Clowes three hundred dollars. He thought it was a gift, but it turns out the money was only a loan, still unpaid. This past Christmas, the vestry gave him one hundred dollars. He insisted he used the money not for himself, but for improvements to the rectory, trees for the front of the church, and decorations for Christmas. For the sake of our church family, I hope the conflict is soon resolved.

Friday, June 17, 1814

A new moon

The Allens, Russells, John Ely, Judge Kent, Mr. Ten Eyck, and Mr. have made early tuition payments. Ebenezer deposited sixty-six dollars in the Mechanics and Farmers Bank.

Thursday, June 23, 1814

Captain Roorback says there was a lunar eclipse on Tuesday evening. This may account for Ebenezer's forgetfulness. Each morning I hand him his hat and bag. Each evening he usually hands them back. Two days ago he left his hat in Troy. Yesterday he left his bag on Mr. Cole's ferry. He said he was distracted by Rensselaer Westerlo asking to enroll Cornelia in our school.

TAPPING REEVE, 1744-1829

Ebenezer is becoming as absent-minded as his Litchfield teacher. One day the students saw Tapping Reeve walk down South Street trailing the reins of his horse. He seemed unaware there was no horse attached. He tied the reins of his phantom horse to the hitching post outside his home and went inside.

Ebenezer and Professor Reeve are not absent-minded. It is the opposite. Their minds are crowded with people and problems. Besides an increase in law cases, Ebenezer has begun weekly supervision of the Union School.

Monday, July 4, 1814

The Declaration of Independence was signed thirty-eight years ago. Two generations of citizens have known freedom. On Independence Day, we put differences aside. We are Americans first. In honor of the birth of our United States, I will use the Ely family recipe for royal cake and call it a democratic cake. The oven will make the kitchen hotter than it is already. That's the price for liberty.

DEMOCRATIC CAKE

one glass of yeast, three quarts of flour, one and one half cups of sugar, one pound of butter, four eggs, one and one quarter cup of raisins, one half glass of wine, one glass of brandy, one half ounce of cinnamon, one quarter ounce of allspice, one pinch of coriander.

Wednesday, July 6, 1814

Ebenezer is forty-one years old today. He says he feels twice that age. He suffers from headaches, likely caused by long work days, and the heat.

He ruminates about his mortality and the fragility of life. His older brother died after he'd been kicked in the head by a horse. His younger brother John died suddenly ten years ago. His father was overcome with melancholia and gradually lost his mental faculties. Eventually, he could not do the simplest chore. He died five years ago.

"He lost his mind," Ebenezer confided. "It is a fate worse than death. Please God, when it is my time to go, grant me a short crossing. I would not want a long preface and preamble."

"Please God," I quickly added, "may you cross over after a long and productive life."

Saturday, July 9, 1814

The hot, humid days of July and August, the sickly months, have begun. River and street smells are strong. The air feels thick. In the morning, the lampposts are wet, and the cobblestones are slippery as wet glass even though there has been no rain for weeks. It is hotter than Tophet.

"It is going to rain, starting tonight," says Penny Postman Winne.

In the morning, mountains.
In the evening, fountains.

"And by the looks of the clouds, the rain will be heavy."

When clouds look like rocks and towers
The earth will have many showers.

I know it will rain when my hair gets curly. Performing the simplest chore, beads of perspiration collect on my forehead, form rivulets that stream down my face and neck, and pool on my breast. Rain would be a relief.

I close my eyes and imagine the beach at Grandmother's. I feel a cool breeze. I inhale the fresh, sea salt air. In my mind, I shed stockings and slippers and wiggle my toes in the sand. Along the beach, sea gulls squabble and sandpipers tease the waves. The ebb and flow rhythm of the ocean calms me.

My quest to give the girls an education is accomplished. What is next for me?

Monday, July 11, 1814

Last night, there was a dramatic display of lightning and thunder. It illuminated the whole room and rattled every window in the house. Samuel moved his chair away from the glass. Horace commenced coughing and went upstairs. Lucretia could not stop laughing. Ebenezer had retired earlier than usual and slept through the storm. He has been overwhelmed with an important trial at Rensselaer County Circuit Court. He takes the early ferry to Troy and returns, exhausted, on the last one at night.

There were so many thunderstorms in Litchfield, I grew accustomed to them, even found them thrilling. At Litchfield I nicknamed Ebenezer "lightning."

Friday, July 15, 1814

St. Swithin's' Day

The heavy rains continue and Penny Postman Winne says,

St. Swithin's day if thou dost rain
For forty days it will remain.

I could not bear rain for forty days and groaned. Together Mr. Winne and I recited, his most frequent refrain.

We weather the weather
Whatever the weather
Whether we like it or not.

Monday, July 18, 1814

Ebenezer arrived home at midday. Despite the heat, he has chills. Cousin John is away and he does not want to bother Dr. Townsend or Dr. Yates. He thinks it is simply over-exertion in the heat. "Rest and a pint of Hamilton's Elixir from Mr. Mancius is what I need."

This is the first time I have seen Ebenezer surrender to his body. Napoleon followed him upstairs and curled up at the bottom of the bed. Ebenezer slept for several hours and woke up thrashing about and talking like he was arguing a case in court. Napoleon stood up, stretched his back and legs, turned around three times, and resumed his watch. Ebenezer fell back to sleep.

Tuesday, July 19, 1814

Ebenezer's fever remains high. I rub Hamilton's Elixir on his chest and cajole him to drink cool tea. He refuses food. Around midday he became agitated and started talking to his deceased father as if he were at the foot of the bed. He says his father is angry at him for leaving the farm. Despite his objections, I sent Mrs. Ellison to fetch Dr. Yates who arrived quickly. He said Ebenezer will be fine after a dose of laudanum. "Like most fevers, it will run its course."

Napoleon does not leave Ebenezer's bed except when "necessary."

Wednesday, July 20, 1814

This morning, Ebenezer is listless. He now says, "Father is pleased that his sons are doing well."

To me he said, "Dear Betsey, we have shared many blessings and found much joy in our family."

"Yes," I answered, "and our blessings will continue."

"Yes, our good works will continue and prosper." He looked into my eyes as if into another world.

Thursday, July 21, 1814

I thought Ebenezer was reviving, but he had made his choice between life and death. He exhaled for the last time at 7:20 this morning. I did not say goodbye. He had already departed.

I know the sexton rang the church bell nine times to announce the death of a male and forty-one times to give his age. No one in our house asks who has passed. No one on Montgomery Street inquires.

I cannot make sense of what people say to me. "Do you need this? Do you want that?" As Ebenezer's spirit ascends to heaven, mine spins about me. I feel dizzy then numb. Tomorrow or next week I will think about Ebenezer. I cannot think about him today.

Samuel covers the mirror with white linen and closes the shutters. A chill creeps into my bones. Mr. Goodrich canceled the end of term examinations.

Mrs. Ellison washed Ebenezer's body and wrapped him in a sheet sprinkled with rosemary. Mrs. Reid offered to sew the grave clothes. Cousin John and Mr. Russell will sit watch after Ebenezer is moved to the front room. Mrs. Russell will order dead cakes from Mr. Lansing.

I do not want Lucretia to see her father and be terrified as I was when I saw my father's lifeless body.

How can I tell Lucretia her father is happy that he has been called to his heavenly home? How could she believe this when she sees my grief and the mournful faces of all who call to pay their respects? Will she think he was not happy here on earth? Does she worry she said or did something to cause his death? Did I? Mrs. Ellison will know what to say to console her.

My world is dark. I am like a frightened child with no safe place to hide.

"Albany Argus, Friday, July 22, 1814,
DIED IN THIS CITY, YESTERDAY MORNING,
EBENEZER FOOT, Esq."

Saturday, July 23, 1814

Before closing the coffin, I kissed Ebenezer's forehead. Samuel, who never showed any affection for Ebenezer while he was alive, took his brother's hand and held it to his cheek. Lucretia would not look at her father and I did not insist. Reverend Clowes said a final prayer and lowered the top of the casket. Ebenezer's mother put her head at the top of his casket and rested there, as if listening to his evening prayer.

Samuel, John, Horace Goodrich, Thomas Russell, Joseph Russell, and William Fowler carried Ebenezer out of our home for the last time. Mrs. Foot, Lucretia and I, the Edward, Gregory, and Ely families, along with many others, followed in a procession to the muddy graveyard west of the church. Heavy rains prevented my mother, sisters, and brothers in Hadley from attending the burial.

Tears stick at the back of my throat.

Monday, July 25, 1814

Mr. Goodrich recommends resuming classes. I do not disagree.

When Captain Roorback returned Napoleon to us this morning, I realized he'd been missing since Ebenezer was buried. He was wet but looked well fed. As usual Napoleon made no apologies for his absence. After grooming himself, he went straight to bed.

Tuesday, July 26, 1814

I feel like I am in Mr. Bushnell's Turtle, adrift. Outside, the water is murky. Which way forward? Which way back? Will I surface or plunge deeper? What will I find if I surface? What will happen if I don't?

Wednesday, July 27, 1814

Is this the fate that all must die?
Will death no ages spare?

All humans suffer the painful loss of a loved one. I know I must surrender to the mystery of God's ways and trust in a heavenly reward for Ebenezer and for me when it is my time. I am thankful to be alone when Lucretia is in school. Seclusion protects me from her over and over questions. They are the same as my own and I have no answers. Napoleon is my constant companion. I stroke his face and he listens to my worries. He has had his three lives to play and three to stray. Is this the three to stay?

Why did God take Ebenezer? How will we live without him? Is he all right? Does he miss us? Is he lonely? Why didn't he sign the subscription document? How will I pay the tuition due August 1? How can I live without him? How can I provide for Lucretia? Who will take care of us? Will we have to move to The Alms' House? Was I a good wife? Did I do everything I could for him while he was sick? Did I wait too long to call Dr. Yates?

Even though I know it is not possible, I expect Ebenezer to return home, answer all my questions, and make everything better.

Friday, July 29, 1814

Kind friends share words of sympathy to comfort themselves. Their condolences upset me.

I know how you feel. It was the will of God. God needed him. The good die young. He is in a better place. He worked himself into the grave. He no longer suffers. He is happy. He is free. He is at peace. You are fortunate you had a good marriage and so many happy memories. You are strong. God never sends us more than we can handle. You are blessed to have your daughter.

Old Mrs. Brown's comment was most disturbing. "Mrs. Foot, you are still young and attractive. I'm sure, in time, you will find an-other..." When she saw my face drop, she hastily revised what she planned to say. "I am sure you will find a way to pass your time. Time heals all wounds."

Passing time is not what I want.

Eventually I will acknowledge the sympathy letters, but not now. When I packed the notes away I found the roll of bills Mr. North gave me one year ago. There were six bills each worth five dollars.

"Put your money away," Mr. Fowler said when I handed him the tuition due August 1.

"The annual fee for Lucretia has been deposited in The Mechanics and Farmers Bank. It will be dispersed quarterly."

Mr. Fowler said banking matters are confidential. He could not divulge details about who made the gift or when.

My life is over but Lucretia has a future.

Monday, August 1, 1814

The full August moon on the Hudson is called the sturgeon moon

All the first-term students returned and there are three new students. Mr. Brinckerhoff enrolled Maria. Mr. Kane enrolled Julia. Mr. Westerlo enrolled Cornelia.

Tuesday, August 2, 1814

The head that was always sunny is overcast. Will the sun rise tomorrow or next week or next year? Will I forever meet each day with a heavy heart? The cemetery gravestone says,

The sky is blue. The grass is green
The days are past which I have seen.
As you are now, so once was I.
As I am now so shall you be.
Prepare for death and follow me.

Why did God take Ebenezer and not me? Why was his life so short? Can I live without him? What will I do with my life now that he is gone?

When I ask these questions, Mrs. Ellison smiles. "Betsey dear, these are the questions you will answer, with time. What is concealed will be revealed."

Saturday, August 6, 1814

I expected Samuel would quickly repay the eight hundred dollars Ebenezer provided for his tuition at Union. Today he told me Ebenezer died with large debts. Samuel says he is responsible for them because he endorsed notes for Ebenezer. One amounts to fifteen hundred dollars. Another is for twelve hundred. There is also the matter of a wager Ebenezer and some others made with four prominent Albany men: a bet on last year's election. Ebenezer's group lost and sued the winners claiming there was fraud. When the court ruled in Ebenezer's favor, Samuel collected and divided the money. In a subsequent appeal, the decision was reversed. The Court for the Correction of Errors ordered the money be returned to the four gentlemen. All complied except Ebenezer. I am sure it was his intent or perhaps he planned an appeal. Samuel owes over five thousand dollars. He must pay or go to jail. He assures me that is unlikely. He will urge the men to consider Ebenezer's poor widow and daughter.

Widow. This is the first time I heard the word. It sounds gray, withered, wasting away. Is this what I am? Is this what I will always be? Discarded and destitute.

Tuesday, August 9, 1814

When will it stop raining? The tears that wouldn't flow, now will not stop.

Bedrenched with tears that flowed from mournful head,
Til nature had exhausted all her store
Then eyes lay dry, disabled to weep more;
And looking up unto his throne on high,
Who sendeth help to those in misery.

Anne Bradstreet

What does it mean to be in mourning? I am still in this world, but feel flung outside it. I am alone, vulnerable, afraid. In the hurly burly everyday world, I seem unchanged, but in two weeks' time my life has totally and forever changed.

No one can help my misery.

Friday, August 12, 1814

In the beginning, three of the four gentleman agreed to forgive the debt. In the end, their love of money prevailed and they changed their mind. Samuel was not surprised. "Some of Albany's finest men are lambs by day and wolves at night."

He will go to jail, but says, "I'm fortunate I will not be subjected to the rack and screw. I'm grateful I will not be branded with a red D because then I could not earn a living. I will not have to sit in the rain in the stocks. I will be warm and dry in jail."

How can Samuel repay the debt when he is in jail? Does jail prevent crimes? Do criminals think they will be caught and punished? Does jail reform them? Samuel will eat and sleep with twelve-year-old pickpockets, lifelong burglars, and serial murderers. Tossed into the mix are the homeless and sick, the deranged, and the intemperate.

Saturday, August 13, 1814

Two of Ebenezer's friends offered to lend Samuel money but he turned them down. He will take responsibility for the loan and serve his time in jail. "Better to go to bed supperless than rise in debt."

Monday, August 15, 1814

The new moon

I prepared food for jail and helped Samuel pack. Sheriff Mancius knows Samuel and trusts he will not escape. He directed the jailer, Mr. Steel, to give Samuel a room on the first floor rather than in a locked cell above. Samuel will be free to meet clients and conduct business in the parlor of the Steel family.

Thursday, August 18, 1814

The British invaded Washington and set fire to the President's House, but not before Dolley rescued Gilbert Stuart's painting of George Washington. The exterior of the house is charred. Since the month has been wet, the house was not destroyed. It will be restored and painted white.

In Albany, the rain finally stopped.

Tuesday, August 23, 1814

Every day, Mr. Winne reminds me there are letters addressed to Ebenezer remaining in the Post Office. According to Samuel, the letters are from New York and should be returned to the sender.

Monday, August 29, 1814

Before I received Miss Pierce's letter, I thought I had exhausted all my tears.

South Street
Litchfield, Connecticut
August 13, 1814

Dearest Betsey,

Please accept my sincere condolences during this time of profound sorrow. I know you grieve alone and in private. You alone know the depth of your loss. There are no words to comfort you.

Loss and suffering are part of life's mystery. Love, joy, and birth are also mysteries that cannot be explained. In time, what is concealed will be revealed. What is hidden will be made known.

Just as every life ends in death, every death brings new life. Under heaven everything happens at the right time. You are forever bound to Ebenezer. However, your work on earth is not finished.

Take your next steps cautiously. In times of mourning, decisions are often driven by fear.

Gnothi Seauton. Your inner wisdom will guide you. Your future will unfold naturally. What is concealed will be revealed. If The Lord leads you to Litchfield, I open my heart, home, and life work to you and Lucretia.

Semper et in aeternum, I am your dear instructress,
Sarah Pierce

Miss Pierce does not understand. There is no life for me. Over and over, day after day, my life is, and will always be, a meaningless dogtrot. She is right: there are no words of comfort or healing. Litchfield Female Academy is what I dreamed of for Lucretia. If I lived with Miss Pierce, I would not be alone. Would returning to Litchfield be a decision made out of fear? Would it be a step back? Can I go back?

Tuesday, August 30, 1814
The second full moon of August

A week ago Samuel sent a letter to the four gentleman appealing for sympathy for the "destitute widow" and daughter. He offered to pay the interest and legal costs of the amount due leaving a balance of nine hundred fifty dollars. After no response, Samuel's only choice was to accept a loan from Ebenezer's friends and pay the debt in full.

All were convinced the gentlemen would not accept the money. They accepted the money and also received a generous lashing of insults from everyone who knows about the situation.

Friday, September 2, 1814

The debt is satisfied. Samuel thanked the Steel family for their many kindnesses and bid them farewell. Mrs. Steel complimented him for his manners. Mr. Steel was grateful for Samuel's legal advice on a personal matter. The Steel children enjoyed learning to play chess. I am relieved he has returned safely to our home.

Wednesday, September 7, 1814

After examination, Judge Kent issued Samuel a license. He is qualified to serve as counsellor in cases where, at the time of death, Ebenezer was the attorney.

Friday, September 9, 1814

Samuel's plan is to sell 36 Montgomery Street and move to a boarding house. He assures me nothing will be done in haste.

"During this period of mourning it is considered proper for you to remain in the home with Mr. Goodrich and myself."

Proper for me to remain in my own home? I never thought I would have to leave the home Ebenezer and I lived in together.

Tuesday, September 13, 1814

A new moon

It is difficult to believe I have accumulated so much over the years. I go from room to room looking at too many possessions. Day after day, room by room, I sift through stuff. Everything demands a decision. What do I keep? What do I give away? Who needs or wants it? What can I toss into the refuse? The work is hard mentally and physically. I go to bed tired and wake up exhausted.

Every night my dreams take me to the homes of my past. Tables, chairs, dish-ware, clothes, books, papers, and an assortment of mystery items are strewn about. Over and over, I attempt to sort, repair, clean, and organize. The job is never finished. Old friends and family long gone order me to clean up.

I want to sweep the mess into a pile and toss everything out. They warn, "You might destroy something of value. You could overlook something important." They offer no help and vanish.

Last night I dreamt the lower right corner of the Union School's subscription paper was torn. I could not find the missing piece. This morning Samuel assured me the document is packed away with his important papers.

Wednesday, September 14, 1814

"My life is over," I confided to Mrs. Ellison. It was the first time I said the words out loud. "My life is over, but Lucretia's is just beginning." Mrs. Ellison listened to the questions I'd not shared with anyone. How will I take care of Lucretia? I have no money and no way to make money. I cannot take in students now that we have the Union School. I don't have the strength to take in washing. I don't have the skills to be a seamstress. I have no patience for baking.

Samuel plans to sell our house and move to a boarding house on State Street. Lucretia and I must find our own place. Where will we go? Should I go back to Litchfield? If I stay in Albany do I have no other choice than to descend to Dock Street and take in gentlemen boarders like Elizabeth Ross? Am I resigned to becoming a slave to strangers?

After sharing my despair with Mrs. Ellison, she was quiet. When I composed myself, she shocked me with the harshness of her reply.

"Nonsense, Betsey. Your life is not over. It is changed. It is changed just as it has every day since the day you were born. The difference is for the first time in your life you are free to direct the change. Managing a boarding house can provide a freedom you have never known. It is true you need to take care of Lucretia and yourself. There are many choices other than Dock Street. Calculate what you need to live comfortably and add a little extra. The total will inform you what to charge potential boarders. Name your price. Good boarding homes are in demand. You will have many applicants from which to choose. Set your terms. What services will you provide and what will not be included? Don't think about what you can't do. You have an opportunity to think about what you can do. Use the gifts you've been given."

She concluded the visit abruptly. "Forgive me, Betsey dear, but I have another engagement."

A changed life? Freedom? Opportunity? Her response shook me. In every drama, including my own, there is a peripeteia: a turn around, a transforming revelation. This was the shift I needed.

Life is a mystery.
What is concealed will be revealed.
What is hidden will be made known.

**"The Albany Gazette, Monday, September 19, 1814.
FOR SALE. A two story dwelling house pleasantly situated.
Two long rooms, three bedrooms, two pantries with kitchen
and cellar. For particulars apply to the printers."**

Tuesday, September 20, 1814

The ink was not dry on the Gazette when Mr. Bladderwort (not his real name) bypassed the printers and came straight to my door. He had a proposition and was sure I'd view it favorably. I had trouble following the details, but it involved his use of our front room as his office. He insisted the family should remain "in the home you love so dearly." In consideration of "our dire circumstances," he would charge us a "modest" amount to occupy the upper rooms. He would consider the difference between this and a fair monthly rental fee as the purchase price for our house.

"Think about it, Mrs. Foot, but don't procrastinate. I am postponing the purchase of another property because Mr. Foot and I were close friends. I had great respect for your husband's business judgement and sense of timing. I owe it to him to help you and your daughter. I know he would support this. We can complete all the arrangements within the week. You can rest in peace. You need not leave your home. You will not accrue further debts. I'm sure you know you will not receive a better offer."

Stunned, I thanked Mr. Bladderwort and said I would consider his offer.

Mr. Groesbeeck must have seen him come and go. Shortly after the gentleman turned the corner, he came knocking.

He was blunt. "Listen to me, Mrs. Foot. I am well acquainted with that man. He thinks he can pull the wool over your eyes. I'm here to tell you, he plans to take advantage of you. In the Groesbeeck family we keep our business private, so you may not be aware Mrs. Groesbeeck has been gravely ill for over a year. Forgive me if I am nosing into your affairs, but if it was me and not my good wife who was at death's door, I would be grateful if someone warned her about men like that scoundrel. He is devoted to the obituaries. He knows what the grieving survivors need. He makes offers too good to be true. Have you received a visit from his friend, the Bible man? He will bring you a leather bound Bible embossed in "real gold." He will say Mr. Foot ordered it for you as a birthday surprise. He will insist on giving it to you free of charge, knowing your pride will not permit it. He will reluctantly settle for a small fee, knowing your pride will not permit it. Finally he will agree to a very, very small deposit now (twice what the cheap Bible is worth) and monthly installments if, and only if, you become financially stable.

This second visit of the day ended as abruptly as the first. "Don't worry, Mrs Foot. I'll see to it you don't receive any more swindlers."

Before he left he said, "I am sorry about Mr. Foot. He was a good man, gone too soon. I don't ask why. My grandfather always told me, 'There are some things 'ya shouldn't need to know!'"

Friday, September 23, 1814

The sun rises further south each morning. Flocks of geese follow. Samuel has rented rooms on State Street. Next to the Tontine Coffee House, it's a good location for his office. He has invited his nephew James Edwards to live with him in Albany and commence the study of law. He encourages Horace to resume the legal work abandoned during the school's first term.

I do not know where I will go or what I will do. Despite what Mrs. Ellison says I have very few options.

Tuesday, September 27, 1814

Mr. Goodrich's college classmate is traveling through Albany and has offered to deliver a lecture on rhetoric to the older girls. "It is a distance back to Ballston Spa. If it would be proper, I would like to invite Mr. Booth to dinner before he leaves for home."

I thought it was an excellent idea. At the mention of Lebbeus Booth's name, Lucretia smiled for the first time in over a month. I'd forgotten about the commencement ceremonies and her infatuation with him.

September 29, 1814
A full moon, the harvest moon

Lebbeus Booth is a charming young man. He and Horace engaged us in a stimulating table conversation about the role of a master teacher. Both agreed an academy education is built on a concrete knowledge of the social, material, and political world. It should then evolve to the more complex and abstract study of math and science principles. The ultimate goal is the development of character, the ability to reason, and ultimately to create. The foundation of a free society rests on an academy education.

Horace has not seemed well the past month. I was happy to see him animated and full of life in the company of his friend, Lebbeus.

Lucretia was uncharacteristically quiet.

Monday, October 3, 1814

My wandering companion returned early this morning in the tight grip of Mr. James Kane.

"Although everyone on the docks loves The Little Captain, we thought it time for him to return home. Captain Roorback informed me 36 Montgomery Street is his legal address."

Napoleon, happy to be released and standing on his own four legs, disappeared inside.

I thanked Mr. Kane and believed he'd be on his way. Instead, he asked if he could have a word with me. Although he was one of the kind men who lent Samuel money, I feared he had a scheme.

He said he and Mrs. Kane recently acquired a home at 35 State Street. "We trade with men who travel for business. They require lodging for a season or two. We need a manager for the property and immediately thought of you. As proprietor, you and Lucretia and, of course, The Little Captain, would live in the first-floor apartment. I only do business with men of character and integrity, men who are accustomed to paying for well-appointed accommodations. It will be your job to assess each applicant's suitability and agree on the terms. The gentlemen appreciate a morning meal, but otherwise expect to dine outside the home. I have engaged Dina Lattimer's sister, Phebe, to help with housekeeping chores. Captain Roorback encouraged me to speak with you. He assured me you would not be offended. Accepting the position is a big decision. I will give you time to think about it."

Minutes after he left, Mr. Groesbeeck appeared. "In the whole city of Albany, you will not find a finer more trustworthy man than Mr. Kane. I know personally of his many benevolent deeds, anonymously given, and with no expectation of return."

Mrs. Ellison confirmed what Mr. Groesbeeck said. "Even the Indians trust Mr. Kane." She offered to accompany me to meet with him at 35 State Street on Thursday.

Thursday, October 6, 1814

Mr. Kane's brick home is in a lovely part of State Street. It is a few doors below the State Bank building with its elegant Palladian window. Newly planted elm trees line both sides of the wide street. There are people waving hello and good bye to arriving and departing coaches, gentlemen on horses, maids selling wafels, cartmen, laborers with buckets, men discussing business, and couples enjoying a leisurely stroll. It is only a short distance from Montgomery Street, but I feel like I have left a small village and arrived in a big city.

Number 35 has a wide front stoop with an iron railing and a covered porch. Next door is Mr. Gill's mercantile business. Just as Mr. Kane opened his door for Mrs. Ellison and me, Mrs. Gill emerged from her door and waved.

In the front hall, on the left, there is a fancy mahogany staircase leading to two upper floors with six furnished bedrooms. To the right is a front parlor painted yellow and two windows facing south. The mantle of the fireplace is carved with urns and garlands. There is a large middle room and in the back, a kitchen and pantry. Below is a cold cellar which Mr. Kane said he would keep fully stocked. Already under the impression I will accept the position, he has removed all the furnishings, "So you can see how well your own fine things will be arranged. Please let me know if there is additional furniture you require."

I still had reservations about the move when Mr. Kane opened the back door to an enclosed garden. A brick path encircled three raised gardens for herbs and flowers. Along the back fence was a bench in front of neatly pruned shrubbery. Mr. Kane promised, "In the spring there will be a wall of azalea, pinkster, and lilac." Next door, Mrs. Gill had moved into her garden and waved again.

STATE BANK OF ALBANY AND STATE STREET

The situation seems ideal for Lucretia and me and I have only one concern. At the northeast corner of State and Pearl is the former Dutch Church parsonage. It was once a handsome four-story gabled structure with brick, iron, woodwork, and tiles imported from Holland. It is now a deteriorating relic occupied by the old curmudgeon, Mr. Lydius. He is a tall, skeletal man with a pale, narrow face and long white hair. He is so cantankerous that people cross the street rather than pass by his house. Boys say he prowls the street on nights of a full moon calling, "Fee, Fi, Fo, Fum, I smell the blood of an Englishman."

Mrs. Ellison had no patience with me. "I've known Balthazar Lydius since he was a boy. Odd, yes. Dangerous, no. He is not looking for blood. He only wants his bottle and pipe. Ever since he took an Indian squaw for a wife, he doesn't leave his house. He is too old to go roaming at night, full moon or not. Besides, there are more street lights on State Street than anywhere else in Albany. Mr. Moore spends most of the night patrolling State Street. It's the safest in the city. It's where the money is."

Her final words before we parted were, "Managing Mr. Kane's property, you will have half the work and twice the money, time, and freedom."

She is right. I will be grateful for the money. As a widow, what would I do with time and freedom?

Monday, October 10, 1814

When Lucretia left for school, Mrs. Ellison delivered the message that Mr. Kane is waiting for my decision.

My only response was not a decision. Something is holding me back. I don't feel ready to move. I feel safe here. I'm too tired to move. I can't see my way. The light has gone out. I want my old life back. I did not tell her the truth. I'm afraid to admit I still expect Ebenezer will come back to Montgomery Street.

Mrs. Ellison understood and recognized what I needed. "Betsey, you are strong, but you cannot change the flow of life anymore than you can change the direction of a river. We are not aware of the wake we leave behind. We don't know what is ahead, around the bend. We can make decisions only on what we see here, what we know now. Your life has changed. What has not changed is the gift with your name. To rekindle the life spark within, you must take the first step. The light will become brighter with each step."

Tuesday, October 11, 1814

A waning moon

An iridescent mother-of pearl seashell of a moon dangles low in the eastern sky this morning. I always viewed the waning moon as a sad moon. When the moon disappears, the next nights will be dark. Today I understand the moon is turning to the morning sun and the promise of a new day.

Samuel supports my decision to take Mr. Kane's offer. He is surprised I made it without consulting him. He will remain on Montgomery Street until the house is sold.

Lucretia is excited we will be around the corner from her new friends on Market. Horace was silent for several days before he asked if he could take one of the rooms at 35 State.

I'm pleased Horace asked to move with us. I've grown fond of him and worry about his health. His cough is unrelenting and he has lost weight since school started in May. It is wise that he is not returning to his former position as law clerk.

Tuesday, October 18, 1814

Mr. Groesbeeck called at 36 Montgomery for a third time. Mrs. Groesbeeck would like to say good-bye before I move away.

I did not know what to expect when I entered her bedchamber. She is frail, but she has the same sweet smile and radiates a peaceful glow.

Mrs. Groesbeeck had two matters on her mind. First, she was happy to tell me that Captain Roorback is training Wilhelm to work with him on the steamboats. Second, she wants me to consider taking Catharine as a writing student. She and Mr. Groesbeeck would like to enroll her in the Union School, but for now, she is needed at home. Because of the circumstances, I do not think there will be a conflict. Mrs. Groesbeeck was visibly relieved when I assured her it would be my honor to tutor her daughter.

"Thank you and good-by" she said and closed her eyes.

Monday, October 24, 1814

The Scovilles offer to send Hannah to help pack our belongings, but it is good for me to keep busy. If necessary Mr. Kane will send Phebe and Dina to help. When I am ready, Mr. Lattimer will transport our possessions.

Friday, October 28, 1814

A full moon, the hunter's moon

Tuesday, November 1, 1814

November is a dark month. I banish thoughts of the cold days ahead and follow the advice of Miss Pierce, "Girls, if you want to be warm, keep moving." I laugh. Today is moving day.

There will be quiet days ahead. Once settled, I will listen to the still small voice within.

Friday, November 11, 1814

A new moon

I have so much to do, I need to make a list.

-Instruct Phebe to prepare a room for Horace Goodrich on the second floor. Next week I will interview Mr. Jesse Buel who requests to rent a room and I will also meet a gentleman from Hudson who plans to stay the winter.

-Write a thank you note to Miss Pierce for her thoughtful offer to move to Litchfield.

-Send a sympathy note to Mrs. Nugent on the passing of her husband.

-Respond to Miss Benton's proposal to teach English to two students from Santo Domingo. The pay is generous.

-Make comments on Catharine Groesbeeck's latest composition.

She needs to provide more details in her writing, especially about the loss of her mother.

-Begin Bible Study at The Ladies Church Society (for those of us who do not like sewing). It will give the women something to talk about besides Reverend Clowes.

-Compile a membership list for The Mothers Association of the Union School.

-Invite Mrs. Gill to tea to discuss her idea about starting a literary circle for ladies.

Saturday, November 26, 1814

A full moon, the frost moon

Thursday, December 1, 1814

My birthday

I celebrate the first of a 365 day journey around the sun: another cycle of sowing, growing, harvesting, and hunting.

Friday, December 2, 1814

The river is closed to navigation.

MRS. JOHN COPELAND AND AAG DAUGHTERS, JOAN '62, LOUISE '60, AND
MIDGE COPELAND '58. 1952 MOTHER'S DAY AT ALBANY ACADEMY
FOR GIRLS, 155 WASHINGTON AVENUE, ALBANY, NY

Wednesday, April 10, 2013

A new moon

Betsey Foot first spoke to me when I was in sixth grade. It was the only terrible, horrible, no good, very bad time of my thirteen years at Albany Academy for Girls. The transition from elementary to middle school was a period of yearning for days gone by and worrying about the future.

We began each morning at AAG with chapel, a time for song, scripture, and words of inspiration. Mr. Hollister played with a flourish the first bars of the processional, the call for students to line up in pairs according to height. On cue, we marched into the Study Hall of the Washington Avenue school singing from the small red Hymnal of the Protestant Episcopal Church. High school girls had assigned desks along the eastern side of the room. Middle school girls sat on the opposite, windowless side. This is where I first saw the framed document that introduced me to Mr. and Mrs. Ebenezer Foot. In black calligraphy with first letters illuminated in gold it read,

OLDEST SCHOOL IN THE WORLD
FOR THE HIGHER EDUCATION OF GIRLS
Albany Female Academy. Albany. N.Y.
Founded AD. 1814.
By Mr. and Mrs. Ebenezer Foot.

Our school's name had been modernized, but I knew this was my school. Oldest school in the world for the higher education of girls? 1814 was a long time ago. Who was Ebenezer Foot? Who was his wife? Did they have a daughter? What was her name? What was she like? Who were her friends? Did she like school? Did she have a nice teacher?

On the document was a drawing of the first school. It was a cozy cottage, and I imagined I would be happier living in the olden days. As one of the first students, I would be special. I would have many friends.

My school work would not be sixth-grade hard. It would be third-grade easy. My teacher would not be demanding. She would be sweet and pretty like my elementary school teacher, Mrs. Fitzgerald. Every day there would be bluebirds and flowers and sunshine and springtime. I wouldn't have any worries.

Hanging near the document was the portrait of a woman. In an ornate gold frame, it was the kind of oil painting you would see in a museum. The woman was dressed in a dark, old-fashioned gown. Her high forehead was fringed with brown curls. She wore a turban and a collar of white frills. When I squinted, it seemed like her face was encircled in a ring of light. She had kind eyes, rosy cheeks, and a serene smile. I imagined she looked directly at me and said, "Good morning, Louise, dear. I hope you have a wonderful day."

I'd seen portraits of famous men; European kings and American presidents. I had never seen a portrait of a woman. I thought she must be very important. Who was she and what did she do? Miss Harris, our headmistress, said she was Betsey Foot. She founded our school in 1814 because there were no schools in Albany suitable for her daughter. What an amazing accomplishment! In social studies, we studied maps and wars and politics. There was little mention of what women were doing.

I did not think about Betsey Foot until many years later when I faced another life transition. Leaving the world of work, I faced changes and choices. I was uncertain about "what's next."

Did Betsey Foot know she had long ago stirred my imagination? Did she call on me because she knew it was an opportune time to tell her story, not because she wanted to be famous, but because she wanted to pass on what she had learned about courage, freedom, and living a life of purpose?

It was not a calling like Moses' burning bush or the flash of lightning that blinded Paul on the road to Damascus. I did not hear Betsey's voice one morning before dawn. The calling happened while my husband Dalton and I were sightseeing along the Coral Coast of Western Australia. We stopped for tea at the seaside town of Fremantle and discovered there was a psychic fair. While Dalton looked at sailboats in the marina, I went to the fair. My first stop was for a foot massage.

After the reflexologist gave my tired feet new life, she said, "Just for fun, check out the booths along the boardwalk. One of the psychics might 'speak' to you."

None of the psychics spoke to me, but one ordinary looking woman made eye contact and smiled. She did not wear a gypsy scarf or gold hoop earrings or look into a crystal ball. When I sat before her I was disappointed because she seemed preoccupied with my jewelry. She noted, "The gold and turquoise at your throat strengthens your ability to communicate. I see you are a writer."

"No," I laughed self-consciously. "I like to write, but I am not a writer."

Turning her attention to the ring on my left hand, she said, "Did your ring once belong to someone else? There is harsh energy coming from it and needs to be cleansed." I'd left my wedding ring at home and wore another for the trip. I cringed because she spoke an uncomfortable truth.

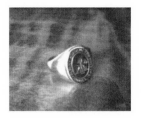

Turning to the AAG ring on my right hand she noted, "There is strong masculine energy coming from that ring. It is very powerful." A girls' school ring with masculine energy? She was wrong about that. Mr. Hollister was the one male teacher in our school. His only power was to reject me from the Glee Club. That was okay. I preferred the stage.

I was polite. "It is from the girls' school I attended for thirteen years." She persisted. "I feel the energy of a powerful man. He is a leader, a minister, or lawyer. He is someone with great oratorical skills. When he speaks, people listen."

I left feeling the session had been a waste of twenty minutes and fifteen dollars. Oh well, she was entertaining, and the foot massage was relaxing. On the next leg of the journey, I thought about projects for back home. I would write stories about my childhood, job experiences, family memories, or my long distance sailing adventures with Dalton. It might be fun to write a children's book about Betsey Foot's daughter. I wanted to pursue an interest in genealogy and learn more about my great-grandmother, Mari Louise Foote. Her last name was spelled with an "e", but I suddenly wondered if her husband was related to Ebenezer Foot.

Back home, our family genealogist, nephew Geoffrey, sent a chart that confirmed our seventeenth century ancestor Nathaniel Foote had two sons. I am descended from the oldest son, Nathaniel. Ebenezer, who dropped the "e" on his last name, descends from the other son, Robert.

After I learned more about my Foote ancestors and wrote a few pages of a children's book, Betsey's voice became more clear. More and more, I sensed her presence. Conversations with people I met, books I read, and places I traveled mysteriously presented pieces of the life and world of Betsey Colt Foot.

According to Samuel Foot, the school owes its existence to his brother Ebenezer. "Whatever was his motive and aim, whether to qualify his own daughter or those of his neighbors and friends for the duties of American ladies, or, more expansive still, to elevate and adorn the female character, and store the female mind with useful knowledge, his name should be kindly remembered by every pupil who has enjoyed or may enjoy the benefits of the institution, and by every friend of female education."

In an 1864 history of the Albany Female Academy, Principal Eben S. Stearns also credits Ebenezer Foot as the school's founder. He poetically exclaims, "How much husbands and children in our city and elsewhere owe to the school's benign influence-how much society is indebted for the virtues and cultivation of many of its chiefest ornaments, no Historian, save the 'Recording Angel,' can write. The Albany Female Academy, esto perpetua!"

I believe it was Betsey Colt Foot's mission, not to provide girls an ornamental education, but one that would elevate the mind. Her story inspires each one to listen to the still, small voice within, and to discover and use the gift they've been given: the treasure that cannot be stolen.

Albany Academy for Girls, may she endureth forever.

END NOTES
• • •

The chronology of events for the two years of the 1813-1814 journal are from Albany newspapers (*The Albany Gazette* and *The Albany Argus*) and Reynolds, Albany Chronicles.

JANUARY 1, 1813. Litchfield Female Academy records before 1800 are incomplete, but several of Betsey's cousins from Lyme, CT attended the prestigious school. It is possible Betsey Colt was one of Miss Pierce's students in 1796 when Ebenezer was at Tapping Reeve's Law School.

SATURDAY, JANUARY 2, 1813. Written by Sarah Pierce for a friend before her marriage. Sizer, et al. To Ornament Their Minds: Sarah Pierce's Litchfield Female Academy, p. 24.

THURSDAY, JANUARY 21, 1813. The Lancaster School, chartered in Albany in 1812, is based on the plan of English educator Joseph Lancaster, 1778-1838.

FRIDAY, FEBRUARY 26, 1813. The NW Corner of State and Pearl in Albany was known as Webster's Corner because it was the site of Websters and Skinners, printers and booksellers. It was also known as Elm Tree Corner because of an elm tree planted by Philip Livingston.

MONDAY, JUNE 7, 1813. Aimwell, Pinkster Ode for the Year 1803.

WEDNESDAY, JUNE 16, 1813. The controversy over Clowes' salary is reported in Hooper, A History of St. Peter's Church, pages 190-201.

WEDNESDAY, JUNE 23, 1813. Lattimer petitioned the New York Legislature for permission to establish a School for People of Color. It was granted by an Act of the Legislature, April 12, 1816.

FRIDAY, JUNE 26, 1813. William Ely, emancipator of his slaves, died in 1760 and is buried in the Ely Family Cemetery on Ely Ferry Road, Lyme, CT.

MONDAY, JULY 12, 1813. The theory is proposed by Richard Cote in his biography of Theodosia Burr Alston.

MONDAY, JULY 26, 1813. Changes in the orientation of The Big Dipper are not visible during the day, but will seasonally appear the same at the same date and time.

TUESDAY, AUGUST 24, 1813. St. Bartholomew's Day. Ely family history. One Ely cup is in the collection of The Metropolitan Museum of Art. Another, with the initials LE and the Ely Coat of Arms, is in the possession of descendent Susan Strange.

TUESDAY, OCTOBER 5, 1813. The shipwreck story is in Beach et. al. The Ely Ancestry.

SATURDAY, OCTOBER 30, 1813. Lucretia Foot Booth died on All Hallow's Eve, 1872. She is buried with Ebenezer and Betsey Foot, Lebbeus Booth, and their children in Ballston Spa Village Cemetery, Ballston Avenue, Ballston, NY.

TUESDAY, NOVEMBER 2, 1813. Samuel Foot's autobiography reports the intervention took place in early 1814.

SATURDAY, NOVEMBER 20, 1813. Before 1863, the date of Thanksgiving was set by individual states.

SATURDAY, NOVEMBER 27, 1813. Foote family story.

WEDNESDAY, DECEMBER 1, 1813. Bryant and Voss, The Letters of William Cullen Bryant, p. 308.

FRIDAY, DECEMBER 3, 1813. In his Memoirs and Letters, James Kent mentions owning the Wollstonecraft book and his agreement with her that the mind has no sex.

THURSDAY, DECEMBER 9, 1813. Lucretia's bracelet is in The Archives and Collections of The Albany Academies. The jeweler is not known.

SATURDAY, JANUARY 1, 1814. The drowning of the Meads boys is fictional.

THURSDAY, JANUARY 6, 1814. The Gregory house still stands in Sand Lake, NY.

SATURDAY, JANUARY 8, 1814. Although Edward Jenner is given credit for being the first to inoculate against cowpox, there were others, including Dr. John Ely, who offered this treatment earlier in the 18th century.

TUESDAY, JANUARY 11, 1814. Two Marvin girls from Albany attended LFA: Emma, 1815-19 and Louisa,1816-17 and 1820.

SUNDAY, MARCH 6, 1814. This story was attributed to P.T. Barnum and cited in Lee, The Yankees of Connecticut, p. 25.

FRIDAY, MARCH 18, 1814. An unsigned painting of Betsey Foot was presented to Albany Academy for Girls by her great granddaughter Sarah Elizabeth Arnold. In Bolton and Cortelyou, Ezra Ames of Albany: Portrait Painter, it is listed as among several Ezra Ames paintings completed by Ames around 1815 but not recorded. The mystery remains: who commissioned the painting and why?

MARCH 19, 1814. Cantonment is now the site of The Red Mill School, Rensselaer, NY. The eye witness account is recorded in Anderson, History of Rensselaer County, Chapter XIX.

WEDNESDAY, MARCH 30, 1814. The wedding announcement was in the Albany Argus. John Ely, Jr.'s relationship to John Ely, MD, was not researched.

FRIDAY, APRIL 15, 1814. Erastus Corning roomed with William Marcy in Troy before moving to Albany.

WEDNESDAY, APRIL 20, 1814. Pettipaug is now Essex, CT.

SUNDAY, MAY 29, 1814. St. Peter's Church records indicate that Leah, a black woman, was a member of the church in 1805.

THURSDAY, JUNE 2, 1814. Abigail Smith, Albany, NY, a student at LFA, 1814-1817. Maria Winne, Albany, NY, a student at LFA, 1819-29. Cornelia Winne, a student at the Union School in 1821.

SATURDAY, JUNE 4, 1814. In Fry's 1815 Directory, Jesse Everett advertises he "applies electricity to disease by the use of his improved electrical apparatus."

FRIDAY, AUGUST 12, 1814. Details of the debt and jail sentence are found in Samuel Foot's biography.

WHO'S WHO IN THE JOURNAL OF
BETSEY COLT FOOT

• • •

Except where noted, the characters in Betsey Foot's journal are not fictional. They are people who lived in 1813-14. To paraphrase The Three Stooges however, any resemblance between the character's actual personalities and the author's description, is a miracle.

Names, addresses and occupations of those who lived in Albany are from the 1814 Albany Directory of J. Fry. First subscribers of the Union School are identified with an *. The number in parenthesis is the number of students pledged. At this time, it was customary for men to keep wives and daughters "behind the veil of domestic privacy" and the girls names are not provided. Certainly Lucretia Foot and Mary Kent were first students and it is likely Maria Ely, Mariam Fowler, and Cornelia Knower were as well.

In 1821, the Board of Trustees of Albany Female Academy awarded premiums for scholarship and behavior. The list contains the names of girls whose last name matches that of a first subscriber. Genealogical research was not conducted to confirm the relationship

*Allen, Moses (2), Not listed in Fry's 1814 Directory. Daughters, Rebecca (fictional first name) and Sarah (fictional).

*Allen, Solomon (1), broker, 71 s. Market. Daughter, Ruth (fictional).

Allen, Mrs., mother of Moses and Solomon. Her funeral on May 31 was reported in the Albany newspapers. The financial gift for her granddaughters education is fictional.

Ames, Ezra, portrait painter, 41 s. Pearl. Daughter Maria Lucretia Ames married Reverend William James in 1824. William James's brother Henry is the father of William James, the psychologist and philosopher, Henry James, the novelist, and Alice James, the diarist.

Backus, E.F., bookseller, 20 Montgomery. Store, 65 State.

Beecher, Lyman (1768-1836), Litchfield, CT. Minister, Litchfield Congregational Church. Teacher, Litchfield Female Academy. Married Roxanna Foote, Guilford,

CT. Daughters, Catharine Beecher, pioneer of female education, Harriet Beecher Stowe, author of <u>Uncle Tom's Cabin</u>, and Mary Foote Beecher Perkins, teacher.

Benne, Henry F., confectioner, 36 n. Market.

Bernard, John, manager theater, 39 Green.

*Bleecker, Nicholas (1), merchant, 32 n. Market. Elizabeth Bleecker won a premium for scholarship and behavior, 1st class, upper school. Catharine Bleecker won a premium for scholarship and behavior, 4th class, upper school, AFA Board of Trustees Minutes, August 1821.

Bloodgood, Frances, attorney, clerk of the NYS Supreme Court, 1797-1825. 119 Washington, office. 122 State. Margaret Bloodgood, Albany, NY is listed as a student at LFA, 1808-1809. In April 1807, Bloodgood was involved in the political "Battle on State Street."

Booth, Lebbeus (1784-1859). Graduate of Union College, 1813. Head Master, Union School, 1815-1817 and 1818-1824. Married Lucretia Foot in 1821. He was 37. She was 17. Lebbeus and Lucretia moved to Ballston Spa in 1824 and founded Ballston Spa Female Seminary.

Boyd, William, jeweler, 9 Steuben. Margaret Boyd won a premium for scholarship and behavior, 3rd class upper school. Jane Anne Boyd won a premium for scholarship and behavior, 4th class, upper school, AFA Board of Trustees Minutes, August 1821.

Brace, John Pierce, Litchfield, CT. Nephew of Miss Pierce. Graduate of Williams College. Teacher at LFA.

Bradford, John M., pastor Dutch Church, 48 n. Market.

Bradstreet, Anne (1612-1672). First American poet to be published in America.

Brenton, Miss, Boarding and Day School, 118 State.

Brinckerhoff, John, 3 Dock. Store 103 n. Market. Maria Brinckerhoff received a premium for scholarship and behavior in the first class of the upper school, AFA Board of Trustees Minutes, August 1821.

Brink, Andrew, captain of the first steamboat, the *North River*, renamed the *Clermont*. Steamboat service between Albany and New York began in 1807. It continued without interruption until the Hudson River Day Line closed in 1947.

Brooks, Jonathan, carpenter, 15 Plain.

Brooks, Jonathan, jun., carpenter, 13 Plain.

Brown, Allen, merchant, 32 Montgomery. Store 43 Quay. His mother, Mrs. Brown, is fictional.

Brown, James, Cheshire, MA., itinerant painter in Western Massachusetts and Eastern New York in the first decade of the nineteenth century. The Lucretia Foot painting is not signed. James Brown is the fictional artist.

*Brown, Edward (1), merchant, 10 Hudson. Store, 1 Hudson. Annabella Brown (fictional). Jane Eliza Brown awarded a premium for scholarship and behavior in the 1st class of the lower school, AFA Board of Trustees Minutes, August 1821.

Buel, Jesse, founder and printer of *The Albany Argus*, January 1813. His house, built in 1820, still stands at 637 Western Ave., Albany, NY.

Bull, Dr. Chauncey Dickinson, Family physician in the village of Stillwater during the early 1800s.

Burr, Aaron (1756-1836). Father, Aaron Burr, president of College of New Jersey (Princeton). Graduate of College of New Jersey. Burr and Foot both studied law with Tapping Reeve. Aaron Burr's sister, Sally, married Tapping Reeve.

Burr, Theodosia (1783-1813), only child of Aaron Burr. Born in Albany and baptized in the Dutch Church. Married Joseph Alston, South Carolina rice planter. She drowned at sea, January, 1813.

Bushnell, David (1742-1824), Saybrook, CT. Inventor of the first American Submarine, *The Turtle*.

Caldwell, James, owner, Albany tobacco plant. Moved to Caldwell, NY (Lake George) in 1811. Tobacco plant operated by Thomas Boyd.

Caldwell, Joseph, teacher, 25 Steuben. Fictional teacher of Orville Roorback. Fictional marriage to Mrs. Wilson.

*Center, Asa (1), merchant, 4 Water Street. Store, 1 State. Jane Agnes Center won a premium for scholarship and behavior, 1st class upper school, AFA Board of Trustees Minutes, August 1821.

*Clark, James (?), merchant, 1 s. Market. Mary Clark from Albany, NY was a student at LFA 1812-1814. First name appears on the subscription document. Last name missing. Named by Munsell and Stearns as a first subscriber.

Clark, William, teacher, 39 Montgomery.

Clowes, Timothy, rector, St. Peter's Church, 1813-1817, Lodge.

Cole, Simon, ferryman, rear of 76 Church.

Colt (Coult), Benjamin, (ca 1698-1754), Lyme, CT. Grandfather of Betsey Colt Foot. Married Miriam Harris, 1724.

Colt, Benjamin, Jr. (ca 1737-1781), blacksmith, Hadley, MA. Father of Betsey Colt Foot.

Colt, Lucretia Ely (1742-1826), Lyme, CT. Mother of Betsey Colt Foot. Married Benjamin Colt, Jr. Mother of ten children. Second marriage to John Walker of Hadley, MA.

Colt, Miriam Harris (1700-1765), Lyme, CT. Grandmother of Betsey Colt Foot.

Cooper, Charles D., 50 State Street. Son-in-law of John Tayler. Combatant in the Battle on State Street.

Cook, John, 33 Church, library and reading room, 6 s. Market.

Corning, Erastus (1794-1872), clerk at Spencer's Hardware in 1814, partner in 1816 and owner in 1823. In 1826, Corning bought an iron mill and in 1831 began investing in a New York railroad system. He is the great grandfather of Erastus Corning II, Albany mayor, 1942-1983.

Crabb, John, teacher, 40 Fox.

Cushman, Paul, potter, 245 Washington Street. His butter urn with the unusual decoration is in the collection of The Albany Institute of History and Art.

Dale, William A. Tweed, teacher, 39 Steuben. Superintendent of The Lancaster School, chartered in Albany in 1812, based on a plan developed by English educator Joseph Lancaster (1778-1838).

Dalton, William, cartman, 173 s. Market.

*Davis, Nathaniel (?), merchant, 6 Water Street. Store, 1 State Street corner of Quay. Sarah Davis won a premium for scholarship and behavior, 2nd class lower school, AFA Board of Trustees Minutes, August 1821. Davis is not on the original subscription document. He is named as a first subscriber by Munsell.

De Witt, Simeon, Surveyor General, 149 s. Market. One of the Regents of the State of New York that granted The Albany Academy Charter, March 4, 1813.

Doortje, Madame, fictional Albany fortune teller in James Fenimore Cooper's novel, Satanstoe.

Edwards, Isaac, Esq., counsellor, Greenfield, Saratoga County. Married Esther Mattoon Foot (1770-1835), sister of Ebenezer Foot.

Elliot, Ethalinda Ely (1762-1829). Sister of Dr. John Ely. Married Dr. William Elliot, Goshen, NY.

Ellison, widow Elizabeth, 34 Montgomery. Fry's 1814 Directory lists the widow of Reverend Thomas Ellison, rector of St. Peter's Church, 1787-1802, at 57 Chapel. The author took the liberty of placing her next to the Foots. The story of the rector's other wife in Newcastle is from Cooper's novel, Satanstoe.

Ely, John, MD, Colonel (1737-1800). Uncle of Betsey Foot. Graduate of Yale College, married Sarah Worthington, daughter of Reverend William Worthington, Westbrook, CT.

*Ely, John (1) (1774-1849), physician and surgeon, 62 n. Market. Surgeon with New York's Fifth Cavalry Regiment during War of 1812. Son of Colonel John Ely, MD. Cousin of Betsey Foot. Married Abigail Lay. Daughter, Maria, presumably a first student. After the war, he returned to Greenville, NY and founded The Greenville Academy that included a library, a primary school, male and female departments.

Ely, John, Jr., dep. compr. 43 Dock. Office, 122 State. His relationship to Betsey Foot and Dr. John Ely was not researched. Married Margaret Lee of Saybrook, CT.

Ely, Richard (1610-1684). First settler. Born in Plymouth, England. Married Elizabeth Fenwick Cullick, Saybrook, CT. Died in Lyme, CT.

Ely, William (1647-1717), Lyme, CT. Son of Richard. Survivor of the shipwreck.

Ely, William, son of William. Emancipated his slaves. He died in 1760 and is buried with other family in the Ely Cemetery on Ely Ferry Road, Lyme, CT.

Ely, Worthington, MD (1759-1804). Son of Colonel John Ely, MD. Cousin of Betsey Colt Foot. Graduate of Yale College. Died in Coeymans.

Everett, Jesse, 78 s. Market. In Fry's 1814 Directory, he advertises American Earthen, Stone and Wooden Ware, Cordials, Children's Toys and Cotton Thread. In 1815, he advertises he is a Medical Electrician.

Fitgerald, Agnes Dugan, AAG '24. AAG Elementary School teacher, 1947-1957. Daughter, Patricia, AAG '55. Son, James, AA '57.

Foot, Betsey Colt (1774-1847). Married Ebenezer Foot in Hadley, MA, 1803. Daughter Lucretia born 1804. Attendance at LFA is a theory proposed by the author.

Foot, Ebenezer (1773-1814), counsellor, 36 Montgomery. After law studies with Tapping Reeve, Litchfield, CT, 1796, he moved to Lansingburgh, NY. Vestryman of Saint Peter's Church, 1809. Drafted the subscription document for The Union School, February 24, 1814, but his name is not listed as a subscriber. Died in July at the close of the school's first term.

Foot, John, Reverend, Cheshire, CT, 1765. Ebenezer's uncle. Graduate of Yale College. Ebenezer studied privately with this uncle to prepare for entrance to Tapping Reeve's law school in Litchfield, CT.

Foot, Lucretia (1804-1872), daughter of Betsey and Ebenezer. First student at Union School. Married Lebbeus Booth, 1821.

Foote, Nathaniel (1593-1644), first settler. Married Elizabeth Deming. Emigrated from Colchester, England around 1630. Settled in Wethersfield in 1634. Seven children: Elizabeth, Nathaniel, Mary, Robert, Frances, Sarah and Rebecca. The author is descended from Nathaniel. Ebenezer is descended from Robert.

Foot, Samuel Alfred (1790-1878), 36 Montgomery. Brother and law partner of Ebenezer. Union College, Class of 1811.

Foote, Eli (1747-1792), shipping merchant in Murfreesboro, NC. Eli's daughter Roxanna Foote, Ebenezer's cousin, married Lyman Beecher, parents of Harriet Beecher Stowe.

Foote, Roxanna (1775-1816), daughter of Eli and Roxanna Foote, married Reverend Lyman Beecher in 1799, died 1816 in Litchfield, CT.

*Fowler, William (1), leather merchant, 33 s. Market. Factory, Ferry. Daughter, Mariam, presumably a first student. Mariam Fowler married Samuel Foot on August 17, 1818. Louisa and Sarah Fowler won premiums for scholarship and behavior, 1st class lower school, AFA Board of Trustees Minutes, August 1821.

Fry, Joseph, 36 Beaver and 99 State, fire inspector. Collected and arranged the first Albany Directory, 1813.

Gansevoort, Maria, daughter of Peter Gansevoort. Married Allen Melvill, October 14, 1814. Son, Herman Melville ("e" added to the last name), attended The Albany Academy. Daughters attended Albany Female Academy.

*Gill, Matthew (2), merchant, 71 n. Market. Store, 37 State. Daughters Martha and Margaret (fictional).

Gillespie, Robert, carpenter, 10 Fox.

Goldberg, John C., professor of music, 22 Hamilton.

Goodrich, Horace, Milton, NY. Graduate of Union College, 1813. Law clerk with Ebenezer and boarder with the Foots. First head of The Union School. "His constitution was feeble, studies and duties were pressing, and he soon sank under their accumulated weight, and died of consumption in the year 1815, while still a member of the family of the widow of his patron." Sketch of the History of the Albany Female Academy, prepared and read by Ebenezer S. Stearns, Principal, 50th Anniversary Commemoration.

*Gould, Thomas (1), merchant, 18 Montgomery. Store, 63 State. Eliza Gould won a premium for scholarship and behavior, 1st class lower school, AFA Board of Trustees Minutes, August 1821.

Gregory, Lucretia Ely (1770-?) married Dr. Uriah M. Gregory, Sand Lake, NY. Cousin of Betsey Foot. The Gregory house is now a restaurant in Sand Lake, NY.

Groesbeeck, C.W., merchant, 39 Montgomery. Store, 95 n. Market. Son Wilhelm and Daughter Catharine are fictional.

Hamilton, Betsy Schuyler (1757-1854), daughter of Philip Schuyler and wife of Alexander Hamilton.

Haney, Jacob, laborer, 34 Montgomery.

Harris, Rhoda, Headmistress, AAG, 1941-1964.

*Henry, John V. (3), counsellor, 19 Columbia. College of New Jersey. Sons in Albany Academy, AA Board of Trustees, Trustee Lancaster School, Board of Trustees, St. Peter's Church. Daughters Emma and Dorothy (fictional). Mary Henry won a premium for scholarship and behavior, 2nd class upper school, AFA Board of Trustees Minutes, August 1821.

Henry, Joseph (1797-1878), developer of the electromagnet, inventor of the electromagnetic telegraph. First Secretary and Director of The Smithsonian Institute and founding member of The National Academy of Sciences. Student at The Albany Academy 1819-1822 and later a teacher at the school.

Henshaw, Martha, LFA student from Albany, 1798.

Hochstrasser, Paul, merchant, 106 n. Market. Organist at St. Peter's Church.

Hollister, Clarence, music teacher at Albany Academy for Girls, 1942-1968.

Hooker, Philip, architect, 7 Church.

Howe, George Augustus, Lord Viscount (1725-1758), Brigadier General in British Army, killed in French and Indian War. There is a commemorative tablet indicating his burial site at St. Peter's Church, Albany.

*Hutton, Isaac (1) (1766-1855), silversmith, 15-17 Columbia Street. Daughter Margaret (fictional).

Jenkins, Elisha (1772-1849), a Quaker and outspoken Anti-Federalist. New York State Assemblyman. Columbia County Treasurer. New York State Comptroller (1801-1806). NY Secretary of State (1806-1807, 1808-1810 and 1811-1813). Mayor of Albany (1816-1819).

Kane, James, merchant, store, 45 Dock. Julia Kane won a premium for scholarship and behavior, 1st class upper school. AFA Board of Trustees Minutes, August 1821. Kane was one of the men who lent money to Samuel and would not accept repayment.

*Kent, James (1) (1764-1847), Chief Justice, 21 Columbia, Yale College, 1781. Married Elizabeth Bailey (Betsy). Daughter Mary Kent Stone was a first student and in 1893 sketched her recollection of the first school building.

*Knower, Benjamin (1), hatter, 41 s. Market. Daughter and presumably first student, Cornelia (1801-1889). In 1825 she married William Marcy in the hat factory and family home that still stands on Route 146, Altamont, NY.

Lansing, John A., baker, 33 s. Pearl.

Lattimer, Benjamin, cartman, 9 Plain. Lattimer was born in Wethersfield, CT and served in the American Revolution. Baptized in First Presbyterian Church, Albany. Dina (last name not known) was a servant in the home of G.W. Mancius, physician. Children Benjamin (1793), William (1805), Betsy (1806), and Mary (1808).

Lee, Ezra (1749-1821), Lyme, CT. Operated David Bushnell's first submarine, *The Turtle*, to attack British ship in New York Harbor, September, 1776.

Lydius, Baltus (Balthazar), 104 n. Pearl at State. There are many Albany tales about Lydius.

M'Donald, D., hair-dresser and bathing house, 7 Beaver.

M'Intyre, Archibald, compr.(sic.) 41 n. Pearl, office 122 State. Chairman of The Albany Academy building committee, 1813.

Mancius, G.W., post office 22 Montgomery, pharmacy, 10 s. Market. Anna Mancius won a premium for scholarship and behavior, 2nd class lower school, AFA Board of Trustees Minutes, August 1821.

Mancius, Jacob, sheriff, 74 n. Market.

Marcy, William (1786-1857), Governor of New York State (1833-1838). Married Cornelia Knower. While Governor, he and Cornelia lived in a home that still stands at the corner of Elk and Eagle Streets in Albany.

*Marvin, Uriah (2), merchant, 2 Water. Store, 3 State. Emma Stevens Marvin from Albany, NY attended LFA 1815-19. Louisa Marvin from Albany, NY attended LFA 1816-1817 and 1820. Genealogy research was not conducted to confirm these two girls are the daughters of this subscriber.

Meads, John, cabinet maker, 29 Maiden Lane. Charlotte Meads, won a premium in the 4th class of the upper school. Louisa Meads, won a premium in the 3rd class of the lower school, AFA Board of Trustees Minutes, August 1821. The boys' drowning story is fictional.

Melvill, Allan, married Maria Gansevoort, October 14, 1814. Son, Herman

Melville attended The Albany Academy. Daughters attended Albany Female Academy. "E" added to surname by Maria after Allan died, bankrupt.

Moore, Richard, lamp lighter, 211 s. Pearl.

Napoleon, Le Petit Caporal, Mr. Kitty. Black and white (now called "tuxedo") cats from Amsterdam were common in Dutch New York.

Niell, William, pastor of Presbyterian Church, 72 Lydius.

North, Samuel, Ebenezer's law partner and boarder in the Foot home. Died 1813, Albany, NY. The Stillwater family is fictional.

Norton, John, mason, 59 Van Schaick.

Nott, Eliphalet, graduate of Rhode Island College (Brown University). President of Union College, 1804-1868.

Nugent, Mrs. John, Seminary for Young Ladies, Van Schee. Her story is fictional.

Pierce, Sarah (1767-1852), Litchfield, CT, founder of Litchfield Female Academy (LFA), 1792-1833.

Price, Lucretia Colt, sister of Betsey Colt Foot, died in Ballston Spa, 1833.

Pye, John, owner of an Inn on the Albany-Troy Road. The robbery story is from Hess, People of Albany.

Redstone, New York City, manufacturer of organs.

Reeve, Tapping (1744-1823), graduate of College of New Jersey (Princeton). Tutored Aaron and Sally Burr. Married Sally Burr. Founded Tapping Reeve's Law School, Litchfield, CT, 1784-1833.

*Reid, John (1), merchant, 79 n, Market. Daughter Emily (fictional).

Robertson, actor at the Green Street Theater. Not listed in Fry's 1814 Directory.

Robinson and Vanderbilt, coachmakers, 27 Church.

*Roorback Arthur (?), steamboat captain, 26 Montgomery. Fanny Roorback received a premium for scholarship and behavior, 4th class upper school, AFA Board of Trustees Minutes, August 1821. On the original subscription document, the lower right hand corner is torn. Only "Roorb---" is visible. Named by Munsell as a first subscriber.

Ross, Mrs. Elizabeth, 38 Dock Street, gentleman boarders.

*Russell, Joseph (1), painter, Water Street. Store, 100 n. Market. Daughter Abigail (fictional).

*Russell, Thomas (3), painter, 38 Montgomery. Store 100 n. Market. Daughters, Julia, Mary and Isabelle (fictional). The three daughters married and remained in Albany and were present at the fiftieth anniversary celebration. Married names not researched.

Scoville, Hannah (fictional). Eliza Scoville, Watertown, CT was a student at LFA in 1802. Silas Scoville married Sabrea Foot and inherited the Foot farm in Watertown.

*Scrymser, James (1), grocer, 40 Montgomery. Daughter Katrina (fictional). In 1864, Principal Eben Stearns erroneously names the subscriber as Seymour.

Skinner, R.C., dentist, 24 Beaver. Credentials provided in Fry's 1814 Directory.

Southwick, actor at the Green Street Theater. Not listed in Fry's 1814 Directory.

*Stearns, John (1), physician, 80 n. Market. Daughter Sally (fictional). James S is visible on the original document. End of last name torn. Named by Stearns and Munsell as a first subscriber.

*Stewart, Gilbert (1), merchant, 69 Hudson. Daughter Elizabeth (fictional).

Spenser, John, merchant, 11 s. Market.

Tayler, John (1742-1829), 50 State. New York State Senator, 1801-02 and 1803-1813. Acting Lieutenant Governor in August 1810 after the death of Lieutenant Governor John Broome until June 1811 when De Witt Clinton was elected. Lieutenant Governor 1813-22. One of the Regents of the State of New York that granted The Albany Academy Charter, March 4, 1813. Vestryman at St. Peter's Church.

*TenEyck, Harmanus (1), 98 n. Market. Daughter Betsey (fictional).

Thompson, Catharine B., Young Ladies School, 38 Columbia.

Townsend, Charles D., physician, 63 n. Market.

Trowbridge, Henry, 51 Hudson, proprietor, The New York State Museum, Old City Hall, s. Market.

Van Antwerp, widow, grocer, 11 n. Pearl. Her story is fictional.

Vander Heyden, Jacob, 85 n. Pearl. The flying iron horse weathervane atop his "palace" was later moved to the southern gable of Washington Irving's home in Tarrytown, NY.

Van Rensselaer, Solomon, adj. general, 76 n. Pearl. Served in War of 1812. Wounded at the Battle of Queenstown Heights. A federalist, he attacked Elisha Jenkins which started the Battle on State Street.

Van Rensselaer, hon. Philip S., mayor.

Van Rensselaer, Stephen III, "The Good Patroon," benefactor of and first President, The Albany Academy Board of Trustees, 1813. Not listed in Fry's 1814 Directory.

*Van Vechten, Abraham (1), 2 n. Market, Attorney General of NY State, Daughter, Kathryn (fictional). One of the Regents of the State of New York that granted The Albany Academy Charter, March 4, 1813.

Watson, Elkanah (1758-1842), born in Plymouth, MA. Moved to Albany in 1790, promoter of public works and development in Albany. Left Albany between 1807-1816.

Wells, Seth, early Albany School master, 1796-1800.

Westerlo, Rensselaer, counsellor, 72 n. Pearl. Cornelia Westerlo won a premium for scholarship and behavior, 2nd class upper school, AFA Board of Trustees Minutes, August 1821.

Willard, Emma Hart (1783-1870). Pioneer of female education. Taught in Berlin, CT, Westfield, MA, and Middlebury, VT. Founded Middlebury Female Seminary in 1814, Waterford Academy (1819), and Troy Female Seminary (1821). TFS name later changed to Emma Willard School.

Willett, Edward, counsellor, 18 s. Pearl, member of St. Peter's Church.

Wilson, widow Martha, teacher, 39 Steuben. Story of marriage to Mr. Caldwell is fictional.

Winne, Cornelia, won a premium for scholarship and behavior in the 4th class of the upper school, AFA Board of Trustees Minutes, August 1821.

Winne, William B., letter carrier, 57 Orange.

Wood, William, printer and silhouette artist, 92 Beaver.

Worthington, Daniel, constable, 184 s. Pearl.

Yates, Christopher C., physician, 71 n. Pearl.

Young, Thomas, comedian, 66 Lydius.

SOURCES

• • •

Aimwell, Absalom. <u>Pinkster Ode for the Year 1803.</u>

Albany Female Academy, Board of Trustees Minutes, August 1821.

<u>Albany's Historic Street: A Collection of some of the Historic Facts and Interesting Traditions relating to State Street and Its Neighborhood,</u> Published in Commemoration of its Fiftieth Anniversary by The National Savings Bank of the City of Albany, 1918.

Allis, M. <u>Historic Connecticut.</u> New York: Grosset and Dunlap, 1934.

Anderson, G. B. <u>Landmarks of Rensselaer County.</u> Syracuse, NY: D. Mason and Company Publishers, 1987.

Beach, M. S., Ely, W. and Vanderpoel, G. <u>The Ely Ancestry, Lineage of Richard Ely of Plymouth, England, who came to Boston, Mass., about 1655 and settled at Lyme, Conn. in 1660.</u> New York: The Calumet Press, 1902.

Beard, L. and Beard, A. <u>The American Girls Handy Book. Centennial Edition.</u> Boston, MA: David R. Godine, Publishers, Inc.,1987.

Beecher, R. <u>Out to Greenville and Beyond, Historical Sketches of Greene County.</u> Coxsackie, NY: Greene County Historical Society Press, 1997.

Beers, J.B., ed. <u>History of Middlesex County, Connecticut.</u> New York: J.B. Beers & Co., 1884.

Beers, S.N & D.G. <u>The New Topographical Atlas of the Counties of Albany and Schenectady, New York.</u> Philadelphia, PA: Stone and Stewart, 1866.

Bennett, A. P. <u>The People's Choice: A History of Albany County in Art and Architecture.</u> Albany, NY: Lane Press, 1980.

Bolton, T. and Cortelyou, I. F. <u>Ezra Ames of Albany: Portrait Painter.</u> New York Historical Society, 1955.

Booth, J.C. <u>Booth's History of Saratoga County, NY</u>. 1858. Reproduced by the Saratoga County Bicentennial Commission, 1977.

Briggs, Rev. C. L. <u>The Story of Roxanna Foote, A Great Soul</u>. Christ Episcopal Church, Guilford, CT. Unpublished remarks, May 4, 1930.

Bryant, W. C.II, and Voss, T. G. The Letters of William Cullen Bryant. Vol.1, 1809-1836. New York: Fordham University Press, 1975.

Child, L. The Mother's Book. Boston, MA: Carter and Hendee, 1831.

Cooper, J. F. The Works of James Fenimore Cooper: Satanstoe. New York: G.P. Putnam's Sons, the Knickerbocker Press. Date not provided.

Cote, R. N. Theodosia Burr Alston: Portrait of a Prodigy. Mt. Pleasant, SC: Corinthian Books, 2002.

Cott, N. F. Bonds of Womanhood: Women's Sphere in New England 1780-1835. New Haven, CT: Yale University Press, 1977.

Cutter, M. L. Life Beside the Connecticut River: A Children's History of Hadley, Massachusetts. Hatfield, MA: Hatfield Printing and Publishing, 1990.

Dexter, F. B. Biographical Sketches of the Graduates of Yale College with Annals of the College History. Vol. III, May, 1763-July, 1778. New York: Henry Holt and Company, 1903.

Fisher, L. The Schools, Nineteenth Century America. New York: Holiday House, 1983.

Foot, S. A., LL.D. Autobiography: Collateral Reminiscences, Arguments in Important Causes, Speeches, Addresses, Lectures, and Other Writings. New York, 1873.

Foote, A. W. Foote Family Compromising the Genealogy and History of Nathaniel Foote of Wethersfield, Conn. Vol. 1. Rutland, VT: Marble City Press, The Tuttle Co., 1907.

Franklin, W. James Fenimore Cooper, The Early Years. New Haven, CT: Yale University Press, 1907.

Fry, J. The Albany Directory. Albany, NY: Websters & Skinners Printers, 1813, 1814, 1815, 1817.

Garrett, E. D. At Home: The American Family 1750-1870. New York: Harry N. Abrams, Inc., 1990.

Goodsell, W. Pioneers of Women's Education in the United States: Emma Willard, Catharine Beecher, Mary Lyon. New York: McGraw-Hill, 1931.

Goodwin, N. The Foote Family or the Descendants of Nathaniel Foote, One of the First Settlers of Wethersfield, Conn. Hartford, CT: Press of Case, Tiffany & Co., 1849.

Gordon, L. Vindication: A Life of Mary Wollstonecraft. New York: Harper Collins Publishers, 2005.

Grondahl, P. Mayor Corning: Albany Icon, Albany Enigma. Albany, NY: Washington Park Press, 1997.

Grose, E. F. Centennial History of the Village of Ballston Spa Including the Towns of Ballston and Milton. The Ballston Journal, 1907.

Habegger, A. My Wars are Laid Away in Books: The Life of Emily Dickinson. New York: Random House, 2001.

Hammond, S. The Colts of Peterson. NJ Historical Society Publication, 1961.

Hedrick, J. Harriet Beecher Stowe: A Life. New York: Oxford University Press, 1994.

Hess, P.J. People of Albany, The First 200 Years. Albany, NY: Albany Steel, Inc., 2009.

Hinman, R. R. A Catalogue of the Names of the Early Puritan Settlers of the Colony of Connecticut; with the time of their arrival in the County and Colony. Hartford, CT: Press of Case, Tiffany and Company, 1859.

Hodges, G. R. New York City Cartmen, 1667-1850. New York: New York University Press, 1986.

Holliday, C. Woman's Life in Colonial Days. New York: Frederick Ungar Publishing Co., 1960.

Hooper, J. A History of Saint Peter's Church in the City of Albany. Albany, NY: Fort Orange Press, 1900.

Horton, J. T. James Kent: A Study in Conservatism, 1763-1847. University of Buffalo: D. Appleton-Century Company, Inc., 1939.

Howard, N. Stories of Wethersfield: Four Centuries of American Life in Connecticut's "Most Ancient Town." Wethersfield, CT: White Publishing, LLC., 1997.

Howell, G. and Tenney, J. Bi-centennial History of the County of Albany, NY from 1609-1886. New York: W.W. Munsell & Co., 1886.

Hughes, M. L. Refusing Ignorance: The Struggle to Educate Black Children in Albany, New York, 1816-1873. Albany, NY: Mount Ida Press, 1998.

Hunt, G. As We Were: Life in America 1814, forward by Jack Larkin, Stockbridge, MA: Berkshire House Publishers, 1993.

Hymowitz, C. and Weissman, M. A History of Women in America. New York: Bantam Books, 1981.

Judd, S. History of Hadley Including the Early History of Hatfield, South Hadley, Amherst and Granby and Family Genealogies by Lucius M. Boltwood. Springfield, MA: H.R Hunting & Co., 1905.

Kenney, A. P. The Gansevoorts of Albany: Dutch Patricians in the Upper Hudson Valley. Syracuse University Press, 1969.

Kent, J. Autobiographical Sketch of Chancellor Kent. The Southern Law Review, July, 1872.

Kent, W. Memoirs and Letters of James Kent, LL.D. Boston, MA: Little Brown and Company, 1898.

Kerber, L. No Constitutional Right To Be Ladies: Women and the Obligations of Citizenship. New York: Hill and Wang, 1998.

Kerber, L. Women of the Republic: Intellect and Ideology in Revolutionary America. Chapel Hill, NC: University of North Carolina Press, 1980.

Knapp, R. M. The History of Albany, New York. Albany, NY: Knapp, 1928.

Larken, J. The Reshaping of Everyday Life: 1790-1840. New York: Harper & Row, 1988.

Lee, W.S. The Yankees of Connecticut. New York: Henry Holt and Co., 1957.

Loeb, R. H. Jr. New England Village, Everyday Life in 1810. Garden City, NY: Doubleday & Co., 1976.

Lomask, M. Aaron Burr: The Years from Princeton to Vice President, 1756-1805. New York: Farrar, Straus, Giroux, 1979.

McClintock, J. T. Albany and its Nineteenth Century Schools; A Research

Report. Harvard Graduate School of Education, 1967.

McCutcheon, M. The Writer's Guide to Everyday Life in the 1800s. Writer's Digest Books, 2001.

McKenna, M.C. Tapping Reeve and the Litchfield Law School. New York: Oceana Publications, Inc., 1986.

Millstein, B. and Bodin, J. We the American Women: A Documentary History. Chicago: Science Research Associates, 1977.

Monaghan, E. J. Literacy Instruction and Gender in Colonial New England. American Quarterly. Vol. 40. No. 1, 1988.

Munsell, J. The Annals of Albany. Vol. 1. Albany, NY: J. Munsell, 1850.

Munsell, J. The Annals of Albany. Vol. 1. 2nd edition. Albany, NY: J. Munsell, 1869.

Nissenbaum, S. The Battle for Christmas. New York: Alfred A. Knopf, 1996.

Norton, M. B. Liberty's Daughters: The Revolutionary Experience of American Women, 1750-1800. Boston, MA: Little Brown and Co., 1980.

Nylander, J. Our Own Snug Fireside. New York: Alfred A. Knopf, 1993.

Parramore, T. C. The Ancient Maritime Village of Murfreesborough, 1787-1825. Murfreesboro, NC: Johnson Publishing Co., 1969.

Proceedings of The Albany Female Academy in Commemoration of Its Fiftieth Anniversary, May 17, 1864, Containing the Welcome Address of the President of The Trustees, The Oration, by Rev. Pres. Stearns of Amherst College, Historical Sketch by the Principal &c. Albany: Weed, Parsons & Company, Printers.

Reynolds, C. Albany Chronicles, A History of the City Arranged Chronologically. Albany NY: J.B. Lyon Company Printers, 1906.

Ring, B. Let Virtue Be a Guide to Thee: Needlework in the Education of Rhode Island Women, 1730-1830. Providence, RI: Rhode Island Historical Society, 1983.

Robertson-Lorant, L. Melville: A Biography. New York: Clarkson Potter Publishers, 1996.

Rugoff, M. The Beechers: An American Family in the Nineteenth Century. New York: Harper and Row, 1981.

Sanford, E. A History of Connecticut. Hartford, CT: S.S. Scranton and Co, 1887.

Sizer, T., Sizer, N., Schwager, S., Brickley, L.T., Krueger, G., Fields, C.K. and Kightlinger, L.C., editors. To Ornament Their Minds: Sarah Pierce's Litchfield Female Academy, 1792-1833. Litchfield, CT: Litchfield Historical Society, 1993.

Sklar, K.K. Catharine Beecher: A Study in American Domesticity. New York: Norton, 1973.

Stowe, H. B. Poganuc People. Hartford, CT: The Stowe-Day Foundation, 1977.

Tenney, J. New England in Albany. Boston: Crocker and Co., 1883.

Weise, A. J. The History of the City of Albany, New York from the Discovery of the Great River in 1524. Albany, NY: E.H. Bender, 1884.

Weise, A. J. History of the City of Troy. Troy, NY: William H. Young, 1876.

Wollstonecraft, M. A Vindication of the Rights of Women.1792. New York: Norton, 1967.

Worth, G. A. Random Recollections of Albany from 1800-1808. Third Edition. Albany, NY: J. Munsell, 1866.

Albany NY newspapers of 1813-1814, The Albany Gazette and The Albany Argus.